HAMISH HENDERSON
COLLECTED POEMS

HAMISH HENDERSON

COLLECTED POEMS

Edited by Corey Gibson

Published in Great Britain in 2019 by Polygon,
an imprint of Birlinn Ltd.

Birlinn Ltd
West Newington House
10 Newington Road
Edinburgh EH9 1QS

9 8 7 6 5 4 3 2 1

ISBN 978 1 84697 486 1

The publisher gratefully acknowledges investment from
Creative Scotland towards the publication of this book.

Typeset in Verdigris MVB by Polygon, Edinburgh
Printed by TJ International Ltd, Padstow

Tail toddle, tail toddle;
Tammie gars my tail toddle;
But-an-ben we diddle-doddle,
Tammy gars ma tail toddle.

– Trad.

CONTENTS

Epigraph   v
Introduction *Rebel Ceilidh:*
    Hamish Henderson's Poetry   xv

THE POEMS

FREEDOM BECOMES PEOPLE

Freedom Becomes People   5
Prologue to a Poem   7
Picture in St Sebaldus Church, Nuremberg   9
The Cell (1)   10
Ballad of the Simeto   13
The Cell (2)   20
Brosnachadh   22
Glasclune and Drumlochy   23
Fuck on, Fuck on, Verlaine, Rimbaud   28
Auldearn   29
Inverey   30
OF EROS AND DUST: POEMS OF C.P.
    CAVAFY AND DINO CAMPANA
    Tomb of Iases   31
    Chimaera   32
THREE POEMS OF HÖLDERLIN
    The Applause of Men   34
    Socrates and Alcibiades   35
    Patmos I   36
    Patmos II   39
Epistle to Mary   41
To Stuart – On His Leaving for Jamaica   44

FOUR CAMBRIDGE POEMS
Bridge St Blues   45
Lost Love Blues   47
X Still = 0   48
High Hedges   49
To Hugh MacDiarmid on Reading
    Lucky Poet   51
So Long   54

BALLADS OF WORLD WAR II – COLLECTED
FOR THE LILI MARLEEN CLUB OF
GLASGOW (1947)

Foreword   57
The Ballad of Wadi Maktilla   59
Ballad of the D-Day Dodgers   61
Ballad of the Big Nobs   63
The Roads to Rome   64
Ballad of the Taxi Driver's Cap   65
The 51st Highland Division's Farewell
    to Sicily   67
Ballad of King Faruk and Queen Farida   69
The Blubbing Buchmanite   72
Ballad of the Banffies   74
Fall of Tobruk   76
Song of the Admiral Graf von Spree   77
A Pioneer Corps Ballad   79
Phoney War – Western Front   80
Ballad of Anzio   81

ELEGIES FOR THE DEAD IN CYRENAICA

Prologue   85
Foreword   87

PART ONE
    Epigraph   89
    First Elegy – End of a Campaign   91
    Second Elegy – Halfaya   93
    Third Elegy – Leaving the City   95
    Fourth Elegy – El Adem   97
    Fifth Elegy – Highland Jebel   99

Interlude – Opening of an Offensive   102

PART TWO
    Epigraph   105
    Sixth Elegy – Acroma   107
    Seventh Elegy – Seven
       Good Germans   109
    Eighth Elegy – Karnak   112
    Ninth Elegy – Fort Capuzzo   117
    Tenth Elegy – The Frontier   118

Heroic Song for the Runners of Cyrene   121

JOURNEY TO A KINGDOM, AND OTHER POEMS

Piron's Epitaph on Himself   129
Epistill   130
To a Free Kirk Minister   131
Journey to a Kingdom   132
Song for an Irish Red Killed in Sicily   140
Sitzkrieg Fantasy   141

Pioneer Ballad of Section Three	145
Sergeant Major Prick Talking	150
Clamavi (or, Serentis in Rebus)	151
Death	152
This is the Exile's Trouble	153
A Wife Ingenrit o the Sea	154
Seascape	155
Dark Streets to Go Through	156
Soldat Bernhard Pankau	159
Mr Jimmy Balgowrie Talking	160
The Salamander	163
When the Teased Idiot Turns	164
Hate Poem	165
Hospital Afternoon	167
Poem for Silvano	168
Ballad of the Stubby Guns	169
We Show You That Death as a Dancer	171
Honest Geordie	172
Strathspey	173
Leaving Brandenburg 1939	174
Ballad of the Creeping Jesus	175
Ballad of the Twelve Stations of My Youth	177
Back from the Island of Sulloon	180
Ballad of Snow-White Sandstroke	181
The Ballad of Gibson Pasha	184
Lines to a Fool	186
You, My Poems, Are My Weapons	187
Requiem for the Men the Nazis Murdered	189
The Serbian Spring, 1941	193
4 September 1939	195
The Highlanders at Alamein	196
Alamein, October 23, 1942	198
The Guillotine	200
Lament for the Son	203
Dialogue of the Angel and the Dead Boy	205
Here's to the Maiden	210

Epitaph for a Barn-Stormer 211
On Two Cambridge Professional Athletes 212
They've got 'ESS! 213
This Island a Fortress 214

'IN THE MIDST OF THINGS': MORE FROM THE ANTI-FASCIST STRUGGLE

Myself Answers 217
Poem 218
A Translation of Nietzsche into Scots 219
Francy 221
Sir Oriflamme Chammlinton 222
Goettingen Nicht 223
Untitled 224
En Marche 225
The Guid Sodger Schweik 226
Speech for a Sensualist in a Play 227
Hate Song Against a Sergeant 228
Brutality Begins at Home 229
Bawdy Scrawled on a Postcard from Egypt 230
Twa Blads frae Africa as Tae a Wheen
    Anglo-Cairenes 231
The Ballad of Zem-Zem 232
The Gods in Exile 234
from The Gods from Greece 236
Poem from the Diary of Corporal
    Heinrich Mattens 239
Nearly Xmas 1941 240
Love Song 241
Primosole: Jul 42 242
Ballad of the Famous Twenty-Third 243
My Way Home 245

TRANSLATIONS OF ITALIAN ARMY SONGS

    Army Life   246

    La Semana Nera   247

    Captain, Captain of the Guard   248

    The Alpine Recruits   249

The Highlanders of Sicily – A Pipe Tune   251

Anzio April   252

The Ballad o Corbara   254

Victory Hey-Down   263

Epitaph   266

Untitled   267

PRODUCTS OF THE FOLK REVIVAL

The John Maclean March   271

The Crowned Heads of Europe   273

Ballad of the Men of Knoydart   277

Song of the Gillie More   280

The Belles o' Marchmont   282

Mains o' Rhynie   284

The Freedom Come-All-Ye   286

Anti-Polaris   287

If You Sit Close Tae Me, I Winna Weary   290

The Flyting o' Life and Daith   294

May's Mou for Jamie   297

Rivonia   298

The Ballad of the Speaking Heart   300

Paddy's Hogmanay   303

A Voice Frae Yont the Grave   305

THE OBSCURE VOICE AND 'OH, THE FADED CHURCHES'

Wind on the Crescent [Eugenio Montale]	311
Colour of Rain and Iron	312
The Sleep of the Virgin	313
In un Momento	314
Letting Go of a Dove	315
Oh, the Faded Churches	316

UNSORTED WORKS

Tae Geordie Fraser on His Waddin Day	319
Comrie Port a Beul	320
Limericks	322
Song	323
Billet Doux	324
Prologue to a Book of Ballads	325
Scottish Childhood	326
Into the Future	327
Death or the Bed of Contention – MacDiarmid or Me?	328
After Churchill	329
Unpublished haiku	330
Unpublished quatrain	331
Unpublished poem fragment	332
Unpublished poem fragment #2	333
Unpublished poem fragment #3	334
Unpublished poem fragment #4	335
Unpublished poem fragment #5	336
Verse of Good Wishes, Collected from Catherine Dix of Berneray	337
The Druid and his Disciple	338
Under the Earth I Go	343
Peccadillo	346

Clanranald's Song to his Wife   347
Written at a Conference   348
Vivamus Mea Lesbia atque Amemus   349
Heine's Doktrin   350
Two Renderings of Psalm 23   351
Auld Reekie's Roses   352
Auld Reekie's Roses II   356
Tàladh Dhomnaill Ghuirm – Blue Donald's
              Lullaby   361

JUVENILIA

After the Battle of Trafalgar – A Thanks
              Giving Service   365
TWO POEMS
    To Ledbury   366
    For Colin Roy   366
Greek Drinking Song   367
Epigram – Z. Marcas   368
As Burns Might Have Translated Catullus's Ode 369
Merrie Ingleton   370
Weltschmerz   376
The Gallowsmountain   377
The Song of a Gallows Brother to Sophie the
              Hangman's Daughter   378
The Spring Song of a Gallows Brother   379
Herr von Korf's Witticism   380
The Aesthete   381
America   382
A Fellow Traveller   384
Homage to Stefan George   388
Ballade des Noms de Plume   389

Acknowledgements   391
Index of Titles   395

INTRODUCTION

REBEL CEILIDH:
HAMISH HENDERSON'S POETRY

In a fond tribute for Hamish Henderson's seventieth birthday, his friend Adam McNaughtan conjured a popular image of 'Big Hamish, Seumas Mór':

> From being the most studious-looking soldier of the forties he grew to be the least academic-looking scholar of the sixties. Over six feet tall, his hair thinning on top but bunching on his collar at the back, that collar unbuttoned but held loosely closed by a tie generously knotted, his eye twinkling and his fists swinging in time to the chorus of 'Tail Toddle', he has sung and lectured with gusto at folk clubs and festivals throughout the country, the most visible symbol of the School of Scottish Studies for almost forty years.[1]

In this short description we get an outline of the trajectory of Henderson's life, from soldier-poet to scholar-revivalist; a dishevelled figurehead for an institution, perhaps also for the folk revival in Scotland, and for a set of sometimes overlapping political ideals – not least world socialism and Scottish independence. The means that Henderson deployed to these ends rested, at least in part, on his ability to make a ceilidh of a moment.

Henderson's champions have come to put great store in the public persona McNaughtan describes – the latter-day folk-hero recreated in countless anecdotes, reminiscences, witticisms, high-jinks, and most importantly, songs. Alec Finlay, editor of Henderson's collected essays and letters, reminds us that we must account for his 'informal pedagogy' and his 'natural conviviality' if we are really to measure his cultural force.[2] The idea that

Henderson's very personality might have been instrumentalised in his cultural-political agenda is not as cynical as it might sound. While he was certainly deliberate in fostering the near folk-hero status he now holds, Henderson's own essays on folk culture and, specifically, questions of authorship and the anonym, make sense of this seemingly contradictory drive at once to be larger than life and to disappear into the currents of an unchecked and unmappable oral tradition.

This book opens with a short epigraph. Transcribed from Hamish Henderson's own rendition at a ceilidh in Kirknewton, West Lothian in 1959, it is the chorus to his party piece, 'Tail Toddle'.[3]

Tail toddle, tail toddle;
Tammie gars my tail toddle;
But-an-ben we diddle-doddle,
Tammy gars ma tail toddle.

This traditional bit of bawdry sung to a jaunty reel of the same name has a pedigree. It can be traced back through Robert Burns' *Merry Muses of Caledonia* (1799) and *The Scots Musical Museum* (1797), and its tune is found in several early eighteenth-century manuscripts. Alan Lomax, the great American folklorist, reportedly thought it was a piece of mouth music on first hearing: a song without words, just rhythmic, suggestive nonsense. But if you understand what it is for a 'tail' to 'toddle' or for a 'doddle' to be 'diddled', and think of the swinging fists of Henderson's performance, it is clear how this song might help us reflect on the most literal sense in which the folk culture to which it belongs is *reproduced*. The songs and stories that make up the tradition move through passing generations, and this intuitively enough implies a great deal of 'tails toddling' down through the centuries. This combination of the long historical view with a sense of living and material urgency is typical of Henderson's approach to poetry and song.

In another tribute to his friend, McNaughtan explained

that Henderson did not collect songs, stories and lore as a 'fly on the wall', anxious about contaminating the recording or the 'discoveries', as though they were pristine and unmediated. Instead, the roles of 'contributor' and 'reporter' were blurred and often inverted in these exchanges. They became ceilidhs and Henderson became a participant: laughing readily, joining in on choruses and carrying songs over from other singers where it seemed like the 'informant' or 'tradition bearer' in question might get a kick out of it.[4] In light of this feature of Henderson's practice as folklorist, this collection has been conceived as a ceilidh of sorts. As such, it seems appropriate to kick off with a turn by Henderson, in his voice, though not in his words. There are many ballads that might have served as a more sombre connection to the long-established traditions that Henderson collected, curated, wrote within and evangelised for: but the vim and vigour of 'Tail Toddle' is an appropriate preface for a body of work that holds to that same energy even through the horrors of the Second World War, which was the backdrop and context for most of these songs and poems.

The ceilidh also suits Henderson's oeuvre as an organising principle because it is intuitively democratic, collective but individuated, egalitarian, participatory and not overly concerned with intellectual property and authorial attribution. Like Hugh MacDiarmid, whom he both venerated and quarrelled with, Henderson drew from a diverse body of source materials in his creative verse: from the folk tradition, the literary canon, classical antiquity, newspapers and popular culture, and perhaps most prominently, from those social spheres he moved through, from the mess halls, battle fields and interrogation rooms of the War, through to the pubs, campfires, kitchens and seminar rooms of his time with the School of Scottish Studies. This collection of Henderson's poetry includes his songs. After all, he thought the distinction a 'false antithesis':

I think of myself as a lyric poet, a satiric poet, a ribald poet, at times a bawdy poet, who thinks not only in terms of words but in terms of music. If at the present moment lyricism, ribaldry, bawdry have been separated from music, it is a passing phenomenon. [5]

In this sense, this might have been a *Collected Songs* that included poetry (rather than the other way around) and in some ways that might have been more in keeping with Henderson's belief that the great 'rebel underground' of folk culture sustains and contains art and literature and is at once more permanent and more elusive and amorphous.

The title of this introduction, 'Rebel Ceilidh', is taken from a series of influential political folk song collections that appeared under the aegis of the Bo'ness Rebels Literary Society in the 1950s and 1960s. *The Rebels Ceilidh Song Book* series featured some of Henderson's most celebrated songs: 'The John Maclean March', 'The Taxi Driver's Cap', 'Ballad of the D-Day Dodgers' and 'Ballad of the Men of Knoydart'. William Kellock's preface describes the full gamut:

> . . . songs of the Popular Hero, and sometimes his girlfriend; Songs of the drama of resistance against impossible odds, Songs of Land-hungry Scots and Alien land-owners, Songs of revulsion against the hypocrites and rogues in our midst, Songs for the Glasgow Irish – both Orange and Green – , Songs of World War II, Songs echoing the heart-cry of farm and city workers for better conditions, Songs of joy, of sorrow, of Scotland's pride, of delight in our beautiful countryside, Sangs o' the Stane that's awa, and Songs on the popular reaction to the fact that London Officialdom just can't count . . . Songs of defiance and rebellion, of Heilans and Lallans all with a beauty of their own. Through it all runs the magic of the Gaeltacht. [6]

Though Henderson's songs and poems sit very comfortably in this loose constellation, this rebel rabble, the case for Henderson's personal-poetical-political ceilidh as *rebellious* can be made in more grounded and biographical terms.

Henderson held that his two most formative influences were his childhood exposure to the 'anonymous song-poetry of Scotland' and the 'comradely solidarity of the anti-fascist struggle'[7]. These twin poles of Henderson's worldview are both nationally and internationally oriented, even hyper-local and near-universal. It was not uncommon for Henderson to reflect on the unbounded qualities of the folk tradition as well as its foundation in interpersonal exchanges. Similarly, as I think his poetry shows, he was conscious of the grand historical and geo-political stakes of the fight against fascism, just as he was cognisant of the injustices of arbitrary authority in the classroom, barracks, city council, or literary establishment. Both of these motivating influences also invoke something of the broad sweep of masses of anonymous historical agents engaged in struggles that are difficult to imagine in their totality or their detail. The poetic voice that these experiences prompted is at once collectivist, radical, romantic, mythic, queer, viciously satirical, lustful, meditative and over-earnest. It reaches always for a way of reconciling the voice of the artist with those whom they presume to speak for, to, or out of; and it wrestles tirelessly with the weight of history and the immediacy of emancipatory struggle. The great majority of the animate voices behind these poems and songs do not speak or sing as though they live outside of those historical contingencies and everyday struggles. Even in the *Elegies for the Dead in Cyrenaica*, where Henderson allows himself some flights into classical myth and antiquity, these are shot through with the terrible, beautiful, grinding everydayness of the War in the North African desert. The intimate and complex interplay between the 'comradely solidarity of the anti-fascist struggle' and the 'anonymous song-poetry of Scotland' in Henderson's early life inspired the life-long search for a notion of the 'folk' (or, *volk*) that was not prescriptive or exclusionary. This 'folk' was to be immune to the reductionism and essentialism that gives fascism its blood and soil-origin myths. His was a New Left socialist humanist 'folk'.

Given Henderson's belief in the transhistorical reach of

'anon' over that of the named 'artist', there is a sense in which publishing all this material – juvenilia, high modernist war poetry, soldiers' songs, reconstituted ballads, bawdy limericks, translations, fragments from unpublished notebooks and rousing anthems – in a sequence and under his name betrays this vision of authorship and historical agency. However, it is hoped that by gathering such diverse work under 'Hamish Henderson' that name might become another conduit for what he termed 'Alias MacAlias': the local habitation and name given to those slippages between the largely anonymous tides of folk culture and the literary arts they carry to the shoreline.

EDITING HENDERSON

Hamish Henderson was a poet and a songwriter. But he was also a soldier, interrogator, translator, song collector, folklorist, folk revivalist, essayist, teacher, political activist, public intellectual, memoirist, and latterly, folk-hero. He was born in Blairgowrie on 11 November 1919, part of a generation born out of war and for war. Never having known his father, Henderson was orphaned at thirteen and spent four years at Ingleton House, a boys' home in Clapham, while attending Dulwich College in South London as a scholarship boy. During the lead-up to the Second World War, Henderson read modern languages at Downing College, Cambridge. And, having initially been refused, he signed up and served in the Pioneer Corps, building anti-tank defences on the Sussex Coast. He was later sequestered to the Intelligence Corps, with whom he saw through the North African and Italian Campaigns. After the War Henderson completed his degree at Cambridge, worked as District Secretary for the Workers' Educational Association in Northern Ireland and published *Ballads of World War II* (1947) and *Elegies for the Dead in Cyrenaica* (1948), winning the Somerset Maugham Award for the latter. Putting some of his prize money on a horse called 'Russian Hero' at the Grand National, Henderson trebled his money and set off to Italy to translate the great Marxist philosopher Antonio Gramsci's prison letters, *Lettere dal Carcere* (1947).

Shortly after returning to Scotland, Henderson began, in earnest, what would become his life's work: the collection of and advocacy for Scottish folk culture, working with celebrated collectors like Alan Lomax during his *Columbia World Library of Folk and Primitive Music* tour and with Calum Maclean (previously of the Irish Folklore Commission) at the nascent School of Scottish Studies at the University of Edinburgh in 1951–3. In 1953 Henderson 'discovered' the great ballad singer Jeannie Robertson; in the summer of 1955 he embarked on his first fieldwork among the travelling people in the Berryfields of Blair; and in 1957 he spent several months collecting from and living with the travellers of Caithness and Sutherland. Throughout these later decades, as Henderson's public profile grew, he continued to campaign and agitate in a range of struggles: for Scottish and international socialism, national independence, republicanism, gay rights and against imperialism, colonialism, racism, apartheid, Christian social conservatism, nuclear proliferation, the Poll Tax and wars of all stripes. He retired from the School in 1987 having built an international reputation as a folk scholar, collector and revivalist. He died on 9 March 2002 in Edinburgh.

Many of these biographical junctures can be traced in the work that follows. Explanatory and contextual notes have been included, almost entirely from Henderson himself (writing from various points, sometimes the time and place a given piece was written, sometimes decades later), with only a very few light-touch clarifications from myself as editor. I have included some lengthy passages of context for some poems where Henderson saw fit to do the same. The most prominent example of this is 'Glasclune and Drumlochy'. Here, Henderson provides a series of crosscutting contexts: the contemporary folk revival of the 1960s, lines from MacDiarmid that were its inspiration, local history, Henderson's own childhood memories, and late medieval chronicles. As noted above, this collection makes no hard or fast distinction between song and poetry. 'Glasclune and Drumlochy' features both spoken and sung elements. Where possible, the appropriate tunes for songs and song-poems have been listed under the title, in a format familiar to the work of generations of antiquarians, collectors and chapbook editors that have come before. There is no musical notation to accompany the lyrics here. Instead, readers are encouraged to look, with Henderson, past the 'false antithesis'. Where the tune is listed, please, look it up if you feel moved to do so. Where the lyrics, lineation, rhyme and metre seem to suggest a tune – as Henderson instructs his readers in a chapbook featuring one of his songs – please, make one up.

Where there are pieces that have appeared under multiple titles they have generally reverted to the original. Exceptions include those where the original title (as evidenced in archives) seems never to have made it to publication. Some pieces that are published here for the first time that did not have titles in the notebooks, manuscripts, or transcripts they come from have been given generic, descriptive titles.

The poems and songs that appear in this collection are, where possible, the first published versions. In some cases, I have been unable to track those down. In this case, the next earliest version is taken as the authoritative source text. Another exception to the first published version guideline is where works later appeared in a coherent collection or cycle. So, for instance, many parts of the *Elegies* were published prior to the complete cycle with Lehmann in 1948 – in magazines based in Cairo during the war and in *Penguin New Writing*, for instance – but the first full edition of 1948 is the copy text here. Where earliest published versions have inconsistencies, missing elements, or other seeming mistakes, I have consulted manuscripts in the archives and later published versions to help correct them. Where material has been lifted from handwritten manuscripts, every care has been taken to compare handwriting samples and establish accurate transcriptions (my thanks to the staff of the Centre for Research Collections at the University of Edinburgh for their help in this). The formatting of poems and songs is an especially slippery business, as so much of this depends on the diverse editorial policies and production conventions of numerous magazines, journals, chapbooks, broadsheets and anthologies. Where possible, these have been standardised according to the templates of first published versions.

In light of Henderson's admiration for the 'folk process', authorship is sometimes difficult to establish. However, the vast majority of poems and songs included here can be unambiguously attributed to Henderson and have been published previously under his name. The proportion of the writing credit that belongs to Henderson is, nevertheless, sometimes difficult to ascertain. Some songs, particularly those associated with the War, but also some of those that came out of the post-war folk revival in Scotland, are likely the product of multiple authors – and this is, of course, a feature that Henderson celebrated in the folk tradition. A fellow soldier-balladeer may have been the first and original author, but then the song is picked up across a company or even a division, before being edited, transcribed and reworked in several directions at once, and perhaps travelling further still. Many of the pieces published in Henderson's *Ballads of World War II* were written solely by Henderson and many at least partially. However, in the original publication we are only told that these songs had been *collected* by Hamish Henderson. Where there is evidence to suggest Henderson's hand in these songs, they have been included. Were it possible to trace every song and poem that Henderson had some hand in across his long life, I imagine this book would be at least three times its current length.

Previously unpublished pieces that are only to be found in Henderson's archive also present a problem in establishing authorship. There are, for instance, full boxes of largely unattributed bawdy material. Much of this is in Henderson's hand – some of it collected and compiled for his friend Gershon Legman as he put together *The Horn Book: Studies in Erotic Folklore and Bibliography* (1964). I have no doubt that Henderson's is the imagination behind lots of this, but I cannot fix the attribution for specific pieces. For a previously unpublished piece to be included here, it means I have found reference to Henderson as author by other commentators and/or very suggestive clues in the archives themselves (his having signed it, initialled it, or listed it among other works whose authorship has been established). I understand that this policy provides no concrete guarantee of authorship and it may transpire with further research that one or two of the pieces I have attributed were merely collected, transcribed and 're-worked' by Henderson. It is worth noting at this juncture that Henderson's estate, the Hamish Henderson Archive Trust and the University of Edinburgh Centre for Research Collections have made a wonderfully rich resource available to future scholars. I look forward to seeing what emerges as dozens of boxes of correspondence, notebooks, manuscripts, photographs, paraphernalia and miscellania are sifted through and studied by future scholars. Raymond Ross' *Hamish Henderson: Collected Poems and Songs* (2000), which is unfortunately now out of print, is an important precedent for this edition. This was the first attempt to collect and collate a substantial proportion of Henderson's creative work in verse, and many previously unpublished pieces found their first airing in that volume. While Ross had access to Henderson's papers, these were not sorted and catalogued as they are now. Furthermore, Ross collaborated with the man himself, who inevitably had final say on what was to be included.

This volume includes some unlikely material. For instance, two pieces in the section titled 'Journey to a Kingdom' are reported speech prose pieces ('Sergeant Major Prick Talking' and 'Mr Jimmy Balgowrie Talking'). I think they merit inclusion, not just because the characters they reveal sometimes have a poetic (sometimes grotesque, sometimes sublime) turn of phrase, but because these were included in a notebook full of Henderson's own poems and songs, numbered and in sequence. As such, I think they must have been intended to appear alongside these more conventionally poetic pieces.

This is not a collection without controversy, challenging language, or historically embedded worldviews. Henderson's earliest work emerges from the mid 1930s, and much of what follows might best be described as unsanitised and unauthorised barrack-room ballads. And there is more than a flavour of the ambient racism, orientalism, sexism and misogyny of those times in some pieces. Perhaps the most shocking example is the 'Ballad of King Faruk [sic] and Queen Farida'. Featured in *Ballads of World War II*, though missing from the *Collected Poems and Songs* (2000), it is a multi-authored piece just like 'Ballad of the D-Day Dodgers'. And, similarly, it seems likely that Henderson was not its originator.[8] Sung to the tune of the Egyptian National Anthem of the time, it is a vicious and scatological attack on the corruption of the Egyptian Royal House, the British Colonial administration that shored it up, and its seemingly loyal subjects. Farouk was known to have Axis sympathies though Egypt was officially neutral. Most Allied forces stationed in North Africa would have at one point or another moved through Cairo and would, reportedly, sing these alternative lyrics wherever the anthem played. It is a genuine piece of soldier balladry and it is not for nothing that Henderson explains in his foreword his refusal to 'insult [the] ballads by bowdlerising them'. As an editorial policy, it seems intuitive enough. But the picture changes slightly when we discover that Henderson himself wrote much of the material he claimed to have 'collected', again muddying the waters of authorship, editorship and curation. This particular song – *both* a critique of tyranny, empire, and corruption, *and* unapologetically racist and mysoginistic – stands to remind us of the apolitical nature of this 'folk process', just as amenable to the forces of reaction as it is to those of revolution, and sometimes, both.

THE COLLECTION

This collection of Henderson's poems is organised, as far as possible, according to Henderson's own design. It opens with a selection of pieces that first appeared in sequence together in a special issue of *Chapman* magazine, edited by Joy Hendry, in

1985. Intended to rectify the relative neglect Henderson's poetry had suffered by this time, it stands as a cross-section of his work: from a series of pre-war poems set in Cambridge, through to translations of C.P. Cavafy and Friedrich Hölderlin from the 1940s, to song-poems that grew out of the post-war folk revival. It is prefaced by a manifesto of sorts, titled 'Freedom Becomes People', written in Edinburgh near the midpoint of Henderson's long life, in 1968. This vision of a poetry that might 'become people', overcoming the isolation of the artist in the twentieth century, is a fitting opening to the collection that follows.[9]

The next two sections of this volume are taken up with Henderson's earliest stand-alone publications: *Ballads of World War II* (1947) – a subversive collection of soldiers' songs from both sides of the conflict – and *Elegies for the Dead in Cyrenaica* (1948) – a cycle of high modernist elegies thick with allusion, reported speech and the landscapes and imagery of Scottish history and classical antiquity. The next section, 'Journey to a Kingdom, and Other Poems', is a sequence of diverse pieces from the mid 1940s, but with corrections and amendments from later decades, as arranged by Henderson in a thick large-format notebook from the archives. It features vicious personal attacks; raucous wartime ballads; translations from Heinrich Heine, Rainer Maria Rilke, Louis Fürnberg and Corrado Govoni; and passages excised from the *Elegies*. The centre piece is the titular 'Journey to a Kingdom', which has appeared in some truncated and excerpted versions, but has not previously been published in as complete a form as it is here. It is a part-biographical, part-mythologised account of the poet as an Ossianic hero, constituted by the stories, song, lore and history of a people. Many later stand-alone pieces were first conceived as part of this dramatic sequence: 'Glasclune and Drumlochy', and 'My Way Home', for instance.

'"In the midst of things": More from the Anti-Fascist Struggle' gathers up the remainder of Henderson's wartime poetry and song, and organises it as far as possible in chronological order, according to its estimated date of composition. The title comes from the foreword to the *Elegies*. It features several previously unpublished works, including translations of four Italian Army songs, gathered while Henderson served as an interrogator in the Intelligence Corps; a translation of Friedrich Nietzsche into Scots; bawdy scrawled on the back of a postcard from Egypt; and two excerpts from a lost long poem titled 'The God from Greece'. After this follows a sequence of translations of modern Italian poetry – Eugenio Montale, Salvatore Quasimodo, Vincenzo Cardarelli and Dino Campana – titled *The Obscure Voice* (1994). To this I have added one further translation, of Alfonso Gatto's 'Oh, the Faded Churches'.

The next section, 'Products of the Folk Revival' deploys a description Henderson often used for his later songs, poems and song-poems. As a turn of phrase, it leaves space for individual authorship whilst giving the revival – and its diverse and decentred models of authorship (workshops, ceilidhs, folk clubs, sessions and field recordings) – its due. It is here that some of the most celebrated works can be found: 'The John Maclean March', 'Song of the Gillie More', 'The Flyting o' Life and Daith', 'Rivonia', and of course, 'The Freedom Come-All-Ye'.

In 'Unsorted Works' I have gathered previously unpublished pieces from the archive that are difficult to date with certainty, miscellaneous texts published in small magazines and other later volumes and fragments first unearthed by Henderson's biographer, Timothy Neat. In the final section, we turn to Henderson's earliest work. The juvenilia therein is mostly from the school literary magazine at Dulwich College, *The Alleynian*, which Henderson edited; and from the small, handmade and infrequent literary magazine, *Ingletonian Raconteur*, that he produced with friends at the boys' home where he lived in the late 1930s. These poems see Henderson playing with pseudonyms (Z. Marcas, Agrippa, Polonius, and even, Omega) and aping Ossianic epics, mock epics, and the Romantic lyric. This section also features several translations from the playful, satirical, metaphysical *fin de siècle* German poet, Christian Morgenstern – including some of the *Galgenlieder* [Gallows Songs] (1905).

There is no consistency in the quality of these collected songs and poems. Some are rightly celebrated and are faithfully reproduced here, some previously unpublished deserve admiration, and some are principally of interest for reasons other than aesthetic or artistic. This is especially true of some of the juvenilia and some of the previously unpublished songs, poems and fragments. At this juncture, I ask the reader to keep in mind that Henderson may never have intended much of this material for publication. As the most comprehensive collection of Henderson's song and poetry yet, this volume reveals a persistent and fascinating preoccupation with the social and political functions of song and poetry. When reading these poems, consider the variety of their contexts and imagined audiences. Some were likely never conceived to last much beyond the night they were written, or to stray further than the margins on which they were scrawled; others have been through countless drafts and are quite consciously arranged for posterity. For Henderson, the folk consciousness did not require everything to be polished, worn, and given over to the stubbornness of time. It meant, more often, that a song-poem might be conjured whole in its moment. To be passed over or forgotten or held in the memories of those who were there, who witnessed its context, its reason and its import. And that nuance, that capacity for the deep history of the oral tradition, and its most responsive and transient manifestations, is chewed over in every line of every lyric.

LEGACY

This is the first collection of Henderson's poetry and song since his death. In that time the neoliberal consensus that had held sway since the late 1970s has collapsed following the 2008 financial crash. Scotland has revisited its constitutional settlement in a referendum in 2014 and independence has emerged as a realistic and seemingly permanent fixture in the political discourse. Poverty has proliferated apace. Elites have consolidated their power. The UK has voted to leave the EU. And an already pervasive imperialist nostalgia and ethno-nationalism in Britain has intensified. New, popular, socialist and anti-capitalist movements have, however, also emerged. The spectre and reality of environmental catastrophe has bloomed in the public consciousness. And our understanding of capitalism's place as its root cause and its guarantor has deepened in concert.

Henderson wrote, sang and agitated for a Scottish socialist republic, for the dissolution of the British empire and for a reckoning with its legacies; and for a conception of human value incommensurable with exploitation under late capitalism. There are those who are already invested in Henderson's legacy, amongst them, those who knew him; those who sustain, promote, study, and teach Scottish folk culture in one form or another; and those who carry the political traditions to which he belonged. There are also those who have only become aware of him more recently, as a latter-day folk-hero, and an increasingly common touchstone in political and cultural discourse in Scotland.

In unpicking Henderson's legacy and its likely direction of movement, I have elsewhere argued for a reappraisal of his theories of art and society.[10] I think they are valuable not just for the high ideals they hold to, but because of the difficulties they reveal in holding to those ideals. Henderson conceived of folk culture as a kind of 'rebel underground', but worried that it would not survive the revolutionary moment he worked towards. Gramsci had taught him that folk culture was always subaltern and opposed to the hegemony of the day, whether that hegemony was in the interest of the capitalist classes or the workers. Henderson believed that the 'folk process' was boundless and untameable, and yet he tried to instrumentalise it, yoking it to a political agenda. He sought a poetry and a freedom that would 'become people', and yet in some of his most celebrated poetry – the *Elegies*, for instance – he indulged in meditations on the role of the artist. Like many in Scotland of his generation, and many since, he was a romantic nationalist and a socialist-internationalist. And though his effort to reconcile those positions was lifelong – sometimes sophisticated, sometimes crude – I would argue that it was never wholly achieved, at least, not to Henderson's satisfaction.[11]

To my mind, it is precisely these tensions and slippages that are among the most valuable legacies Henderson might leave us. The famous phrase of Romain Rolland's (a favourite of both Gramsci's and Henderson's) sums it up well: 'pessimism of the intellect, optimism of the will'. My own critical work on Henderson gives much of its attention over to the first half of this formula. I think it appropriate, however, that the collected poetry is oriented in favour of the latter.

Henderson's most celebrated works give us supreme examples of the 'optimism of the will' holding off the 'pessimism of the intellect' for just long enough to get out a song. Consider the final stanza of 'The Freedom Come-All-Ye':

So come all ye at hame wi freedom,
    Never heed whit the hoodies croak for doom;
In your hoose aa the bairns o Adam
    Can find breid, barley bree and painted room.
When Maclean meets wi's freens in Springburn
    Aa the roses an geans will turn tae bloom,
An a black boy frae yont Nyanga
    Dings the fell gallows o the burghers doon.

In this closing image of the song, which as a whole imagines a post-imperial, and therefore post-capitalist world, the former colonial subject is the one to strike the final blow against the machinery of the bourgeois state. This hopeful vision of a revolutionary moment of rupture, international yet imagined from and through Scotland, is the highest example of this earnestness and idealism that cuts through in Henderson's best songs and poems.

This optimism and sincerity was, however, to be sharpened against the 'hoodies [who] croak for doom'. In an undated notebook likely from the late 1940s, a young Henderson vents his impatience with the shallow thinking and self-serving cowardice that leads to the drift rightward with age:

> I am sick of hearing mercenary and cynical old men telling me, in order to excuse to themselves their complete moral impoverishment and surrender, that 'the high ideals of youth often have to yield, in this hard world, to less exalted but more practical policies.'
>
> This merely means that they have abdicated human dignity – that they are numbered for ever among the big battalions.
>
> Fuck them.[12]

One explanation I would hazard for the intractable optimism Henderson stokes against such 'mercenary' attitudes in poetry and song is that the folk-inspired model of authorship he most emulated precludes that unforgiving cynical edge (though it does not forsake satire). That angle of mind belongs squarely to the individual consciousness, and not to the communitarian element baked into the 'folk process'. In other words, the ideology of the 'big battalions' is unable to penetrate the balladeer's 'rebellious house' without conceding to some kind of radical, transformatory potential. With few exceptions, Henderson's poetry and song is generous and humane, concerned with empowering the dispossessed with a voice and with a sense of historical agency while directing righteous condemnation at the powerful. The personal philosophy that underpins this project finds its most abstracted and spiritual expression in another passage from an unpublished notebook, this time from 1959. In it, Henderson describes the antidote to his own 'fears and hatreds'. It is the kind of revelation on love that we might all be familiar with, one that is thoroughly emancipatory – for as long as it lasts. The scales seem to fall from our eyes. But, without wanting to sound like a cynical mercenary for the big battalions, its truth is much harder to hold to and to extrapolate. Perhaps the transient yet transcendental solidarity of the 'Rebel Celidh' is made of the same stuff. Either way, I think it is worth keeping in mind as we savour the collected poems of Hamish Henderson:

Love is the only god that I'll ever believe in. The books of the Holy Bible never say but one time just exactly what God is, and [in] those three little words it pours out a hundred million college educations, and says: God is love. And that is the only real definite answer to ten thousand wild queries and questions that I, my ownself, tossed at my Bible – I mean to say, that is the only real sensible easy honest warm plain quick and clear answer I found when I was too ready to throw so-called fearful cowardly thieving poisoning religion out of my back door. It was those three words that made not only religion but also several other sorts of superstitious fears and hatreds in me meet one very quick death. God is love. God is really love . . . love casts out hate. Love gets rid of all fears. Love washes all clean. Love forgives all debts. Love forgets all mistakes. Love overcomes all errors, and excuses and pardons and understands the key reason why the mistake, the error, the stumble was made. Love heals all. Love operates faster and surer than space or time or both. Love does not command you, order you, dictate to you. Love asks rather for you to tell its forces what to do, and where to go, and how to build up your planet here by the blueprint plan of your warmest heart's desire. Love can't operate on your behalf as long as your own sickly fear will not permit love to operate on your behalf. Your love commands must for ever be just exactly the direct opposite of war's crazy baseless hatreds. Peace, peace, and sweet sweet peace must be the song of thy tongue tip . . . Peace is love. Love is peace . . . Your love command must for all eternity be your peace command.[13]

Corey Gibson, 2019

1. Adam McNaughton, 'Hamish Henderson', *Tocher* 43, 1991, pp. 2–5.

2. *Alias MacAlias* (Polygon, 2004), p. xvii.

3. The audio can be accessed at the Tobar an Dualchais (Kist o Riches) site, where recordings from the School of Scottish Studies (University of Edinburgh), BBC Scotland, and the Canna Collection of the National Trust for Scotland are digitized. <http://www.tobarandualchais.co.uk>

4. Adam McNaughton, 'Hamish Henderson – Folk Hero', *Chapman* 42, Vol. 8, No. 5, Winter 1985 (pp. 22–9), p. 22.

5. *Alias MacAlias*, p. 451.

6. The Bo'ness Rebels Literary Society, *The Rebels Ceilidh Song Book* (1953), pp. 1–2.

7. *Alias MacAlias*, p. 454.

8. Henderson's biographer, Timothy Neat, suggests that this ballad did belong primarily to Henderson. See Timothy Neat, *The Making of the Poet (1919–1953)* Vol. 1, *Hamish Henderson: A Biography* (Birlinn, 2007), p. 95.

9. Duncan Glen first put the phrase together, 'Hamish Henderson: Poetry Becomes People', in *Selected Scottish and Other Essays* (Akros, 1999), pp. 60–8.

10. Corey Gibson, *The Voice of the People: Hamish Henderson and Scottish Cultural Politics* (Edinburgh University Press, 2015).

11. It is in this spirit that Henderson features in Cailean Gallagher, Rory Scothorne, and Amy Westwell's *Roch Winds: A Treacherous Guide to the State of Scotland* (Luath, 2015) – a refreshing defence of 'organised pessimism', Marxist critique, and persistent invective directed at Scottish politics in the twenty-first century.

12. Hamish Henderson Archive.

13. Hamish Henderson Archive and as cited by Timothy Neat, *Poetry Becomes People (1952–2002)* Vol. 2, *Hamish Henderson: A Biography* (Polygon, 2009), pp. 327–8.

THE POEMS
(Songs, and Song-poems)

FREEDOM BECOMES PEOPLE

Chapman 42 (1985)

FREEDOM BECOMES PEOPLE

Freedom, which has hitherto only become man here and there, must pass into the mass itself, into the lowest strata of society, and become people.

– Heinrich Heine

The idea of the poem:

What Heine says of freedom applies also to poetry. Poetry becomes everyone, and should *be* everyone. But in fact, at any rate in the Western World, it is only a few individuals here and there. Our most urgent task, as I see it, is to make poetry 'become people'.

How to start? First, we must not be ashamed to go to school with the folksingers – I mean the traditional singers – because in the past, and breenging into the present, it is their work which has 'become people'. I think Yeats was getting at the same thing when he wrote, not long before his death: 'Before the night ends you will meet the music. There is a singer, a piper and a drummer. I have picked them up here and there about the street, and I will teach them, if I live, the music of the beggar man, Homer's music.'

In Scotland we luckily have many forerunners in the practice of this strategy. Robert Burns set up a folksong-workshop of his own, and transformed, without seeming effort, our whole conception of the meaning of traditional art for society. Of course there were many minor writers who could not comprehend what he had done, and, trying to ape his excellence, landed in a slough. This spectacle must not be allowed to deter us. Hugh MacDiarmid, for all his great services, is totally at sea on this approach which throws into sharpest relief the reasons for the murderous alienation of the poet in contemporary society. We must abjure self-gratificatory elitism – and particularly the quasi-solipsistic elitism which one senses in much of MacDiarmid's work – and make poetry 'become people'.

My aim is to write a long, unified, connected poem which would argue these ideas. It would no longer (like my desert war *Elegies for the Dead in Cyrenaica*) be a poem of endurance, of in the main passive suffering; it would rather represent the moment of resolve, of transformation, of insurrection. It would leave the desert behind, and find a likelier landscape in Italy (or rather Italy and Scotland combined, as in 'Banks of Sicily'). It would celebrate the 'vulgar' Italy so hated and despised by its bourgeoisie – its bounding voracious popular culture, its secrecy, its turbulence, its victorious gaiety, and above all its unbeatable lust for life.

The central figure of the poem, however, would have to be the self-sacrificing political champion of the *rossa bandiera*: in this setting, Antonio Gramsci – like John Maclean, hero and martyr – whose ideas, articulated in the solitude of his prison cell, are still working away like yeast in the consciousness of the West. They provide us, for the first time, with an acute and visionary Marxist analysis of the potentialities of a genuine 'people's culture', and spell out, for up and coming generations, the modern implications of Heine's revolutionary humanism.

Edinburgh, 1968

Note: The translation of Heine comes from 'Lutezia', *Vermischte Schriften*, Vol. 3 (Hamburg, 1854): 'Die Freiheit, die bisher nur hier und da Mensch geworden, muß auch in die Massen selbst, in die untersten Schichten der Gesellschaft, übergehen und Volk werden.' I am grateful to Beth Potter for this reference. The lines from Yeats come from *The Death of Cuchulain*, a play Yeats completed from his death bed. [Editor]

[*Chapman* 42, Vol. 8, No. 5, Winter 1985. ed. by Joy Hendry]

PROLOGUE TO A POEM
(for Peter Duval Smith)

Jokers abounding
    who jouk the wuddy
and fly for refuge
    to the horned mystery,
I'll acclaim the accomplished
who wield two-edged history.

In council or ambush
    adroit and graceful
or for twenty years
    their barred sky scanning,
the apollyon abysses
with their bodies spanning,

they learn in due time
    to take the measure
of bumpkin death
    and his uncouth dalliance.
Ay, brought to the ring
they'll dance a galliard.

To jouk in the leeside
    of lumpen Jesus –
or walk alert
    without guide or ally
through glowering ravine
and too-silent valley:

Peter, facing that journey
    my wish is yours
to emerge with luck
    from history's ambuscades,
and surely to encompass
the crossed sword-blades.

Note: *jouk the wuddy* – 'dodge the gallows' – like Flattery in *The Three Estatis*, by sacrificing his comrades. I was also thinking of a sentence in the *Letters of Samuel Rutherford*: 'I thought it manhood to play the coward, and jouk in the lee-side of Christ.'

brought to the ring: Wallace's words to the Scottish army before the Battle of Stirling Bridge: 'I have brought you to the ring, now you must dance.'

[*New Statesman*, Vol. 45, Iss. 1151 (28 March 1953)]

PICTURE IN ST SEBALDUS CHURCH, NUREMBERG

There is the crowning with thorns
       and one stands under
our whole lives long

       Not like the spectators
they were here ahead of time
most half disillusioned already
maybe trying to summon up a little blood-lust.

       (here and there some genuine sadists)

          One sees them often
       they are always with us:
       trying to jump the queue
some intent on private concerns
       yawning from sheer satiety
              capering
       shooting out their lips

They are hurrying around
       seeing to their affairs
          loving
             begetting children

But with Christ one always feels:
this is something which takes much longer.

[*Chapman* 42, Vol. 8, No. 5, Winter 1985. ed. by Joy Hendry]

THE CELL (I)
(pro memoria Antonio Gramsci)

Evening is the worst
   years as long as hours

Night's better
   the heart's rebellious
arguing the toss

whether at a given point
   forestalling counter-measures
but allowing for come-backs
        one should have

        could have

And never wearies:
uphill and downhill
toting its cargo
question and anger
make-believe and memory
up along   down along

whether 'at a given point'
   the objective situation
weighed up, found wanting
      might not
        might not

And never wearies:
crossing and re-crossing that disputed land
sizing up the obstacles, the features,
   sly dips and hummocks

patches of good ongoing
     impassable depressions

pits holding history's refuse

       white earth
            not earth

blunt contours
hummocks of the dead –
and the heart joins issue
with the betrayed betrayers:
ballocky death's eager beavers
randy panders of the hoors of night
complaisant bawds of the nothing

(and this stagey night!
   all organdie and spangles
the sickly moon malingering

what was it Pound wrote
  moon my pin-up)

think and think long
mouths full of blood
limbs full of weals
eyes full of excrement

And never wearies
uphill and downhill
toting its cargo
question and anger
make-believe and memory
up along   down along

And never wearies
    til dawn, noon and evening
bring years as long as hours.

[*Lines Review*, No. 18, 1962]

BALLAD OF THE SIMETO
(for the Highland Division)

I

Armament, vehicles and bodies
make heavy cargo that is checked and away
        to Sicily, to Sicily
    over the dark moving waters.

The battalions came back
        to Sousse and Tunis
through the barrens, and the indifferent
        squatting villages.

Red flower in the cap
        of Arab fiesta!
and five-fold domes
        on the mosque of swords!

We snuffled and coughed
        through tourbillons of dust
and were homesick and wae
        for the streams of Europe.

But the others were blind
        to our alien trouble
they remembered the merciful
        the Lord of daybreak.

Launches put out
        from palm-fuzzed coastline
to where landing craft lay
        in the glittering sea-roads.

The ships revolved
            through horizons of dust –
then foregathered like revenants
            from the earth near fresh graves.

Och, our playboy Jocks
            cleaned machine-guns, and swore
in their pantagruelian
            language of Bothies

and they sang in their unkillable
            blustering songs,
ignoring the moon's
            contemptuous malice.

All the apprehensions, all the resolves and the terrors
and all the longings are up and away
            to Sicily, to Sicily
    over the dark moving waters.

II
Take me to see the vines
    take me to see the vines of Sicily
for my eyes out of the desert
    are moths singed on a candle.

Let me watch the lighthouse
    rise out of shore mist. Let me seek
on uplands the grey-silver
    elegy of olives.

Eating ripe blue figs
    in the lee of a dyke
I'll mind the quiet of the reef
    near the lonely cape-island

and by swerve of the pass
    climb the scooped beds of torrents
see grey churches like keeps
    on the terraced mountains.

The frontier of the trees
    is a pathway for goats
and convenient sanctuary
    of lascive Priapus.

Over gouged-out gorge
    are green pricks of the pines:
like strict alexandrines
    stand the vertical cypresses.

O, with prophetic grief
    mourn that village that clings
to the crags of the west
    a high gat-toothed eyrie

for the tension in the rocks
    before sunset will have formed
a landscape of unrest
    that anticipates terror.

A charge has been concealed
    in the sockets of these hills.
It explodes in the heat
    of July and howitzers.

We are caught in the millennial
    conflict of Sicily.
Look!   Bright shards of marble
    and the broken cornice.

III

On the plain of dry water-courses
    on the plain of harvest and death
the reek of cordite
    and the blazing stooks!

Like a lascar keeking
    through the green prickly pears
the livid moon kindled
    gunpowder of the dust

and whipped to white heat
    the highland battalions
who stormed, savaged and died
    across ditches called rivers.

Battle was joined
    for crossing of the Simeto.
Pain shuddered and shrieked
    through the night-long tumult.

But aloof from the rage
    of projectiles and armour
our titan dreamed on
    into brilliant morning,

and suspended from clouds
    was asleep like a bat
in the ocean of summer
    a blue leviathan.

Yes, Etna was symbol
    of the fury and agony.
His heart was smouldering
    with our human torment.

– Drink up your fill
    parched trough of the Simeto
for blood has streamed
    in too wanton libations

and tell of the hills
    hard-mastered Dittaino
where broke with our onslaught
    the German iron.

A bonnet on two sticks
    is tomb for the Gael.
A Sgiathanach mor, be making
    moan for Argyll.

IV
Through doon-tummelt clachans
    platoons of scozzesi
with tongues like fir-cones
    and eyes like hidalgos.

Panache of pipes
    and the tasselled swagger
doddle of drums
    and a jig for danger!

The balconies, fountains
    and children greet them:
the hungry, the hating
    the weak will know them.

Who lift in their arms
    the sloe-eyed bambini
whose laugh crosses gulfs
    of the lapse of language.

Their dirks in the wames
    of sniftering bonzes
the lusty Jocks
    who desire signorine

and castrating tyrants
    in search of vino
our drouthy billyboys
    in tartan filibegs!

 – Gay pierrot plumes
    on the horses greet them:
guitarists and hawkers
    and hoors will know them.

Where faro armed
    keeps an eye on the straits
they'll strip for a swim
    in debatable waters

then loose on Calabria
    the sons of the hounds
to exult in red fangs
    of vicious artillery.

Ballads and bullets
    and reels to fire them!
The hangmen, the hornies,
    the deils will fear them!

Note: This poem was spoken by James Grant as part of the Commentary for the television film, *The Dead, The Innocent*. 'Tomb for the Gael' – the accompaniment to 'Ballad of the Simeto', composed by Ken Hyder for his folk-jazz group Talisker – can be heard on their LP T*he White Light* (Vinyl Records, VS009).

['Ballad of Sicily', Nicholas Moore, ed., *New Poetry* 2 (London: Fortune Press, 1944)]

THE CELL (2)
(*pro memoria D.S. Mirsky*)

Memories of the undone
   on narrow shoulders lean their atrocious weight

history's refuse, mass graves, the murdered

   corpse obedience
       filing past
         (saluting even!)
           mattocks at the port

      Our own, the others,

And never wearies
     up along down along
the objective situation
     doom of the dialectic
weighed up and found wanting . . .

Think and think long
     on all that horror, history's saturnalia:
the torturous power-webs,
         the boxes, the alcoves,
the souped-up ideologies,
         the lying   memoranda,
the body count,
         the tenders for the crematoria,
the wire, the ramp,
         the unspeakable experiments

White earth   not earth

Evening
      the fall
            and despair gathers
like a stain on the white loin of the wall.

[*Chapman* 42, Vol. 8, No. 5, Winter 1985. ed. by Joy Hendry]

BROSNACHADH
(for the partisans of peace)

Break the iron man. Forsake
The arrogant robot's rule. Take
Peace down from the wall. Make
Waste the fenced citadel.

Tell of the rebellion's truth. Foretell
At street corners the awakening. Swell
The insurgent armies of knowledge.
Foregather on field and fell.

Face the imperative choice. Base
On huge rock your building. Trace
With strained bodies a new legend,
This human house greatly to grace.

Hold to the reasonable faith. Mould
Gently to mind's unreason. Shield
From calculated illusions our children
And bring them back to the hedge and field.

Know how the country lies. Throw
Your shadow across valleys. Blow
A summons over the whaup's mountain
To claw the gorging eagle low.

Above all be quick. Love
Never outlasts its moment. Prove
That with us is no 'villainy of hatred'
And history will uphold us – justify and forgive.

Note: *Brosnachadh* (Gaelic): incitement to rise

['Poem for Partisans', *Conflict*, May 1949]

GLASCLUNE AND DRUMLOCHY

From the crest of Cnoc-mahar
                    I look on the laigh:
On fat Strathmore, and its braw
    largesse of lochs;
Black Loch and White Loch, Fengus, Marlee, Clunie
    Where the bolstered curlers come . . .

But back I turn
northward, and stand at nightfall under Glasclune,
by the canyon cleft of the shaggy shabby Lornty
(the shaggy shabby, the dowdy, duddy Lornty)
that marked the clannish confine.

There were two castles,
two battled keeps, Drumlochy and Glasclune,
that kept a bloodfeud bienly on the boil.
They sat on their airse and they girned fell gyte at ither
('I'll paisley your fit', 'I'll Brackley your Invereye')
. . . and atween, the scrogs of the dowdy duddy Lornty.
Drumlochy's laird was a slew-eye dye-blue bloodhound
who fought, as his sires had fought, with steel (cold steel!)
and said the other mugger couldn't take it.
But Glasclune knew six of that: he was progressive,
and to be in tune with the times was all his rage.

Now, one day he went out and bought a cannon
(a quare old toy unknown to the lad next door):
with this he gave Drumlochy a thorough pasting –
dang doon his wall, gave his stately pile the shakes:
in fact, blockbust him quite.

'The moral of this,' said Glasclune, with 'ill-concealed'
hidalgo satisfaction, 'is that Right
– unready starter in the Donnybrook stakes –
must still rise early to possess the field.'

Now wae's me Glasclune
    Glasclune and Drumlochy
They bashed ither blue
    By the back side o' Knockie.

Drumlochy focht fair,
    But Glasclune the deceiver
Made free wi' a firewark
    Tae blaw up his neebor.

Then shame, black shame, ay, shame on the bluidy Blairs!
    Shame on the Blairs, an' sic wuddifu races.
They think nae sin
    when they put the boot in
In the eyes of all ceevilized folk tae disgrace us.

Ochone Drumlochy
    Glasclune and Drumlochy –
Twa herts on ae shiv

    An' a shitten larach.

Note: This poem is a product of the folk revival – it grew and developed as spoken (and sung) poetry at Edinburgh Festival readings in the mid sixties. These took place mainly at the original Traverse Theatre building in the Lawnmarket, and in the Crown Bar (now demolished) in Lothian Street, where the EU Folksong Society held its reunions.

Right from the earliest period of the 'People's Festivals' in Edinburgh (1951, 1952, 1953) poetry readings were an integral part of the growing 'folk scene'. The first of these were organised by the late Alan Riddell, founder of *Lines Review*. Excerpts from Hugh MacDiarmid's *A Drunk Man Looks at the Thistle* were given at the 1951 People's Festival ceilidh, between the rumbustious ballad singing of John Strachan and the vivacious piping sprees of John Burgess. Young poets were encouraged to contribute to these sessions. Much of the work of Alan Jackson and Tom Leonard has its ultimate origin in this particular creative blend of oral poetry and traditional Scottish song. Matt McGinn's work was also to a considerable extent inspired by it.

(Alan Jackson's version of 'The Minister to his Flock', an ancient orally transmitted joke which can be found in Richard M. Dorson's *Folk-Tales Told Around the World*, p. 43, was given by him at one of the Traverse ceilidhs in 1963.

> Aye, ye're enjoyin' yoursels noo wi' your drinkin' and your women and your women and your nights oot at the pictures, and never a thought given to the Word of God, and his great and terrible laws.
>
> But ye'll change your tune when ye're doon below in the fiery pit, and ye're burnin' and ye're sufferin', and ye'll cry: 'O Lord, Lord, we didna ken, we didna ken.' And the Lord in his infinite mercy will bend doon frae Heaven and say: 'Well, ye ken noo.'

This joke, which epitomises the barbaric black humour of Calvinist Scotland, was energetically applauded by a predominantly English youthful audience which assumed that it was by Alan himself – and indeed it fell naturally into place between such poems as 'Knox' and 'Lord Save us, it's the Minister'. It appears – attributed to anon – in Alan's collection *Well, Ye Ken Noo*, produced in Bristol with the aid of the CND duplicator i n 1963.)

'Glasclune in Drumlochy' is based on an historical tale which I heard in Glenshee, Perthshire, when I was a child. The subject matter is clearly blood-brother to many tales of Appalachian feuds. As children we naturally believed the story to be true, and indeed it may well be founded on fact.

The ruins of the castle of Glasclune are about three miles north-west of Blairgowrie, home of the 'Stewarts of Blair'. Glasclune is described in the *Ordnance Gazeteer of Scotland* (Edinburgh, 1884) as 'an ancient baronial fortalice on the border of Kinloch parish, Perthshire, crowning the steep bank of a ravine at the boundary with Blairgowrie parish. The stronghold of *the powerful family of Blair*, it was once a place of considerable strength, both natural and artificial, and is now represented by somewhat imposing ruins.' The ruins were decidedly less imposing when we played around them – and in them – as children in the 1920s, and since then decay has proceeded apace. Indeed, Glasclune has gradually become for me a symbol like the mill which Hugh MacDiarmid apostrophises in 'Depth and the Chthonian Image' (a long poem which is subtitled 'On looking at a ruined mill and thinking of the greatest'):

> The mills o' God grind sma', but they
> In you maun crumble imperceptibly tae.

However, Glasclune is still there: the keep of Drumlochy, which bore the brunt of cannon fire, had disappeared off the face of the earth. (The Mains of Drumlochy is a farm.)

Glasclune appears once – and dramatically – in medieval Scottish history. It was the scene of a battle in 1392, when one of the sons of Alexander Stewart – son of Robert II, and well known to history as 'The Wolf of Badenoch' – made an incursion into Stormont and the Braes of Angus. This foray was a kind of curtain raiser to the more famous Highland invasion of 1411, when Donald of the Isles, leading a large army of 'Katherans', was fought to a standstill at Harlaw. In Wynton's *Original Cronykil of Scotland* (Book IX, Chapter XIV) there is a graphic account in verse of the battle of Glasclune, including an episode in which a knight from Dundee called Sir Davy de Lyndesay speared a Highlander, and was himself wounded by the dying cateran who writhed up the spear-shaft and cut Lyndesay's boot and stirrup leather and his leg to the bone.

> Sua, on his hors he sittand than,
> Throw the body he strayk a man
> Wytht his spere down to the erde:
> That man hald fast his awyn swerd
> In tyl his neve, and wp thrawand
> He pressit hym, nocht again standand
> That he wes pressit to the erd,
> And wylh a swake thare off his swerd
> The sterap lethire and the bute
> Thre ply or foure, abone the fute
> He straik the Lyndesay to the bane.
> That man na straike gave bot that ane

For thaire he deit: yeit nevirtheles
That gude Lord thare wondil wes,
And had deit thare that day,
Had nochl his men had hym away
Agane his wil out of that pres.

Wynton locates the battle at 'Gaskclune', but this is certainly the Glasclune of my childhood, for it is referred to as being in the Stermond (Stormont); furthermore Bower, in the *Scotichronicon*, locates the conflict in 'Glenbrereth', probably Glen Brerachan, which is the same general area. Bower informs us that Walter Ogilvy, Sheriff of Angus, was slain *per Cateranos quorum caput fuit Duncanus Stewart filius domini Alexandri comitis de Buchan* (by caterans whose leader was Duncan Stewart, son of the lord Alexander, Earl of Buchan).

(It is interesting to note that it was a brother of this same Duncan, leader of the 'caterans', who as Earl of Mar led the Aberdeenshire army against Donald of the Isles at Harlaw. So much for the oversimplified view of these conflicts as being simply and solely between 'Highlands' and 'Lowlands'.)

My poem is, as it were, an echo of this old warfare, as it still remotely pulsates in the folk memory. The 'clannish confine' lies in jagged outline across Scottish history. I was thinking also, of course, of the millennial internecine conflict of humankind, which in our century bids fair to write *finis* to the 'haill clanjamfrie'. – The sung part of the poem is the ballad pastiche, and is in italics. The tune is a variant of 'Cam ye by Atholl'.

['Blairgowrie Bloodfeud', *Chapbook*, Vol. 5, No. 3, 25 Sept 1968 and Edward J. Cowan, ed., *The People's Past* (Polygon, 1980)]

FUCK ON, FUCK ON, VERLAINE, RIMBAUD

Mock on, Mock on, Voltaire, Rousseau;
      Mock on, Mock on, 'tis all in vain.
You throw the sand against the wind,
      And the wind blows it back again.

– William Blake

Fuck on, fuck on, Verlaine, Rimbaud;
      You blissful buggers, fuck again.
For on my heart, as on the town . . .
      The small drops of your poems rain.

– Hamish Henderson

[*Chapman* 42, Vol. 8, No. 5, Winter 1985. ed. by Joy Hendry]

AULDEARN

Amorous Hornie summons to his dance
long-buried elders sure of their election:
and glowering clouds advance.

The bells foretell no woodland resurrection
no sticky-eyed awakening among midges.
                    The unholy manse
slavers afternoon terrors under the hill.
While black man Clootie crawls among fern-scruffed ridges
the hairy witch sits on the window-sill.

[*Chapman* 42, Vol. 8, No. 5, Winter 1985. ed. by Joy Hendry]

INVEREY

Over the low hills gropes a muffled hate
With slouch hat over brow and eyes – dark eyes
Sightlessly cruel in the intricate ways.
No lightening soon or late.

[For Colin Roy]

[*Chapman* 42, Vol. 8, No. 5, Winter 1985. ed. by Joy Hendry]

OF EROS AND DUST: POEMS OF C.P. CAVAFY AND DINO CAMPANA
(for Hayden and Kate Murphy, married 11th July 1981)

These two translations together form a kind of Janus-poem. I seldom think of the one without thinking of the other. They seem to me to express the psychological ambivalence of much poetic creativity, the interpenetrative ambiguity of its very nature.

Androgyne mon amour

TOMB OF IASES
(C.P. Cavafy)

Iases lies here. In this city of cities
A boy renowned for his grace and beauty.
Scholars admired me, and also the people –
The rough and the ready.
   To all sorts I gave pleasure.

But because the world thought me Narcissus
 and Hermes,
Abuses consumed me and killed me.
    Passer-by,
If you are from Alexandria, you will not
 blame me.
You know the fury, the pace of our life here –
 What ardour there is, what extreme pleasure.

CHIMAERA

[Dino Campana]

Ignorant whether your pale face
appeared to me among rocks,
or if you were
a smile from unknown distances,
your bent ivory forehead gleaming,
young sister of the Gioconda:
or whether you were
the smile of extinguished springtimes,
mythical in your paleness,
O Queen, Queen of our adolescence:
but for your unknown poem
of voluptuousness and grief
marked by a line of blood
in the circle of your sinuous lips,
musical bloodless girl,
Queen of melody:
but for your virginal head
reclined, I, poet of the night,
kept vigil over the bright stars
in the oceans of the sky;
I, for your tender mystery,
I, for your silent blossoming.
Ignorant whether the pale fire
of your hair was the living
mark of your paleness,
or was a gentle vapour
drifting over my pain,
the smile of a face by night alone.
I gaze on the white rocks, the
          silent sources of the winds,
and the immobility of the firmament,
and the swollen rivers that flow
          lamenting

and the shadow of human labour
        stooped over the cold hills,
and again through limpid skies towards
        far-off free-coursing shadows
again
    and yet again
            I call you
                Chimaera

[*Broadsheet National Library* (1983)]

THREE POEMS OF HÖLDERLIN

THE APPLAUSE OF MEN
[Friedrich Hölderlin]

My heart is holier now, and filled with a lovelier life,
Since I have loved. Why then did you esteem me more
      When I was proud and wild,
        And free with most empty words?

Och, the mob is content with what counts in the market place,
And the god of the slave is the man who kicks him around.
      In the divine believe
      Only the gods themselves.

[*Chapman* 42, Vol. 8, No. 5, Winter 1985. ed. by Joy Hendry]

SOCRATES AND ALCIBIADES
[Friedrich Hölderlin]

'Why do you always pay, holiest Socrates,
Homage to this mere boy? Is there no higher thing?
    Why do you look on him
    With love, as if on the gods?'

He who has thought the most loves the fullest of life;
Highest virtue is prized by him who has looked on the world;
    And often the wisest turn
    To beauty in the end of all.

[*Chapman* 42, Vol. 8, No. 5, Winter 1985. ed. by Joy Hendry]

PATMOS I
[Friedrich Hölderlin]

Near is
And hard to catch hold of
God.
But where danger is, grows
That which can save.
In the darkness the eagles
Have habitation, and fearless
The Sons of the Alps cross
      over the abyss
On narrow flimsy bridges
Therefore,
Since around us are heaped
The peaks of time
      and our beloved
Live, near, yet
      far spent.

On the furthest of mountains,
Give to us holy water
O wings give us, that we may truly
Cross over and come back again.

I spoke, and was carried away
Quicker than my thought, and further
Than I had looked to go, by a familiar
From my own house. In twilight
Lay the shadowy woods, and the nostalgic
Streams of my homeland. And no longer
Knew I countries . . .

But there swell around Asia's gates,
Drawn backwards and forwards
Over the uncertain plain of the sea

Enough of shadeless streets,
Yet the sailor knows the islands.
And as I heard
That one of the nearby isles
Was Patmos,
I longed greatly
To go thither, and there
To visit the dark grotto. For not
Like Cyprus, rich in fountains
Or another among them
Lives Patmos in honour.

Yet hospitable is she
In her poorer house,
And if a stranger
By shipwreck comes, or lamenting
Lost home or a friend departed,
Then she rejoices, and her children,
The voices of the parched grove
And the noises where the sand
Falls, and the field's surface
Is divided, they hear him
And lovingly
They echo the stranger's grief. So welcomed
She formerly the beloved of God,
The seer who in his blessed youth had
Walked with the Son
Of the Highest, from him inseparable.
For He, the God of Thunder, loved
                         his disciple's
Simplicity, and the observant man
Saw in its fullness the face of the god,
When, at the mystery of the vine, they
Sat together, at the hour of the Passover,
And the Lord, knowing in his soul calmly
That Death was near, spoke to them

And his final love – for never
Enough of words had he, to speak of
                    goodness
And to lighten, when he saves it
The anger of the world.
For all things are good. So he
                Died. Much could
Be said of this. And as he rose in
                Triumph
His friends watched him at the end,
                then also . . .

Note: This poem, which I consider one of the finest in German literature, had a great effect on me when I first read it in 1938, for I was then troubled by a conflict of mythologies. Such conflicts are in danger of making you mad, but they generate poetry.

[*Orientations*, May 1942 and Hamish Henderson Archive]

PATMOS II
[Friedrich Hölderlin]

And if the immortals still,
As I believe, love me,
How much more then
Must they love you; for this I know,
That the will of the eternal father
      is of account to you.
Silent his sign
In the thundering sky. And One stands under
His whole life long. For Christ lives still.
And the heroes that are his sons
Have all come, and holy writings
From him, and the deeds on earth
Explain the lightning to this day.
They run an unceasing race. But
        he is present in it. For his works
Are all known to him from before.

Too long, too long already
Is the honour of the immortals invisible.
For almost they must guide
Our fingers, and shamefully
With violence are our hearts torn from us.
For the immortals must have a sacrifice
Every one. And if ever it was grudged,
Then evil came.
We have given worship to our mother the earth,
And lately we gave up worship to the sun's light
In our ignorance, but the Father rules
Over all, and he most loves
That the abiding letter
Be written down, and what is lasting
Clearly pointed to.
        Thus spake German song.

Note: In this poem, one of the greatest in the German language, can be seen in its highest expression the sensitive and imaginative genius of the German people – a people whose great traditions have been debauched by an abominable tyranny. [1941]

[*Chapman* 42, Vol. 8, No. 5, Winter 1985. ed. by Joy Hendry]

EPISTLE TO MARY

'Epistle to Mary' was written (to Mary Macdonald, wife of the late Fionn MacColla) on receiving an invite to the 21st birthday party of the School of Scottish Studies in 1972. Mary had invited Robert Garioch – then working for the Dictionary of the Older Scottish Tongue as a 'lexicographer's orra'man' (his own expression) – to compose the invite, which was couched in the following terms:

17th January, 1972.

Dear Sir or Madam, as the case may be,
We request the pleisor of yir companee
At the
              21st BIRTHDAY PAIRTY
                  of the School of Scottish Studies,
DRESS INFORMAL, i.e. the usual orra duddies,
           ON THE 29TH JANUAR AT 7PM.
Sae ye can easy get there efter the gemm.
We'd better tell ye, no to be mair circumstantial,
That ye'll maist likely get something gey substantial,
For, be it said, the Schule of Scottish Studies
Kens mair about cookery than jist hou to byle tatties and haddies.
There's to be Haggis and Clapshot, Stapag, and parritch caad
    Brochan,
That thick, ye'll maybe can tak some o't hame in yir spleughan.
Atholl Brose, very nice, to make yir thochts mair effervescent,
Frae a genuine Atholl recipe – we mean the Forest, no the
    Crescent.
            R.S.V.P. BY THURSDAY, 27TH JAN.
Or maybe sometime suiner, if ye can.
And if ye come to
          27 GEORGE SQUARE, EDINBURGH
            frae aa the airts,
Ye'll find parking space fir yir cawrs, caravans and cairts
Richt forenenst the Schule of Scottish Studies,
And, in the Meedies, guid grazing fir yir cuddies.

The invite was, of course, unsigned, and as Mary Macdonald was chiefly responsible (along with the then secretary, Mrs Anna Belfourd) for arranging the culinary attractions listed, my reply was sent to her.

'Epistle to Mary'
(on receiving an invite to cross the Meedie.)

Dear Mary, ye'll hae heard the baur
A news-hound peddled near and faur
That hobnailed tramplins in the glaur
      Or punch-ups bluidy
Await the hardy souls wha daur
      Tae cross the Meedie!

A thowless game they skellums play
Wha manufacture scares for pay.
Guid kens the donnert things they'll say
      Tae pad an article,
Although it's plain o' sense they've nae
      The sma'est particle.

A hangin' Judge, by name MacQueen,
In Twenty-Eicht dwalt snod and bien.
Frae's wark he'd wander hame his leen
      Nor mak it speedy!
And whiles, tae ceilidh on a freen,
      He'd cross the Meedie.

What he could dae, and freely did,
When croods were yellin' for his bluid,
We honest fowk, for Scotland's guid
      (And oor ane tummies)
Will shairly dae, seein' we are bid,
      And pree yir yummies!

Though noddies gether in the mirk
Wi' gullie knives, tae dae a Burke;
Thouh a' Young Niddrie Terrors lurk
                Wi' een sae beady –
For them I winna gie a firk.
                I'll cross the Meedie!

We'll step it oot tae George's Square
And sample a' this 'hamely fare' –
Although exotic's mebbe mair
                The word I'm seekin'!
We'll pree the fleshpots, while they're there,
                And never weaken.

Though in oor path the lichtnins flash,
Or Orange bowsies sing the Sash,
We'll run the risk o' bein' ca'd rash
                – Or just plain greedy!
Wi'oot a doot we'll hae a bash.
                We'll cross the Meedie.

George's Square and the Meadow (in the singular) are the original – 18th-century – appellations. Robert MacQueen (better known as Lord Braxfield) lived at No. 28 during the great Sedition Trials of the 1790s. The present [in 1970s] Director of the School is Professor John MacQueen, and another MacQueen, Neil, is one of the technicians. In 1971/2 there was a scare, blown up out of all proportions by the newspapers, about muggings on the Meadows; hence the references to 'Young Niddrie Terrors', etc.

[*Chapman* 42, Vol. 8, No. 5, Winter 1985. ed. by Joy Hendry]

TO STUART – ON HIS LEAVING FOR JAMAICA

Gae fetch tae us twa bolls o' malt,
The best that Sandy's can provide us,
And syne anither twa lay doon
As sune's we get the first inside us.
Scotch drink and sang hae aye been fieres;
Whisky and Stuart gang thegither:
Sae when the partin' gless we've drained,
We'll no' be sweir tae hae anither!

The boat that rocks aside the pier
Will rock some mair when ye are on it.
Its deck will tilt o' Stuart's bonnet.
On Kingston strand the dusky dames
For sportive romps will soon prepare 'em;
Spyin' the shape o' things to come,
They'll soon resolve tae grin an' bear 'em.

Stuart, atween us braid maun roll
'A waste of seas' – a vale o' water.
(What signifies a waste o' seas?
A waste o' beer's anither maitter.)
But, in their cups, in auld Bell's bar,
The Legion o' the Damned will mind ye;
And howp that, noo and then, ye'll toast
The gallus crew ye've left behind ye.

Note: In March 1972, the poet and novelist Stuart MacGregor left for
Jamaica, where he was to take up a temporary medical post. As a student at
Edinburgh University in the 50s, Stuart had been a vital driving force in the
early days of the Scottish Folk Revival, and was the effective founder of EU
Folk Song Society; one of his songs ('Sandy Bell's Man') is still popular. He
was tragically killed in a car crash less than a year after arriving in Jamaica.
The song is, of course, a Burns pastiche, to the tune of 'The Silver Tassie'.

[*Chapman* 42, Vol. 8, No. 5, Winter 1985. ed. by Joy Hendry]

FOUR CAMBRIDGE POEMS

BRIDGE ST BLUES

(Given its premiere in the clubrooms of the Cambridge University Socialist Club in May 1939, to the jazz guitar accompaniment of Peter Paston Brown)

I was reading Malherbe
       and your smile came into my mind,
So I left Malherbe
       and his starchy verse behind.
I put on a mac; then I paused
          and I grinned with pain.
From one end of this town to the other
          I walked in the rain.
I knew what I'd say when I found you.
          It's quite absurd.
You smiled, and I stammered,
          a totally different word.

This is the road
       now blocked
          with a rickle of rubble
Old ballads and bones
       piled high
          in one heap of trouble.
To Bablyon's walls
       I walk
          in my pea-packed sandals.
Going through to the end
       seems hardly
          worth the candle.

A sabre you need
         and a great big blubbery glove
To cut your way through the undergrowth
To cut your way through the undergrowth of love.

[*Chapman* 42, Vol. 8, No. 5, Winter 1985. ed. by Joy Hendry]

LOST LOVE BLUES
(1939)

The island that answered our call lies under the waves.
The stubble is bare where once were fulsome sheaves.
Now pride tries building his ineffectual rampart.

Great death is free with his non-committed comfort.
He sits in the skull and plays his mandoline.
He plucks away at one numb and deadened string.

[*Chapman* 42, Vol. 8, No. 5, Winter 1985. ed. by Joy Hendry]

X STILL = 0
(written during the air raid on Cambridge, June 13/14, 1940)

There are planes in the sky, but a healthy distance away.
Every now and again I can hear the muffled humming,
and think how the searchlight's fingers stroke the sky.

I am sure that a bomb dropped then – may be others coming? –
for this frail place shook with a faint but perceptible tremor.
(Like Jericho's walls it'd fall if a bomb dropped nearer).

The song that the sirens sing makes the night go gay,
makes the fenlands bright with a bloody illumination
of blazing bomber – (in dogfight had its day).

and we've had it, and all, this poor bloody generation. Still,
for 'history' the verdict is easy. Poor mugs, they bought
a pig in the same old poke. X still equals nought.

Note: Expecting my call-up papers daily, I stayed on in my Cambridge
digs at 6 Round Church St, after the end of the summer term of 1940. I
was sitting reading Cyril Connolly's *Enemies of Promise* one night in June
when the warning sirens sounded, the ack:ack guns opened up – and the
unmistakable throbbing sound of enemy aircraft was heard overhead. The
bombs I heard – the first to fall on Cambridge – fell in the area of the railway
station.

A rumour circulated that Baldur von Schirach, Hitler's youth leader,
had said that bombs on Oxford and Cambridge would bring Britain to
her knees. Oddly enough, this, and the equally preposterous rumour that
Hitler had only one testicle, turned out to be true.

[*Chapman* 42, Vol. 8, No. 5, Winter 1985. ed. by Joy Hendry]

HIGH HEDGES
(Hardwicke, Cambridge, June, 1940)

'I am hoping these hollyhocks
will grow higher before the summer is over.
Last year – can you guess how high they were?
They overtopped the thatch of the cottage.'

Spruce white-walled cottage with its hollyhocks,
and its orange lilies for Ireland;
the parlour always warm, and Palm Sunday crosses
twined in the pictures of Madonna and Redeemer.

'There are still high hedges, look – rare now in England.
I am glad to live here, as we still have these hedges . . .
Were you out on the river since you last came to see me?
I really can't remember such a splendid summer.

'D'you know what I'll do if the planes pay us a visit?
If Hitler gives me time, I shall run down the path
and lie down in the ditch. I believe you are safe there,
you are safe in the ditch if you stay there, so they tell me.

'Look at this rug. It's from Kesh in Fermanagh.
My mother used to say it was older than the Union.
When you ride down the road, looking so grand on your horses,
I shall come to the gate and watch.'

Frail old lady with eyes like a starling,
bird-like old teacher in the Cross's comfort,
Who often told the Board school girls of Jesus
and are now unafraid with him as saviour.

'They change so much, they are hard to recognise.
I always try, forgetting so hurts them.
They show me their first-born, and other lovely things.
Yes, I have many children.'

She speaks from a world I am helping to deforest,
Where our job is to level and to clear, for the building
of our human house on the level, in the sunlight.
We have boasted our Universe ghostless and godless.

So what? – I'll not slacken in the necessary labour
with handsaw and axe, with trowel and with mortar,
but must freely acknowledge Christ to live among gods
while that white cottage can boast its high hedges.

[*Chapman* 42, Vol. 8, No. 5, Winter 1985. ed. by Joy Hendry]

TO HUGH MacDIARMID ON READING
LUCKY POET

Ich bin dir wohl ein Rätsel?
So tröste dich – Gott ist es mir.

        – Heinrich von Kleist

You admit acting out a superb comedy
Before the Scots burghers, that blubbing company.
Panache weel cockit, sharp sgian in stocking,
But conscious of something (your fighting tail?) lacking,
You strut and you gaelivant before them.
Powerless with your piping fancies to fire them
You spurn their blind-alley ways
        their shuttered faces
And gar your muse kick high her paces.

If there were just two choices ...
      mine would be yours, MacDiarmid!

You tilt against 'Englishism': the words sleek and slick,
The smoothing fingers that add trick to trick;
The admirable refusal to be moved unduly
By the screaming pipe. The desire to speak truly
With a middle voice; the acceptance of protection;
The scorn for enthusiasm, that crude infection ...

That's all very well.
      But what about 'Scotchiness',
This awful dingy bleary blotchiness?
You list 'Anglophobia' as your recreation,
But it's Scotland that's driven you to ruination!
Why not admit it? The meanness, the rancour,
The philistine baseness, the divisive canker,
The sly Susanna's elder-ism, McGrundyish muck-raking,
Are maladies of Scottish, not of English making.

If we think all our ills come from 'ower the Border'
We'll never, but never, march ahead 'in guid order'.

I try to make sense of your tortured logomachy,
For there *is* a sense in which England's our enemy.
Though to her we seem boorish
                              or just plain funny
She can buy the 'wee Jocks', and get value for money.
Although 'let us prey' is the text the Scots glory in
(It's the paper we'll wrap up our blood-boltered story in)
The licence to roam through the world for plunder
We received on a plate from the big boss down under.

And does *that* let us out? No, not on your life, sir!
We've fought England's battles to the dreepin' knife, sir!
And after the gougings, the thumpings, the kickings,
We've never been averse to the jackal's pickings.
And, when we're gabbing, and have a drink to spout with,
'Here's tae us, wha's like us' is the toast we come out with.
I know you've been living in the isles like a hermit,
But you know bloody well this is true, MacDiarmid!

And have said it all before. So we're back where we started.
Yes, you've said it all before.
                              And are broken-hearted?
You've shown up the shame of our idiot Burns Suppers
Which – when poetry's skint, stony broke, on its uppers –
Spend more on a night of befuddled bard-buggering
Than a poet can earn in a year's hugger-muggering.
The couthy Wee McGreegors can still goad you to fury.
You tear coloured strips off their twee tasselled toories.
And as for our brass-hats, and their anti-Red slaverings,
You've done more than most to put paid to their haverings.
So why all this other junk? Man, I don't get it.
This problem would soon lay me low – if I let it.
Amidst all the posturings, tantrums and rages,

Is there something you haven't said, in all these pages?
Is there some secret room, and you don't want to show it?
Did an unlucky break befall the Lucky Poet?

Just what *do* you stand for, MacDiarmid?
                                    I'm still not certain.
I don' wanna step behin' dat tartan curtain . . .

Merano
September–October, 1945

[Duncan Glen, ed. *Poems Addressed to Hugh MacDiarmid* (Akros, 1967)]

SO LONG

(Re-crossing the Sollum frontier into Egypt, 22nd May, 1943, in a lorry carrying captured enemy equipment.)

To the war in Africa that's over – goodnight.
    To thousands of assorted vehicles, in every stage of
decomposition,
    littering the desert from here to Tunis – goodnight.
To thousands of guns and armoured fighting vehicles
    brewed up, blackened and charred
from Alamein to here, from here to Tunis – goodnight.
To thousands of crosses of every shape and pattern,
        alone or in little huddles, under which the unlucky
bastards lie –
        goodnight.

        Horse-shoe curve of the bay
        clean razor-edge of the escarpment,
        tonight it's the sunset only that's blooding you.

Halfaya and Sollum: I think that at long last
    we can promise you a little quiet.

So long. I hope I won't be seeing you.

To the sodding desert – you know what you can do with yourself.

To the African deadland – God help you – and goodnight.

[Victor Selwyn, ed., *From Oasis into Italy* (Shepheard-Walwyn, 1983)]

BALLADS OF WORLD WAR II
COLLECTED FOR THE
LILI MARLEEN CLUB
OF GLASGOW (1947)

Collected by Seamus Mór Maceanrug
(Hamish Henderson)

Issued by
THE LILI MARLEEN CLUB OF GLASGOW
To Members Only

(Printed by the Caledonian Press, 793 Argyle Street, Glasgow. C.3.)

Promotional Blurb:

We rejoice to announce to all present and prospective members of
the Lili Marleen Club that Hamish Henderson's collection of War
Balladry is now ready.

This collection, which can truthfully be called unique, is already
celebrated among Jocks and swaddies from Alamein to Anniesland.
To acquire it, the collector (who is also a creator) has wandered
further than the Brothers Grimm, drunk harder than the Bishop
Percy and told more ingenious tales than Ossian MacPherson. It
now appears in print for the first time.

Copies are available only to Members of the Lili Marleen Club.
The Membership Fee for the Club is FIVE SHILLINGS each.
No copies will be available to the public, and no review copies will
be distributed.

FOREWORD (BY SEAMUS MÓR):

The balladry of World War II developed in conditions quite unlike
those of previous major wars. It grew up under the shadow of – and
often in virtual conflict with – the official or commercial radio of
the combatant nations.

The state radio in time of war does not encourage dissidence
from the straight patriotic line. It regards most expressions of the
human reaction to soldiering as a drag on the national war effort.

Accordingly it does not allot a great deal of time to the genuine Army ballad.

For the Army balladeer comes of a rebellious house. His characteristic tone is one of cynicism. The aims of his government and the military virtue of his comrades are alike target for unsparing (and usually obscene) comment. Shakespeare, who ran God close in the matter of creation, knew him well and called him Thersites.

Of course, the state radio was wrong about the morale effect of the Army ballad, as about nearly everything else. Perhaps the most cynical ballads of the war were produced by German troops in Italy at the same time that they were fighting an exemplary rearguard action right up the peninsula.

The only ballad I have included which was also a radio hit is 'Lili Marlene'. This song, with its haunting tune, gained a currency among both Axis and Allied troops in the desert which entitles it to inclusion. It also sprouted variants and parodies galore in the authentic ballad manner.

Needless to say I have refused to insult these ballads by bowdlerising them.

[*Ballads of World War II* (1947)]

THE BALLAD OF WADI MAKTILLA

(Describing a somewhat abortive raid by the 2nd Camerons on an Iti outpost about 12 miles East of Sidi Barrani – 1940)

(Tune: 'Villikens and His Dinah', alias 'The Ould Orange Flute')

Now here is my story, it happened one night,
How the Seventy Ninth they went into a fight.
They were carried in lorries over the bump, rock and cranny –
Many arses felt sore on that road to Barrani!

   Chorus:
      What the hell
      'S all the fuss?
    O wouldn't you, wouldn't you like to be us?

Then we hoofed it along, lads, to Musso's armed villa
 – A stronghold it was, and named Wadi Maktilla.
We tip-toed along, as we came near our mark –
Not a sound could be heard, all was silent and dark.

Then suddenly the Itis let go all they had;
It's a bloody good job that their aiming was bad.
We got down on the ground and lay as if dead,
While the shells and the whizzbangs flew over our head.

Many lads prayed to heaven, which before they'd forsaken,
And they thought that they'd eaten their last of tinned bacon.
But the Itis felt worse as they lay in the sangars,
And their guns roared in fear, for it wasn't in anger.

There were Libyans against us, both filthy and black
But we yelled *Cabar Feidh!* as we pressed the attack.
Then the Wops shouted 'Bruno' on whom they are nuts,
But they got for their pains our cold steel in their guts.

Now most of the Camerons, there isn't a doubt,
Got corns on their knees from this crawling about.
But the blokes that lay flat brought us many a grin,
For the most of their bellies were all hackit-skin.

When at last we emerged from that *un*healthy zone,
We got on the trucks and we headed for home.
You can say what you like, you have plenty of scope,
Do you think we enjoyed it? My Christ! What a hope!

[*Ballads of World War II* (1947)]

BALLAD OF THE D-DAY DODGERS

(A rumour started in Italy that Lady Astor had referred to the boys of the C.M.F. [Central Mediterranean Force] as D-Day dodgers.)

(Tune: 'Lili Marlene')

We're the D-Day Dodgers, out in Italy –
Always on the vino, always on the spree.
>8th Army scroungers and their tanks
>We live in Rome – among the Yanks.
We are the D-Day Dodgers, way out in Italy.

We landed at Salerno, a holiday with pay;
The Jerries brought the bands out to greet us on the way . . .
>Showed us the sights and gave us tea.
>We all sang songs – the beer was free,
To welcome D-Day Dodgers to sunny Italy.

Naples and Cassino were taken in our stride,
We didn't go to fight there – we went there for the ride.
>Anzio and Sangro were just names,
>We only went to look for dames –
The artful D-Day Dodgers, way out in Italy.

On the way to Florence we had a lovely time.
We ran a bus to Rimini right through the Gothic Line.
>Soon to Bologna we will go
>And after that we'll cross the Po.
We'll still be D-Day dodging, way out in Italy.

Once we heard a rumour that we were going home,
Back to dear old Blighty – never more to roam.
>Then someone said: 'In France you'll fight!'
>We said: 'No fear – we'll just sit tight!'
(The windy D-Day Dodgers, way out in Italy).

We hope the Second Army will soon get home on leave;
After six month's service it's time for their reprieve.
>   But we can carry on out here
>   Another two or three more years –
Contented D-Day Dodgers to stay in Italy.

Dear Lady Astor, you think you know a lot,
Standing on a platform and talking tommy-rot.
>   You, England's sweetheart and its pride,
>   We think your mouth's too bleeding wide
That's from your D-Day Dodgers – in far off Italy.

Look around the mountains, in the mud and rain –
You'll find the scattered crosses – (there's some which have no
    name).
>   Heartbreak and toil and suffering gone,
>   The boys beneath them slumber on.
Those are the D-Day Dodgers who'll stay in Italy.

Note: This is my version of a Ballad which was circulating among the '8th Army scroungers' at the time. [Henderson]

Roy Palmer identifies the original version as having been written by Harry Pynn of the Tank Rescue Section, 19th Army Fire Brigade in November 1944, *What a Loverly War!: British Soldiers' Songs from the Boer War to the Present Day* (1990), pp. 177–81. Though it is difficult to identify the first, it is clear that Henderson's is one among many. [Editor]

[*Ballads of World War II* (1947)]

BALLAD OF THE BIG NOBS
(Sung by the 8th Army, September 1942)

There's Wavell, there's Wavell
And he contemplates his navel
   But he *was* some fuckin' use
                to the Eighth Ar-mee.

There's the Auk, there's the Auk
And although some bastards talk
   Och, he didn't do so bad
                for the Eighth Ar-mee.

There's Ritchie, there's Ritchie
And his arse is feeling itchie
   For he wasn't much fuckin' use
                to the Eighth Ar-mee.

There's Stalin, there's Stalin
That the worker's got a pal in,
   And he *is* some fuckin' use
                to the Eighth Ar-mee.

There's Winston, there's Winston
And he ought to be in Princetown
   But he is some fuckin' use
                to the Eighth Ar-mee.

O we had two Heilan laddies –
Now we've got two Irish paddies.
   Let's hope they're some fuckin' use
                to the Eighth Ar-mee.

[*Ballads of World War II* (1947)]

THE ROADS TO ROME

(Tune: 'The Roads to Rome' – A pipe march composed by Pipe
Major MacConnochie of the Royal Scottish Fusiliers)

The Caesars were a randy crew –
   Ye ken the story o'm.
They tauld this tale tae Goy and Jew
   That a' roads lead tae Rome.

But for a' the haverin o' the runts,
   An' the bletherin blarney o',
Ye heard ae sang frae a' oor fronts:
There's nae road leads tae Rome.

 – But noo ye'll hear the pipers play
   Afore St Peter's Dome
And Scotland tells the world today
   That *oor* road led tae Rome.

[*Ballads of World War II* (1947)]

BALLAD OF THE TAXI DRIVER'S CAP
(to a refrain by Maurice James Craig)

(Tune: 'The Lincolnshire Poacher' or 'MacNamara's Band')

O Hitler's a non-smoker
and Churchill smokes cigars
and they're both as keen as mustard
on imperialistic wars.
But your uncle Joe's a worker
and a very decent chap
because he smokes a pipe and wears
a taxi-driver's cap.

When Rommel got to Alamein
and shook the British line
the whole of Cairo beat it to
the land of Palestine.
But Moscow's never raised a yell
and never had a flap
because Joe smokes a pipe and wears
a taxi-driver's cap.

That Hitler's armies can't be beat
is just a lot of cock,
for Marshal Timoshenko's boys
are racing through von Bock,
the Fuehrer makes the bloomers
and his Marshals take the rap;
meanwhile Joe smokes a pipe and wears
a taxi-driver's cap.

The Fascist drive on Stalingrad
is going mighty slow.
They've got a room in Number Nine

of Slobberskaya Row.
When Fascist Armies start to run
old Goebbels fills the gap.
Meanwhile Joe smokes a pipe and wears
a taxi-driver's cap!

At home those beggars publicise
the deeds of 'our Ally'
whose dearest wish was once to biff
the Bolshie in the eye.
Your uncle Joe is wise to this;
he isn't such a sap
although he smokes a pipe and wears
a taxi-driver's cap!

[*Ballads of World War II* (1947)]

THE 51ST HIGHLAND DIVISION'S FAREWELL TO SICILY

(Tune: 'Farewell to the Creeks', a well-known Gordon Pipe March composed by Pipe-Major James Robertson, Banff)

I
The pipie is dozie, the pipie is fey,
   He winna come roon for his vino the day.
The sky ower Messina is antrin an' grey,
   And a' the bricht chaulmers are eerie.

   Then fare weel ye banks o' Sicily,
      Fare ye weel ye valley an' shaw.
   There's nae Jock will mourn the kyles o' ye
      Puir bliddy bastards are weary.

   And fare weel ye banks o' Sicily
      Fare ye weel ye valley and shaw.
   There's nae hame can smoor the wiles o' ye
      Puir bliddy bastards are weary.

Then doon the stair and line the waterside
   Wait your turn, the ferry's awa'.
Then doon the stair and line the waterside,
   A' the bricht chaulmers are eerie.

II
The drummie is polisht, the drummie is braw
   He cannae be seen for his webbin ava.
He's beezed himsel up for a photo an' a'
   Tae leave wi' his Lola, his dearie.

Then fare ye weel ye dives o' Sicily
   (Fare ye weel ye sheiling an' ha'),
And fare weel ye byres and bothies
   whaur kind signorinas were cheerie.

And fare weel ye dives o' Sicily
   (Fare ye weel ye sheiling an' ha')
We'll a' mind shebeens and bothies
   Whaur Jock made a date wi' his dearie.

Then tune the pipes and drub the tenor drum
   (Leave your kit this side o' the wa')
Then tune the pipes and drub the tenor drum –
   A' the bricht chaulmers are eerie.

[*Our Time*, Vol. 4, No. 11, June 1945 and *Ballads of World War II* (1947)]

BALLAD OF KING FARUK AND QUEEN FARIDA

(Tune: Egyptian National Anthem – 'Salam el Malik')

O we're all black bastards, but we do love our king.
Every night at the flicks you can hear us fuckin' sing:
> *Quais ketir, King Faruk,*
> *Quais ketir, King Faruk,*
> *O you can't fuck Farida if you don't pay Faruk.*

O we're just fuckin' wogs, but we *do* love him so,
And we all do without just to keep him on the go;
> From Sollum to Solluch,
> Tel el Kebir to Tobruk,
O you can't fuck Farida if you don't pay Faruk.

O we're just damned niggers that a bugger brought to birth,
But when we have a bint, then we want our money's worth.
> You may have a tarboosh,
> A gamel, a gamoos,
But you can't have Farida if you ain't got filoos.

O it's no use to say, if you want to have it in,
'Be a sport, King Faruk,' he would only fuckin' grin.
> You may beg on your knees,
> He would just say 'Mafeesh.'
O you won't get Farida if you don't give baksheesh.

O his subjects all tell of the fame of King Faruk
From Gezira to the Turf, from Helwan to Bab-el-Louk.
> They can tell what a sell
> Hangs their balls on a hook
For they can't fuck Farida if they don't fuck Faruk!

If her boudoir you pass 'tween the hours of ten and two
You will see all the Wafd standing waiting in a queue.

Though Nahas ain't an ass,
Though Nahas *is* a crook,
Still he can't fuck Farida if he don't pay Faruk.

O it's not hard to see poor Delilah's up a tree,
For the 'She' wears the horns in the Lampson familee.
Old Sir Miles with his wiles
In advance tries to book –
Still he can't fuck Farida if he don't pay Faruk.

If you feel like a grind when you've had a pint of beer,
To the Berka wend your way, where it ain't too fuckin' dear.
Quais ketir, mangariyeh,
Quais ketir gonorrhoea.
Shufty kus. Got filoos? Shove it up – from the rear!

Queen Farida's very gay when Faruk has got his pay,
But she ain't so bleedin' glad when she's in the family way
Stanna shwaya! O desire!
Stanna shwaya! Pull your wire.
Pull your pud. Does you good. Send it higher! Send it higher!

King Faruk! King Faruk! Hang your bollocks on a hook!
King Faruk! King Faruk! Let the swaddies have a look.
Quais ketir Abassia!
Bags o' beer. Shit and fear!
Up your pipe! Take a swipe! Quais ketir! Quais ketir!

O this song that you've heard is the song the Gippos sing,
And they'd sing just the same if we made old Nahas king.
Quais ketir, Nahas Pash,
Quais ketir, Nahas Pash,
O we won't mind your morals if you hand out the cash.

And this song that you've heard is the song the Gippos sing,
And they'd sing just the same if they'd Rommel for a king.
     Quais ketir, Rommel dear,
     Quais ketir, Rommel dear,
O we're glad you've won the battle, and we're so bucked you're
  here!

FINALE

Then sing Sieg Heil for Egypt's king
And to his feet your tributes bring.
     Quais ketir, King Faruk,
     Quais ketir, King Faruk,
O you can't fuck Farida if you don't pay Faruk.

Note: Chiefly the authentic version as sung (1942) in the First South
African Division, Second New Zealand Division and Fifty-First Highland
Division.

Glossary (Arabic):

Quais ketir:	plenty good
bint:	woman
tarboosh:	fez
gamel:	camel
gamoos:	water buffalo
filoos:	money
mafeesh:	'there ain't none'
Bab-el-Louk:	Cairene railway terminus
stanna shwaya:	take it easy (lit. stay a little)

THE BLUBBING BUCHMANITE

When Moscow sends the call at night
'Workers of the world unite!'
The lads begin to wonder when
The human race will act like men.

And Tam (from Greenock) tells us why
The bosses send us out to die.
He says: 'We Scots have gone to seed –
A revolution's what we need!'

But Micah Grant (from Schotts) starts in
To tell us how to deal with Sin –
He calls on us to turn again,
And then resumes his old refrain:

> 'A revolution in the mind
>   will be more couthie, will be more kind.
> A revolution in the brain
>   will not annoy the boss again.'

'At times' he says 'the workers feel
They've had a pretty rotten deal;
But if they search their inmost hearts
They'll find that's due to Satan's arts.

'I see what few have understood –
God tries the worker for his good;
Each lustful keek at Katie Brown
Will dock his wages half a crown!

'So don't provoke the Mighty God
Too sore, or you will feel the rod.
The Lord destroys that fool who fights
For earthly things like workers' rights.'

> 'A revolution in the mind
>   will be more couthie, will be more kind.
> A revolution in the brain
>   will not annoy the boss again.'

But Tam gets back his breath and cries:
'You creeping Jesus, damn your eyes!
It's canting cunts like you who sap
The worker's spirit. Shut your trap!

'A revolution in the soul
Will leave the bosses' profits whole.
A revolution in the heart
Won't help the workers' cause a fart.

'We cannot have too blinking few
God-awful bums the like of you!
If just once more you try to wreck
The workers' fight, I'll wring your neck.'

[*Ballads of World War II* (1947)]

BALLAD OF THE BANFFIES

(adapted from Piper Frank Stewart of the Sixth Battalion, the Gordon Highlanders)

(Tune: 'The Gallant Forty Twa')

Ye can talk aboot your Moray loons,
   Sae handsome and sae braw;
The Royal Scottish Fusiliers,
   A scruffy lot an a'
The Cameronians frae the South,
   They sure are mighty fine,
But in the Battle of Anzio
   'Twas the Banffies held the line.

The crofters' sons o' Banffshire,
   The cooper frae the glen,
The weaver frae Strathisla,
   Aye, and shepherd frae the ben;
The fisher lads alang the coast,
   They a' made up their min'
Tae fecht an' save their country
   In Nineteen Thirty-Nine.

Von Arnim knew that he was beat
   When he capitulated.
The mistake he made was the Banffies
   Whom he underestimated.
They chased them frae the Atlas hills
   And threw them in the sea;
Then across tae Pantellaria,
   Some mair territory to free.

Then Alex said: 'Oor troops maun land
    A few miles Sooth o' Rome;
The Banffies are my strongest point,
    They sure can send it home.'
They landed up at Anzio
    In January Forty Four
And havena captured Rome yet
    But are knockin' at the door.

Ye can talk aboot your Scots Guards
    Sae handsome and sae strong,
But unlike oor wee Banffies
    They canna haud on for long.
In years to come, when Italy
    Is free, an' the Balkans too
Your bairns will read in history
    How the Banffies pulled us through.

ENVOI

Where'er ye be, by land or sea
    Or hirplin' in the road
If ye can meet a Banff, ye'll find
    He sure can bum his load.

[*Ballads of World War II* (1947)]

FALL OF TOBRUK

Tommy thinks he holds Tobruk.
   Along the road comes Rommel.
Inside two shakes Tobruk is took
   And Tommy's on the bummel.

He's on the bummel to the Rhine
   Where sylphs will drive him barmy.
I think old Timoshenko's fine.
   Thank God for the Red Army.

(June 1942)

[*Ballads of World War II* (1947)]

SONG OF THE ADMIRAL GRAF VON SPEE

(I heard this ballad sung in a Sussex pub (1940) and have compared the text with a written version I got in Libia (1942).)

(Tune: 'Casey Jones'-ish.)

This is the saga of the *Graf von Spee*
Pocket-battleship of the German navee.
Full up with Nazis and their nasty tricks –
All of them afraid of Himmler and his dicks.

> Chorus:
> *Graf von Spee*
>   *feelin' mighty windy*
> *Graf von Spree*
>   *feelin' mighty low*
> *Graf von Spree*
>   *kickin' up a shindy*
> *Davy Jone's locker, Hun, that's where you'll go!*

Off she went a-sailing one September night,
Slipped the British Navy, lads, before it was light.
'I'm concerned with piracy, not anything my size.
Merchantmen and neutral ships, Gott damn their eyes!'

Newton Beach and *Alice*, *Travanian* and more
Little ships she sank them to the wild sea floor.
'Hoch,' the pirates shouted, 'we're the Fuehrer's last trick.
Guess the British Navy must be feeling mighty sick.'

Sailing east of Punta el Estec on a day,
Sighted they a Frenchy, a likely bit of prey.
Ajax, in attendance, mounted very small guns.
'Just the thing for Hitler' said these bastard Huns.

Gleeful they fell on her, till they spied afar
Exeter – Achilles – British ships of war.
Gaping, they shouted, getting in a blue funk,
'Are we the *Rawaldpindi*? Better do a bunk.'

Three little cruisers spat their little ship's guns
At the battleship *Spee* manned with far bigger ones.
This way she twisted, and that way she ran –
Never was such running since the war began.

Into Montevidéo limped the great *Graf Spee*,
The Heines' pride and the terror of the sea.
The spry little cruisers were in great fighting trim,
Singing *Deutschland ueber Alles*, such a truthful hymn!

'Nobody loves us,' the Commander cried.
'If Harwood gets us, we'll be taken for a ride.
Uruguay don't want us, but mein Gott who'd dare
To fight those British Schweinehunds who're waiting out there.'

Out of Montevidéo did the *Graf Spee* sail,
But as she went under you could hear her wail:
'Sink me in the fairway, to teach 'em the *von Spee*
Can still do her bit as a menace to the sea.'

[*Ballads of World War II* (1947)]

A PIONEER CORPS BALLAD

(Sung 1940 by the A.M.P.C. – Auxiliary Military Pioneer Corps – now the Royal Pioneer Corps.)

O we cut down the old pine tree
And we gave it to the A.M.P.C.
To make a coffin of pine
For old Hitler the swine
Yes we cut down the old pine tree.

> For Hitler's sleepin' sound in his grave tonight,
> And that's where old Musso ought to be.

O the A.M.P.C. are the finest in the land
And they cut down the old pine tree.

[*Ballads of World War II* (1947)]

[79]

PHONEY WAR – WESTERN FRONT

It was Christmas Day in the Workhouse
And dangerous Dan McGrew
Was fighting to save the pudding
For a lady by the name of Sue.

All was quiet on the Western Front,
The waves were beating on the shore;
So send for the life-boat at Wigan –
We've never had it from there before.

[*Ballads of World War II* (1947)]

BALLAD OF ANZIO

When the M.G.s stop their chatter
And the cannons stop their roar
And you're back in dear old Blighty
In your favourite pub once more;
When the small talk is all over
And the war tales start to flow,
You can stop the lot by telling
Of the fight at Anzio.

Let them bum about the desert,
Let them talk about Dunkirk,
Let them brag about the jungles
Where the Japanese did lurk.
Let them boast about their campaign
And their medals till they're red:
You can put the lot to silence
When you mention – the beachhead.

You can tell of Anzio Archie
And the Factory, where the Huns
Used to ask us out to breakfast
As they rubbed against our guns.
You can talk of night patrolling
They know nothing of at home
And you can tell them that you learned it
On the beachhead – south of Rome.
You can tell them how the Heinies
Tried to break us with attacks,
Using tanks, bombs and flamethrowers
And how we flung them back.
You can tell them how we took it
And dished it out as well.
How we thought it was a picnic
And Tedeschi thought it hell.

And when the tale is finished
And going time is near
Just fill your pipes again, lads,
And finish up your beer.
Then order up another pint
And drink before you go
To the boys that fought beside you
On the beach at Anzio.

[*Ballads of World War II* (1947)]

ELEGIES FOR THE
DEAD IN CYRENAICA

for our own and the others

John Lehmann (1948)

PROLOGUE
(for John Speirs)

Obliterating face and hands
The dumb-bell guns of violence
Show up our godhead for a sham.
Against the armour of the storm
I'll hold my human barrier,
Maintain my fragile irony.

I've walked this brazen clanging path
In flesh's brittle arrogance
To chance the simple hazard, death.
Regretting only this, my rash
Ambitious wish in verse to write
A true and valued testament.

Let my words knit what now we lack
The demon and the heritage
And fancy strapped to logic's rock.
A chastened wantonness, a bit
That sets on song a discipline,
A sensuous austerity.

These elegies and the Heroic Song in which they culminate were written between March 1943 and December 1947 in North Africa, in Italy and in Scotland. Four of them already existed in fragmentary form in the Autumn of 1942.

It was the remark of a captured German officer which first suggested to me the themes of these poems. He had said: 'Africa changes everything. In reality we are allies, and the desert is our common enemy.'

The troops confronting each other in Libya were relatively small in numbers. In the early stages of the desert war they were to a large extent forced to live off each other. Motor transport, equipment of all kinds and even armoured fighting vehicles changed hands frequently. The result was a curious 'doppelgaenger' effect, and it is this, enhanced by the deceptive distances and uncertain directions of the North African wasteland, which I have tried to capture in some of the poems.

After the African campaign had ended, the memory of this effect of mirage and looking-glass illusion persisted, and gradually became for me a symbol of our human civil war, in which the roles seem constantly to change and the objectives to shift and vary. It suggested too a complete reversal of the alignments and alliances which we had come to accept as inevitable. The conflict seemed rather to be between 'the dead, the innocent' – that eternally wronged proletariat of levelling death in which all the fallen are comrades – and ourselves, the living, who cannot hope to expiate our survival but by 'spanning history's apollyon chasm'.

Above all, perhaps, the doppelgaenger symbol allowed me to re-state in dialectical terms the endless problem of how to safeguard our human house. It is not enough surely to repeat or to re-phrase the words of the great makar –

No state in Erd here standis sicker;
As with the wynd wavis the wicker
So wannis this world's vanitie.

As the processes of history become clearer, one must, in spite of all disorientation and despair, have the courage to be consequent and to acclaim the 'runners' who have not flinched before their ineluctable exploit.

In the first part of the cycle, echoes of earlier warfare and half-forgotten acts of injustice are heard, confusing and troubling the 'sleepers'. It is true that such moments are intended to convey a universal predicament; yet I was thinking especially of the Highland soldiers, conscripts of a fast vanishing race, on whom the dreadful memory of the clearances rests and for whom there is little left to sustain them in the high places of the field but the heroic tradition of *gaisge* (valour).

Before leaving Italy I discussed the ideas I have outlined above with one of my Roman friends, the editor of a literary quarterly. His comment was: 'Surely, having been so much in the midst of things, you must find it very difficult to be impartial.'

He was, I suppose, quite right. It certainly *is* terribly difficult, if one has been (to use his phrase) in the midst of things. However, as I gradually get the hang of how people form their opinions, I begin to feel that it is next to impossible if one has not.

PART ONE

Alles geben die Götter, die unendlichen,
Ihren Lieblingen ganz.
Alle Freuden, die unendlichen,
Alle Schmerzen, die unendlichen, ganz.

The gods, the unending, give all things
without stint to their beloved:
all pleasures, the unending,
and all pains, the unending, without stint.

– Johann Wolfgang von Goethe

Note: Goethe's quatrain was frequently included in small anthologies 'for the Front' carried by German soldiers in the field – and indeed its thought lies very near the mood of many of them.

FIRST ELEGY

END OF A CAMPAIGN

There are many dead in the brutish desert,
      who lie uneasy
among the scrub in this landscape of half-wit
stunted ill-will. For the dead land is insatiate
and necrophilous. The sand is blowing about still.
Many who for various reasons, or because
      of mere unanswerable compulsion, came here
and fought among the clutching gravestones,
      shivered and sweated,
cried out, suffered thirst, were stoically silent, cursed
the spittering machine-guns, were homesick for Europe
and fast embedded in quicksand of Africa
      agonized and died.
And sleep now. Sleep here the sleep of the dust.

There were our own, there were the others.
Their deaths were like their lives, human and animal.
There were no gods and precious few heroes.
What they regretted when they died had nothing to do with
      race and leader, realm indivisible,
laboured Augustan speeches or vague imperial heritage.
(They saw through that guff before the axe fell.)
      Their longing turned to
the lost world glimpsed in the memory of letters:
an evening at the pictures in the friendly dark,
two knowing conspirators smiling and whispering secrets; or else
a family gathering in the homely kitchen
with Mum so proud of boys in uniform:
      their thoughts trembled
between moments of estrangement, and ecstatic moments

of reconciliation: and their desire
crucified itself against the unutterable shadow of someone
whose photo was in their wallets.
Then death made his incision.

There were our own, there were the others.
Therefore, minding the great word of Glencoe's
son, that we should not disfigure ourselves
with villainy of hatred; and seeing that all
have gone down like curs into anonymous silence,
I will bear witness for I knew the others.
Seeing that littoral and interior are alike indifferent
and the birds are drawn again to our welcoming north
why should I not sing *them*, the dead, the innocent?

SECOND ELEGY

HALFAYA
(for Luigi Castigliano)

At dawn, under the concise razor-edge
of the escarpment, the laager sleeps. No petrol fires yet
blow flame for brew-up. Up on the pass a sentry
inhales his Nazionale. Horse-shoe curve of the bay
grows visible beneath him. He smokes and yawns.
Ooo-augh,
       and the limitless
shabby lion-pelt of the desert completes and rounds
his limitless ennui.

At dawn, in the gathering impetus of day, the laager sleeps.
Some restless princes dream: first light denies them
the luxury of nothing. But others their mates more lucky
drown in the lightless grottoes. (Companionable death
has lent them his ease for a moment).
       The dreamers remember
a departure like a migration. They recall a landscape
associated with warmth and veils and pantomime
but never focused exactly. The flopping curtain
reveals scene-shifters running with freshly painted
incongruous sets. Here childhood's prairie garden
looms like a pampas, where grown-ups stalk (gross outlaws)
on legs of treetrunk: recedes: and the strepitant jungle
dwindles to scruff of shrubs on a docile common,
all but real for a moment, then gone.
       The sleepers turn
gone but still no nothing laves them.
O misery, desire, desire, tautening cords of the bedrack!
Eros, in the teeth of Yahveh and his tight-lipped sect

confound the deniers of their youth! Let war lie wounded!
Eros, grant forgiveness and release
and return – against which they erect it,
the cairn of patience. *No dear, won't be long now*
keep fingers crossed, chin up, keep smiling darling
be seeing you soon.

On the horizon fires fluff now,
further than they seem.

      Sollum and Halfaya
a while yet before we leave you in quiet
and our needle swings north.

      The sleepers toss
and turn before waking: they feel through their blankets

the cold of the malevolent bomb-thumped desert,
impartial
hostile to both.

The laager is one.
Friends and enemies, haters and lovers
both sleep and dream.

THIRD ELEGY

LEAVING THE CITY

Morning after. Get moving. Cheerio. Be seeing you
when this party's over. Right, driver, get weaving.

The truck pulls out
along the corniche. We dismiss with the terseness
of a newsreel the casino and the column,
the scrofulous sellers of obscenity,
the garries, the girls and the preposterous skyline.

Leave them. And out past the stinking tanneries,
the maritime Greek cafes, the wogs and the nets
drying among seaweed. Through the periphery of the city
itching under flagrant sunshine. Faster. We are nearing
the stretch leading to the salt-lake Mareotis.
Sand now, and dust-choked fig-trees. This is the road
where convoys are ordered to act in case of ambush.
A straight run through now to the coastal sector.
One sudden thought wounds: it's a half-hour or over
since we saw the last skirt. And for a moment we regret
the women, and the harbour with a curve so perfect
it seems it was drawn with the mouseion's protractor.

Past red-rimmed eye of the salt-lake. So long then,
holy filth of the living. We are going to the familiar
filth of your negation, to rejoin the proletariat
of levelling death. Stripes are shed and ranks levelled
in death's proletariat. There the Colonel of Hussars,
the keen Sapper Subaltern with a first in economics
and the sergeant well known in international football
crouch with Jock and Jame in their holes like helots.

Distinctions become vain, and former privileges quite pointless
in that new situation. See our own and the opponents
advance, meet and merge: the commingled columns
lock, strain, disengage and join issue with the dust.

Do not regret
that we have still in history to suffer
or comrade that we are the agents
of a dialectic that can destroy us
but like a man prepared, like a brave man
bid farewell to the city, and quickly
move forward on the road leading west by the salt-lake.
Like a man for long prepared, like a brave man,
like to the man who was worthy of such a city
be glad that the case admits no other solution,
acknowledge with pride the clear imperative of action
and bid farewell to her, to Alexandria, whom you are losing.

And these, advancing from the direction of Sollum,
swaddies in tropical kit, lifted in familiar vehicles
are they mirage – ourselves out of a mirror?
No, they too, leaving the plateau of Marmarica
for the serpentine of the pass, they advancing towards us
along the coast road, there are the others, the brothers
in death's proletariat, they are our victims and betrayers
advancing by the sea-shore to the same assignation.
We send them our greetings out of the mirror.

Note: The quotations in this poem are from 'The God Leaves Anthony' by
the Greek Alexandrian poet, C.P. Cavafy (1868–1933). In Cavafy's poem,
Alexandria is a symbol of life itself.

FOURTH ELEGY

EL ADEM

Sow cold wind of the desert. Embittered
reflections on discomfort and protracted absence.
Cold, and resentment stirred at this seeming
winter, most cruel reversal of seasons.
The weather clogs thought: we give way to griping
and malicious ill-turns, or instinctive actions
appearing without rhyme or reason. The landsknechte
read mail, play scat, lie mute under greatcoats.
We know that our minds are as slack and rootless
as the tent-pegs driven into cracks of limestone,
and we feel the harm of inaction's erosion.
We're uneasy, knowing ourselves to be nomads,
impermanent guests on this bleak moon-surface
of dents and ridges, craters and depressions.
Yet they make us theirs: we know it, and abhor them,
vile three in one of the heretic desert,
sand rock and sky . . . And the sow wind, whipping
the face of a working (or a dying) unit
who shoulders his shovel with corpse obedience.

The sons of man
grow and go down in pain: they kneel for the load
and bow like brutes, in patience accepting the burden,
the pain fort and dour . . . Out of shuttered Europe
not even a shriek or a howl for its doomed children
is heard through the nihilist windvoice. Tomorrow's victors
survey with grief too profound for mere lamentation
their own approaching defeat: while even the defeated
await dry-eyed their ineluctable triumph.
Cages are crammed: on guard crouch the fearful oppressors

and wait for their judgement day.
　　　　　Therefore recollecting
the ice-bound paths, and now this gap in the minefields
through which (from one side or the other) all must pass
shall I not speak and condemn?

Or must it always
seem premature: the moment always at hand,
and never arriving, to use
our rebellious anger for breaking
the vicious fetters that bind us?

Endure, endure. There is as yet no solution
and no short cut, no escape and no remedy
but our human iron.
　　　　　And this Egypt teaches us
that mankind, put to the torment, can bear
on their breast the stone tomb of immolation
for millennia. The wind. We can build our cairn.

FIFTH ELEGY

HIGHLAND JEBEL
(for John Lorne Campbell)

Was ist es, das an die alten seligen Küsten mich
fesselt, dass ich sie mehr liebe als mein eigenes Land?

– Friedrich Hölderlin

Our eyes, fatigued by the unsearchable desert's
moron monotony, lifted to the hills.

Strong-winged
our homing memory held us
on an unerring course: soared, leaving behind it
in an instant camp, coast-line and city,
sea, imbecile wasteland and the black sierras
for a well-known house.
             It found the treeless machair,
took in bay and snub headland, circled kirkyard and valley
and described once again our love's perfect circuit
till, flying to its own,
it dashed itself against the unresponsive windows.

So we waited
and lifted our eyes to
the hills, whence comes aid.

In our ears a murmur
of wind-borne battle. Herons stalk
over the blood-stained flats. Burning byres
come to my mind. Distance blurs

motive and aim. Dark moorland bleeding
for wrong or right.
*Sons of the hounds
come here and get flesh.* Search, bite!

In what deep antre
of death is there refuge
from this living rock?

Beyond the gate of the pass
are a high and low road: but neither
is the road back. No, laochain, they must lead us
in the hauteur of battle. Must array, enroll us
among listening cohorts. Where both vaunting and atonement
remain muffled for ever. The caverns will number
our momentary cries among the stounds and echoes
of this highland's millennial conflict.
Another falls for Hector.
                    Again there!
                             Aye, in spite of
the houses lying cold, and the hatred that engendered
the vileness that you know, we'll keep our assignation
with the Grecian Gael. (And those others.) Then foregather
in a gorge of the cloudy jebel
older than Agamemnon.

Travelling light, and making the most of
the early coolness, we'll come before morning
to the raw uplands, and then by evening greet you
in the wilderness of your white corries, Kythairon.

Note: *Laochain.* Literally means 'little hero'. Familiar term of endearment
for a young lad in Gaelic. *Another falls for Hector.* Patroclus. – I was thinking
also of the warcry of the Macleans who died in defence of their chief at

Inverkeithing: *Fear eile airson Eachainn* (Another for Hector).

The Grecian Gael. Term occasionally used by the old bards for the Scots and Irish – cf. the *Brosnachadh* (*Incitement to Rise*) addressed to Argyll before Flodden. (Book of the Dean of Lismore.)

INTERLUDE

OPENING OF AN OFFENSIVE

(a) the waiting

Armour has foregathered, snuffling
through tourbillions of fine dust.
The crews don't speak much. They've had
last brew-up before battle. The tawny
deadland lies in a silence
not yet smashed by salvoes.
No sound reaches us
from the African constellations.
The low ridge too is quiet.
But no fear we're sleeping,
no need to remind us
that the nervous fingers of the searchlights
are nearly meeting and time is flickering
and this I think in a few minutes
while the whole power crouches for the spring.
X–20 in thirty seconds. Then begin

(b) the barrage

Let loose (rounds)
the exultant bounding hell-harrowing of sound.
Break the batteries. Confound
the damnable domination. Slake
the crashing breakers-húrled rúbble of the guns.
Dithering darkness, we'll wake you! Héll's bélls
blind you. Be broken, bleed
deathshead blackness!
            The thongs of the livid

firelights lick you
                    jagg'd splinters rend you
                                        underground
we'll bomb you, doom you, tomb you into grave's mound

        (c) the Jocks

They move forward into no man's land, a vibrant sounding board.
        As they advance
the guns push further murderous music.
Is this all they will hear, this raucous apocalypse?
The spheres knocking in the night of Heaven?
The drummeling of overwhelming niagara?
No! For I can hear it! Or is it? . . . tell
me that I can hear it! Now – listen!

        Yes, hill and shieling
sea-loch and island, hear it, the yell
of your war-pipes, scaling sound's mountains
guns thunder drowning in their soaring swell!
– The barrage gulfs them: they're gulfed in the clumbering guns,
gulfed in gloom, gloom. Dumb in the blunderbuss black –
lost – gone in the anonymous cataract of noise.
Now again! The shrill war-song: it flaunts
aggression to the sullen desert. It mounts. Its scream
tops the valkyrie, tops the colossal
        artillery.

Meaning that many
German Fascists will not be going home
meaning that many
will die, doomed in their false dream

We'll mak siccar!
Against the bashing cudgel
against the contemptuous triumphs of the big battalions

mak siccar against the monkish adepts
of total war against the oppressed oppressors
mak siccar against the leaching lies
against the worked out systems of sick perversion
mak siccar
          against the executioner
against the tyrannous myth and the real terror
mak siccar

Note: *Scaling sound's mountains.*

> Wi' nocht but the cry o' the pipes can Earth
> Or these – or silence – meet.
>> Hugh MacDiarmid.
>> 'Coronach for the End of the World'

Mak siccar (Make sure). One of the famous phrases of mediaeval Scottish history.

After Bruce had stabbed the Red Comyn in Dumfries Kirk he was found outside the building by Lindsay and Kirkpatrick. Lindsay asked if Comyn were dead. Bruce replied that he didn't know.

'Aweel,' said Kirkpatrick, 'I'll mak siccar.'

PART TWO

'Na shuidhe marbh an 'Glaic a' Bhàis'
fo Dhruim Ruidhìseit,
gille òg 's a logan sìos m' a ghruaidh
's a thuar grìsionn.

Smaoinich mi air a' chòir 's an àgh,
a fhuair e bho Fhurair,
bhith tuiteam ann an raon an àir
gun éirigh tuilleadh . . .

Ge b'e a dheòin-san no a chàs,
a neo-chiontas no mhìorun,
cha do nochd e toileachadh 'na bhàs
fo Dhruim Ruidhìseit.

       – Somhairle MacGill-Eain

Sitting dead in 'Death Valley'
below the Ruweisat Ridge,
a boy with his forelock down about his cheek
and his face slate-grey.

I thought of the right and joy
He had from his Fuehrer,
of falling in the field of slaughter
to rise no more . . .

Whatever his desire or mishap,
his innocence or malignance,
he showed no patience in his death
below the Ruweisat Ridge.

       – Sorley MacLean

Note: Set at the beginning of the second part is the sceptical ironic spirit of a Gaelic poet who fought in the desert and was wounded at El Alamein.

SIXTH ELEGY

ACROMA

Planning and execution
recede: the preliminary inertia,
the expectation, the lull, the relaxing and the encounter's
suddenness recede, become history: thrusts, sieges and feints
that still blood maps with arrows
and left dead like refuse, these are the basis
of battle studies. And we're no better. The lying films
contain greater truth than most of our memories.

And the participants? – Staff Officers consider,
discuss and record their provisional verdicts.
These were go-getters, professional outflankers,
capable assault troops, or specialists in night warfare;
while those others had guts and lacked training, yet put up
a decent enough show at Himeimat or Munassib.
Occasionally there are doubts, dispute becomes acrimonious,
the case is not proven, judgement must be deferred.
On one point however there is unanimity: their sacrifice
though hard and heroic was on the whole 'necessary'.
I too have acquiesced
in this evasion: that the unlucky
or the destined must inevitably fall
and be impaled on the basalt pinnacles of darkness.

Yet how can I shame them, saying that they
have died for us: that it was expedient
a generation should die for the people?
To justify them, what byways must I follow?
Into what inaccessible sierras
of naked acceptance, where mere reason cannot live,

where love shines like a glacier. Could I ever attain it?
Neither by dope of reportage, nor by anodyne of statistics
is *their* lot made easier: laughing couples at the tea-dance
ignore their memory, the memoirs almost slight them
and the queue forming up to see Rangers play Celtic
forms up without thought to those dead. – O, to right them
what requiem can I sing in the ears of the living?

No blah about their sacrifice: rather tears or reviling
of the time that took them, than an insult so outrageous.
All barriers are down: in the criss-crossed enclosures
where most lie now assembled in their aching solitude
those others lie too – who were also the sacrificed
of history's great rains, of the destructive transitions.
This one beach where high seas have disgorged them like flotsam
reveals in its nakedness their ultimate alliance.

So the words that I have looked for, and must go on looking for,
are worlds of whole love, which can slowly gain the power
to reconcile and heal. Other words would be pointless.

SEVENTH ELEGY

SEVEN GOOD GERMANS

The track running between Mekili and Tmimi was at one time a kind of
no-man's-land. British patrolling was energetic, and there were numerous
brushes with German and Italian elements. El Eleba lies about halfway
along this track.

                    Of the swaddies
          who came to the desert with Rommel
there were few who had heard (or would hear) of El Eleba.
They recce'd,
          or acted as medical orderlies
or patched up their tanks in the camouflaged workshops
and never gave a thought to a place like El Eleba.

To get there, you drive into the blue, take a bearing
and head for damn-all. Then you're there. And where are you?

– Still, of some few who did cross our path at El Eleba
there are seven who bide under their standing crosses.

The first a Lieutenant.
          When the medicos passed him
for service overseas, he had jotted in a note-book
to the day and the hour   keep me steadfast   there is only
the decision and the will
                    the rest has no importance

The second a Corporal.
          He had been in the Legion
and had got one more chance to redeem his lost honour.
What he said was

Listen here, I'm fed up with your griping –
If you want extra rations, go get 'em from Tommy!
You're green, that's your trouble. Dodge the column, pass the buck
and scrounge all you can – that's our law in the Legion.
You know Tommy's got 'em . . . He's got mineral waters,
and beer, and fresh fruit in that white crinkly paper
and God knows what all! Well, what's holding you back?
Are you windy or what?

      Christ, you 'old Afrikaners'!
If you're wanting the eats, go and get 'em from Tommy!

The third had been a farm-hand in the March of Silesia
and had come to the desert as fresh fodder for machine-guns.
His dates are inscribed on the files, and on the cross-piece.

The fourth was a lance-jack.

     He had trusted in Adolf
while working as a chemist in the suburb of Spandau.
His loves were his 'cello, and the woman who had borne him
two daughters and a son. He had faith in the Endsieg.
THAT THE NEW REICH MAY LIVE prayed the flyleaf of
his Bible.

The fifth a mechanic.

    All the honour and glory,
the siege of Tobruk and the conquest of Cairo
meant as much to that Boche as the Synod of Whitby.
Being wise to all this, he had one single headache,
which was, how to get back to his sweetheart (called Ilse).
– He had said

   Can't the Tommy wake up and get weaving?
If he tried, he could put our whole Corps in the bag.
May God damn this Libya and both of its palm-trees!

The sixth was a Pole

     – or to you, a Volksdeutscher –

who had put off his nation to serve in the Wehrmacht.
He siegheiled, and talked of 'the dirty Polacken',
and said what he'd do if let loose among Russkis.
His mates thought that, though 'just a polnischer Schweinhund',
he was not a bad bloke.

On the morning concerned
he was driving a truck with mail, petrol and rations.
The M.P. on duty shouted five words of warning.
He nodded
laughed
revved
and drove straight for El Eleba
not having quite got the chap's Styrian lingo.

The seventh a young swaddy.

Riding cramped in a lorry
to death along the road which winds eastward to Halfaya
he had written three verses in appeal against his sentence
which soften for an hour the anger of Lenin.

Seven poor bastards
dead in an African deadland
(tawny tousled hair under the issue blanket)
wie einst Lili
dead in an African deadland

einst Lili Marlene

EIGHTH ELEGY

KARNAK

Er lächelt über die ganze Welt hinaus

Surely it is a holiday
or a day of national thanksgiving. – Observe the King
as he offers up the spoils of Syria to Osiris.
No doubt he is acknowledging
the conclusion of some war to preserve civilization.

Insolence of this civilization,
to counterfeit with such assurance the eternal!

Yes, here among the shambles of Karnak
is Vollendung unknown to the restless Greeks.
Here, not in Elis and Olympia
are edle Einfalt und stille Grösse.
They bore many children
but their triumphal barque of civilization
was weighed down with a heavy ballast
of magnetic death.
There is the Schwerpunkt, not here,
there across the river that made it all possible
the dead were taken across death
(listen to the waves of the flowing symbol,
lisping death) were taken to temporary slumber
and were introduced with courtesy to Osiris
and the immortal macabre company

        But the envious desert
held at arm's length for millenia
had its own way at last –

   in the name of Mohammed
the nomads conquered:

   though not for the first time.
It had all happened before, as is the confounding way of history:
when the shepherd kings, Yaakeb and Yusuf,
heavy breathing with their hairy gutturals,
stood incredulously in the courts of Amun.
They looked down their noses at the phallic Min
and took up stones against impassive Osiris.
(Not of them hawk Horus, or the clerkish Thoth,
not of them the complacence on the lips of Pharaoh
not of them the capitals of lotus and papyrus.)

Those who go a-whoring after death
will assuredly find it. Will be sealed in, confined
to their waste palaces. And Karnak the temple
be 'stalls for the nomads'.

   Puff of dust
on the blurred horizon means the imminent approach
of the solution, of subjection-deliverance.
These horsemen are merciful, they bring
the craved annihilation.
These are 'my servants, the Assyrians',
   these the necessary antithesis,
these the standard-bearers of the superb blasphemy,
felling gods, levelling cities,
death-life grappling with life-death, severing
the umbilical cord of history.
These are the trampling migrations of peoples,
the horsemen of Amr, the 'barbarians' of Cavafy
and Rommel before the gates of Alexandria.

But still, in utter silence, from bas-relief and painted tomb
this civilization asserts

its stylised timeless effrontery.
Synthesis is implicit
in Rilke's single column, (die *eine*)
denying fate, the stone mask of Vollendung.
(Deaf to tarbushed dragoman
who deep-throatedly extols it).

Yes, pinned with paint to walls, deep in stone carved, they cannot
resent the usurper. They fix and hold motionless
a protracted moment of time, a transitory eon.

The sun-boat travels through the hours of darkness
and Ra mounts heavenwards his chosen path.

What will happen during this day?
                                            Will the King's Vizier
find time to be present at his public function?
Will silly girls fight among the stooks: will a sailor
be beaten for insubordination?

Is the harvest home yet: will stewards be computing
in the household office the extent of their surplus?
Will patient labourers work the shadouf?
Is fruit on the branch: and will ripe pomegranates
be shipped down to Thebes? Will rough Greeks land on Pharos?
Will prisoners of war drive the shaft for a tomb?

Is scaffolding up? Will the subsidized craftsmen
work diligently still on their couple of colossi,
all masters of the chisel, its calculated cutting?
Are Bedouin herds moving up from the South?

Will it be a feast-day: will the smooth priests
in bell-bottomed robes process between the sphinxes?
Detesters of the disk, possessors of the mystery,
shrewd guardians of the vested interests of Amun!

Where will the King be? Out boating for his pleasure;
while his boat shears through the Nile reeds
he aims at wild fowl with a boomerang –
can he be sure of bringing home a bag?
            No doubt the court
will see to it, being solicitous.

In the evening he will return to Thebes, in his state
chariot, with the music of many instruments.
To his fellaheen a vision of flower-strewn godhead
the scourge and the crook, under the sycamore leaves of life

            of life
            o unheeding
            the long ambiguous shadow
            thrown on overweening temple
            by the Other, the recurrent
            the bearded
            the killer in the rhythmical tragedy
            the heir   the stranger

Welcome O Hussein
When you enter Karbala

Note: 'This civilization was filled, so great was its unshaken complacence
on this earth, with a profound death-longing – it longed, dreamed, lusted,
went a-whoring after death.

    'Karnak, smashed, is the ironic image of Vollendung. The tombs in the
Valley of the Kings are as good a sketch as man has made of "the eternal".

    'I do not let myself be weighed down by the impassive timeless
effrontery of this civilization. I realise that all of us, from Hellenes to
Gaelic outlanders of the western world are in a sense beside Thebes
half-civilized clod-hoppers, hairy men with a lop-sided slant on time,
half-baked hurried ignorant Yank tourists with a kink about progress
mechanical or social.

'But you can have Luxor – it solves none of the problems, it doesn't even pose them. If we of the modern west devote a tenth of the time to life that Karnak devoted to death, we'll bring a tangible hope, even to the inhabitants of the Nile Valley.'

– Extract from my notebook, 17 January 1943.

The 'barbarians' of Cavafy. I was thinking of these lines in the poem 'Waiting for the Barbarians':

> And now what is to become of us without barbarians?
> These barbarians were a kind of solution.

He aims at wild fowl with a boomerang. If any one doubts the authenticity of this reference, he should pay a visit to the tomb of Menna, which is among the nobles' tombs at Thebes.

NINTH ELEGY

FORT CAPUZZO

For there will come a day
when the Lord will say
– Close Order!

One evening, breaking a jeep journey at Capuzzo
I noticed a soldier as he entered the cemetery
and stood looking at the grave of a fallen enemy.
Then I understood the meaning of the hard word 'pietas'

(a word unfamiliar to the newsreel commentator
as well as to the pimp, the informer and the traitor).

His thought was like this. – Here's another 'Good Jerry'!
Poor mucker. Just eighteen. Must be hard-up for man-power.
Or else he volunteered, silly bastard. That's the fatal,
the – fatal – mistake. Never volunteer for nothing.
I wonder how he died? Just as well it was him, though,
And not one of our chaps . . . Yes, the only good Jerry,
as they say, is your sort, chum.
                    Cheerio, you poor bastard.
Don't be late on parade when the Lord calls 'Close Order'.
Keep waiting for the angels. Keep listening for Reveille.

Note: *The newsreel commentator*. I was thinking particularly of one
whose mic-side manner when referring to the area targets of Bomber
Command or when delivering ignoble gibes at the expense of enemy
front-line soldiers filled me (and plenty of others) with shame and fury.

TENTH ELEGY

THE FRONTIER

One must die because one knows them, die
of their smile's ineffable blossom, die
of their light hands

But dust blowing round them
has stopped up their ears
           o for ever
not sleeping but dead

The airliner's passengers,
crossing without effort the confines
of wired-off Libia, remember
little, regret less. If they idly
inspect from their windows the ennui
of limestone desert
        – and beneath them
their skimming shadow –
        they'll be certain
they've seen it, they've seen all

(Seen all, maybe, including
the lunar qattaras, the wadis like family trees,
the frontier passes with their toyshop spirals –
seen nothing, and seen all

And the scene yields them? Nothing)

Yet that coast-line
could yield much: there were recces and sorties,
drumfire and sieges. The outposts

lay here: there ran the supply route.
Forgotten.

      By that bend of Halfaya
the convoys used to stick, raw meat for the Jabos.

And here, the bay's horseshoe:
how nobly it clanged through laconic communiqués!

Still, how should this interest the airborne travellers,
being less real to them than the Trojan defence-works
and touching them as little as the Achaean strategies?
Useless to deny. The memorial's obsequious
falsehoods are irrelevant. It has little to arrest them,
survivors by accident
      that dried blood in the sangars.

So I turn aside in the benighted deadland
to perform a duty, noting an outlying
grave, or restoring a fallen cross-piece.
Remembrancer.
    And shall sing them who amnestied
escaped from the tumult to stumble across sand-dunes
and darken their waves in the sea, the deliverer.

Run, stumble and fall in their instant of agony
past burnt-out brennpunkt, along hangdog dannert.
Here gutted, or stuck through the throat like Buonconte,
or charred to grey ash, they are caught in one corral.
We fly from their scorn, but they close all the passes:
their sleep's our unrest, we lie bound in their inferno –
this alliance must be vaunted and affirmed, lest they condemn us!
Lean seedlings of lament spring like swordsmen around us;
the coronach scales white arêtes. Bitter keening
of women goes up by the solitary column.
Denounce and condemn! Either build for the living
love, patience and power to absolve these tormented,

or else choke in the folds of their black-edged vendetta!
Run, stumble and fall in our desert of failure,
impaled, unappeased. And inhabit that desert
of canyon and dream – till we carry to the living
blood, fire and red flambeaux of death's proletariat.
Take iron in your arms! At last, spanning this history's
apollyon chasm, proclaim them the reconciled.

Note: *Stuck through the throat like Buonconte*. Dante, *Purg. V.* 88–129.

The episode of Buonconte was quoted to me by a Tuscan partisan in the hills north of Florence.

HEROIC SONG FOR THE RUNNER OF CYRENE
(to Gregorio Prieto)

> *Without suffering and death one learns nothing.*
> *We should not know the difference between the visions*
> *of the intellect and the facts.*
> *Only those ideas are acceptable that hold through*
> *suffering and death . . .*
> *Life is that which leaps.*

– Denis Saurat, 'Death and the Dreamer'

I

The runners who would challenge
　　　　the rough bounds of the desert
and strip for the test
　　　　on this barbarous arena
must have sinews like hounds
　　　　and be cunning as jerobas.

Rooting crowds 'll not hail them
　　　　in boisterous circus
nor sleek fame crown their exploit
　　　　with triumph and obelisk.
Sún beats their path
　　　　down the hours of blank silence:
each knows that in the end
　　　　he'll be lucky to have respite.

Freely they'll run
　　　　to the chosen assignation;
ineluctable role,
　　　　and they ready to accept it!
Going with élan of pride
　　　　to the furious onset
they'll reclaim the dead land
　　　　for their city of Cyrene.

Sún beats their path:
　　　　this no course measured plainly
between markers on the beach,
　　　　no event for the novice.
The gates open: are closed.
　　　　And the track leads them forward
hard by salt-lake and standing stone
　　　　blind as by the cyclops.

While keeping the same pace
      neither slower nor faster
but as yet out of sight
      behind plateau and escarpment
is history the doppelgaenger
      running to meet them.

II
Stroke of the sun means the hour that's to lay them
is present once more on the dust-blurred horizon.
They start, and awake from their stupor of rhythm –
and think, as they catch glimpse of sea beyond watch-tower
they cannot be far from . . . a place they'd forgotten.

At last it is sure. O, they know that they'll never
be hesitant feet on the marches of darkness
or humped Epigonoi, outliving the Fians.

No matter what hand stirs the dust, questions gently
with curious touch the grazed stones of the city
yon stroke of the sun vaunts their exploit for ever.

They quicken their pace. (And those others too.) Faster,
and livelier now than at jousts of the Toppo.
The goal is in sight. Simultaneous the onrush,
the clash close at hand, o incarnate dialectic!
The runners gain speed. As they hail their opponents
they can hear in the air the strum of loud arrows
which predestined sing to their point of intersection.
Blaze of harsh day stuns their human defiance;
steel beats their path with its pendulum brilliance.

Sun's thong is lifted. And history the other
emerges at last from the heat's trembling mirror.

III
        Their ruin upon them
they've entered the lip of the burning enclosure.
Each runs to achieve, without pause or evasion
        his instant of nothing

        they look for an opening
grip, grapple, jerk, sway
and fall locking like lovers

down the thunderous cataract of day.

        Cyrene, 1942 – Carradale, Argyll, 1947.

Note: Cyrene in this poem is for me the symbol of civilized humanity, of our 'human house'.

    The legend of the brothers Philaeni who competed against athletes from Cyrene suggested the symbol of the runners.

History the doppelgaenger.

        Spectre of Albion! Warlike fiend!
        In clouds of blood and ruin rolled,
        I here reclaim thee as my own!
        My selfhood! Satan! Arm'd in gold.

        – William Blake

They cannot be far from. I had in my mind here a line which introduces the Skaggerrak motif in Reinhold Goering's play *Seeschlacht* (Sea Battle) – 'We cannot be far from the Skaggerrak.'

Seeschlacht, which appeared in 1917, was inspired by the Battle of Jutland fought the previous year – a battle known in German as the

Skaggerrakschlacht. The opening scenes recreate with real skill the atmosphere of suspense before battle.

The play, incidentally, is well worth reading for its delineation of the German military mentality. Here are the dying words of a would-be mutineer who has after all distinguished himself in the fighting:

> I've done good work firing, eh? –
> And I'd have mutinied well, too, eh? –
> But the firing was nearer our hearts, eh? –
> Ay, it must have been nearer our hearts.

After the Fians.
Oisein an déigh na Feinne (Ossian after the Fians) is a Gaelic proverbial expression. Ossian is reputed to have outlived his compeers, the Fingalian heroes.

Jousts of the Toppo.
Dante, *Inferno, XIII.* 118–21. The fugitives in the Wood of the Suicides.

JOURNEY TO A KINGDOM,
AND OTHER POEMS

from the Hamish Henderson Archive

PIRON'S EPITAPH ON HIMSELF

Here lies poor old Piron   Now gone to Perdition
Who was nothing – not even   An Academician.

Note: Alexis Piron (1689–1773), French dramatist celebrated for his epigrams. [Editor]

[Hamish Henderson Archive]

EPISTILL
(aureate style)

Peter, of Cambridge makars all the flour,
For that to mak amend ye did nocht tarrie
I am appeasit. Sweit apothecarie
Your ounce of civet is ane richt guid cure.

Remissioun to auld Emmanuel's tour,
My saulis croun, all luvingly I carrie;
And glaid acceptance – through my thanks be puir,
And I maun be mine ain bauld emissarie.

Note: This letter was sent (by hand) to Peter Paston Brown, who had sent me (by post) an apology, and an invitation to tea. – Peter, a close friend of mine at Cambridge, accompanied some of my early song-poems on guitar. – A bomber-pilot in the RAFVR, he was shot down over France on 20 June 1943. He was 23.

[*Pervigilium Scotiae* (Etruscan Books, 1997)]

TO A FREE KIRK MINISTER

You, brother, are too fond of talking about Sin,
By which you mean, of course, Sex.
There would in the population be fewer rakes and wrecks
If more of the population entered in.

The female spinster is a hump on the world's back
And a monster like the male virgin of thirty.
Och, I know; this land would be less dirty
And your poor damned parish less bleak and black

If sex were acknowledged to be the chief good of life,
(As it is), and the fountain of spirit:
The most sweet root of love, treasure of most merit
And if our human kindness loved mother and wife.

[Hamish Henderson Archive]

JOURNEY TO A KINGDOM

'That guy? He's one of the wandering Kings of Scotland.'

– Paul Potts

I

Going to Exeter, the faithful city,
The fat canaille swept through their several ruts.
I left my curses in their purpled guts
Though most escaped my cromak, more's the pity.

Hell wither your soul! So the sallow trees
That stand in the evening storm-light purpled and eerie
Must turn the spit for me; the fulsome sheaves,
Tumbling like new republics in the shocks,
Now make me welcome.
                          Vandalism of time
That makes irrelevant the spinning sun
And crumbles all my purpose!

            'Back to your vinegar, you gherkin, go!
            Your sour carbuncle on the feet of Marx!
            You chambermaid's delight! The coppers' narks
            Will snitch me where the pimps and fiddlers go.'

Och, to your stinging words, get your great ways.
Go to the Mameluke, and tread the tarmac
With his rambustion, Paul!
                    Meanwhile I follow my thumb
Under air-routes where the moaning bombers fly.
Big-wombed with death. The soldier's whore dissemble
In sections mormels in the coaxing corners.
Prussian the sky-blue over this isle-reich, rolling
Rich cumuli in as yet unnumbered columns.
('I have four columns marching on the city

And one that's gone before, to which the conquest')
Now in the clammy egg-white light of the country
Dawning, I hug my thoughts between shivering hedges
Whistling the dew. And, at strategic turns
I find him – bragging that age's rust
Is battle-blood, our surly Cerberus stands,
The untamed traction engine.
                                    Merry murder
when farmers bear their plough-shares into swords
And twirl invasion's stripes! . . .
                                    Alone and alonie
I climb Balmano Street. The haggard houses
Spew out their wizened withered aged children
On to the dirty stone. They puke and sprawl
And play, while in the fetid passage-ways
Coated with venomed slime, our hairy marys
Lick poison out from bloody blackened nails.
So howl, ye ships from Clyde!
                                    Alone and alonie
I climb Balmano Street. They graze and grieve me,
The harsh and hacking accents of my people.
(And yet in the early morning, by Schiehallion,
I heard their lovely tongues' wave-beating language.)
Your metaphysics is not brazed to this,
Nor can your sly, cold analytic phrases
Disprove this canon – he who makes his bed
On velvet coal-dust must cut out his eyes
And impale them on a pin.
                                    You think you live.
The demon crooks himself into your bones
And snaps them. So you are dead. But you in time,
Redeemer of us, will tear him from your branches
And tread him down into the fetid slime.
  . . . The spindle tocks and turns. Alone and alonie
I climb Balmano Street and climb to the Highlands.

II

Stranger, troubled and older
My eyes look north, now search for no charmer
Among magus mountains. For the fire
In my brain's socket burns colder
And cold brings sleep.

But alone, an alien
Among ferns and squirrels . . .

Through the mummy swathings
Of numb and swaddled sleep, my country's
Phantom slips into mind's last inlet.

The ships have sailed
Past Tomnahurich hill, where men with shoes
On dry land walked. Brigades of innocent sheep
Have put a race to rout: The glens are theirs.
Seaforth has gone. His doom that filled the Lews
Forgotten.
                    Coinneach Odhar is revenged
For his phosphorescent end. The tub's burnt out . . .

The happy seer that saw not Leverhulme,
The Brahan Seer, with all his prophesies
Is gone. And with him gone the luckless Gael.

III

But some there are, a remnant, lingering yet
Rich only in song and story, among the hills.
And four I'll mention, both to do them honour
If any honour springs from a poet's speech,
And also to recall them, to define them
From the peopled gloaming of my memories.

Murdo of Clachan.
For you of all I'll first strike Lucifer
And take you by the hair, Murdo of Clachan
To start and stare into your luminous eyes.
There was word went out a daft-like lad
                              went shambling
In the rimy morning mist by thistle and thorn
Along your half-ploughed field, but that's a lie
That's sprouted evilly. A rock of torment
Has formed, Murdo, and split inside your skull,
And yet your eyes are gentle, and your ways courteous.
They called you *bàn*, the fair-haired, bonny boy
Who call you mad now.

Inverey cam doon Deeside, whistlin' and playin'

Spitch. The flare. Who's this?
I am Duncan MacMaster
And wish to speak to you, Canon, most urgently
About most urgent matters, Canon. The tinker,
Who's to be married, do you remember, must be taught
The details of the service, Canon. He must say
'With all my worldly goods I thee endow'
And *will* say 'woollen goods'. O Canon, Canon . . .

Who's this?
                    Och, by the Solomon, I knew
That you'd be here tonight – I knew you'd climb
The painful stairs out of damned Hieland pride!
                    Welcome then
The high hidalgo nose and humorous eyes
And welcome the indomitable heart.
You gallant, grey-haired, gracious old Diana,
I greet you. Catherine Macdonald Grant!
How well we understood each other. When
I joked, you'd laugh and ask where was our Boswell

To scribble us down and put us in a book.
Your speech had dignity, wit and easy knowledge
Quoting Rob Donn and expounding Swedenborg –
But you were best on your neighbour's characters
(that loathing broth of Hieland cauld and hunger)
And your sly tod enemies in Newtonmore.

Nous naissons, nous vivons, bergère;
Nous mourrons, sans savoir comment . . .

On the road from Lochgilphead to Inverary
I had your company, Peter; though the road was hard
And your feet were sore,
There was light enough going for us – the
whole drum-thundering host
Of heaven was with us. Ours of the Pilgrims
In your bundle came archangels and
the flaming angels
To go before us. O, on your noble head,
Grey-haloed like a covenanting saint's
A hand (whose hand!) has rested –
                    Which no fell,
No fiend's fingers could clutch or claw away.
O, Peter, in a corner of my brain
That knows the Universe ghostless and godless
I knew your vision, Peter, and my own heart.

IV
From the height of Cnoc-makar I look on the townlands,
On fat Strathmore, and its braw largesse of lochs.
Black Loch and White Loch, Fengus, Marlee, Clunie
Where the bolstered curlews come.
                    But back I turn
Northwards, and sit at nightfall under Glasclune,
Nearby the canyon cleft of the shaggy shabby Lornty
That marked the clannish confine.

There were two castles,
Two battled keeps, Drumlochy and Glasclune,
That had an eternal blood-feud with each other.
They sat on their bums, girned raucle wrath at each other
And between, the scrogs of the dowdy, duddy Lornty.

Drumlochy's lord was a broiled and curried die-hard
Who fought, as his fathers fought, with steel (cold steel)
And said the other fellow couldn't take it.
But Glasclune had marched with the times –

he was progressive

And felt in tune with the Spirit of the Age.
Now one day he went out and bought a cannon
(An instrument unknown to the chap next door).
With it he gave Drumlochy a thorough pasting –
In fact, smashed him to hell.

'The moral of this,' said Glasclune, with satisfaction,
'Is: you gotta keep ahead of the other fellah.
Everything's fair in love and total war.'

Now wae's me, Glasclune
Glasclune and Drumlochy,
They bashed thirsels blue
By the back side o Knockie.

Drumlochy focht fair
But Glasclune, the deceiver
Made free wi' a firework
Tae blaw up his neebur.

Then shame on the Blairs
An' sic wuddifu races
I' the eyes of a' *ceevilized*
Fowk tae disgrace us!

Ochone, Drumlochy,
Glasclune and Drumlochy –
An arrow, twa hearts and a broch o rubble.

V
A path through the black-cored moorland
Is my way home, where no voice calls my name.
Only the weasel
Running a nimble courier
Starts from my stride and flees.
Now the west knows
I have come. Now night has lowered its barrier
I can take my rest.

But I can have no quiet
For still in my dream
I am harried.
It comes on me to arise
And ride the nightmare: to carry
The bundle of my words
To the Hebrides.

Not slow to rise
I am up and away.
I leap early
To winged islands
And get of them mastery.
Sgurr and Quirang
My fanatic grip they feel:
            Over to Uist
            I'll carry my song of steel.

            O Eilein mhóir, m'eileir, mo chiall . . .

Look, I have grasped it! See how it burns,
Maclean's candle he got from Lenin's.
This glim has still to shine through Scotland.
Thick darkness is over the moorland, but wait. –
                    But wait.

Note: Fragments of this poem were published in Andrew R. Hunter's 'Hamish Henderson: The Odyssey of a Wandering King', *Aberdeen University Review*, No. 178, Autumn 1987. The version here is from the Hamish Henderson Archive and is dated to August 1940. It seems to be the last attempt at the complete poem before segments were separated as stand-alone pieces. [Editor]

[Hamish Henderson Archive]

SONG FOR AN IRISH RED KILLED IN SICILY

Comrades onward
The raging sunward
The fleeing moonward.
      Our rifles thunder
      The stars asunder
            Till the axe falls.

Down we'll tumble
The wormwood lumber
The clutterclumber.
      Their straw and wicker
      'll frisk and flicker
            Till the axe falls.

For us no moaning
No wakes and keening
No whines and screaming.
      We'll mind the heroes
      That fell before us
            Till the axe falls.

[Hamish Henderson Archive and Raymond Ross, ed. *Hamish Henderson: Collected Poems and Songs* (Curly Snake, 2000)]

SITZKRIEG FANTASY
(a Gallimaufry)

MacSporran laments his filibeg; nightly
   He makes his moan:
Potbelly Abe pulls long pants over
   His old shin-bone.
The girls from Paree teach Jock and swaddy
   To bill and coo
But holy Lenin sings on Orion
   Till all is blue.

A whiff of grape-fruit proclaims the Lieutenant
   has taken tea
While Corporal Crump spikes with testudo
   The stoat-skin sea.
My aunt Eulalia spurs the battalion
   To derring-do
But holy Lenin sings on Orion
   Till all is blue.

Dancing the oka with an aspidistra
   Is Harry P.
He declares that a polony's aroma
   Is not for he,
And employs with effect the dialectic
   To prove this true
But holy Lenin sings on Orion
   Till all is blue.

Latimer screeched when his toes were scorching
   And the candle burned.
Gentleman Oates, lashed fast to the coat-tail
   Got what he'd earned.
Tolstoy, Tartuffe and Savonarola
   Are playing loo,

But holy Lenin sings on Orion
  Till all is blue.

The Eireann censor demands that O'Casey
    Cross self and pray,
But Peadair O'Donnell's sign is a sickle
    And rosary.
Our playboy Dev consults at a séance
    Brian Boru
But holy Lenin sings on Orion
  Till all is blue.

Scotland reveals that war in the isles is
    Most certain sure
For Hugh MacDiarmid has buried the hatchet
    – In Edwin Muir.
And Compton Mackenzie is seen to reach for
    His sgian dubh
But holy Lenin sings on Orion
  Till all is blue.

Huxley and Heard, secure in Nirvana
    Look down on dirt,
But Spender relates how Aeneas went and
    Pulled off his shirt.
Dylan was shocked, but Wystan Hugh Auden
    Just whispers 'Coo!'
And holy Lenin sings on Orion
  Till all is blue.

Paul Potts requests that I dial October
    One Nine One Seven
And find from a Comrade Middleton Murray
    If earth *is* heaven –

Though Count Potocki swears by Apollo
     That he's a Jew,
Our holy Lenin sings on Orion
     Till all is blue.

Tambi relates somes scandalous stories
     concerning Joad,
Alleging he used to smother his daughter
     With coats of woad,
And then kick the gong around with the Brains Trust
     That *Godless* crew,
But holy Lenin sings on Orion
     Till all is blue.

Frank Pitcairn suspects that Moscow gold has
     Just crossed the sea,
For Nancy Astor invites to Cliveden
     The whole C.P.
He hints that she has bitten off more now
     Than she can chew,
But holy Lenin sings on Orion
     Till all is blue.

Roy Campbell, though fond of cracking up Franco
     Sure is no fool.
Some say that a flowering rifle is not
     His only tool.
The sons of Mithras have *luck*, but so have
     The sons of Lugh
And holy Lenin sings on Orion
     Till all is blue.

And Lenin had luck – luck, faith and reason,
     The holy three,
When he opened wide an historical door with
     History's key,

Professor Laski reads 'War and the Workers',
     Murmurs 'Sez you' –
But holy Lenin sings on Orion
     Till all is blue.

(1940)

[Hamish Henderson Archive and Raymond Ross, ed. *Hamish Henderson: Collected Poems and Songs* (Curly Snake, 2000)]

PIONEER BALLAD OF SECTION THREE

(Tune: 'O We're Rusty Bums')

O, I'll sing you a song, and a damn good song,
    Of the good old Section Three.
We carry the pipes, we carry the clamps,
    And put 'em together, do we.
We jerrymander the bloody things up
    And we sling them into the sea.
Then covered in muck we bum on the truck
    And bugger off home to tea.

>   Chorus:
>   *O, we're rusty bums, and jolly good chums,*
>   *We live like Royal Turks,*
>   *And when we're in luck we bum on the chuck*
>   *And pity the guy that works.*

                              (repeat after each verse)

We get gobbets of meat, and veg to eat
    That tastes like sweaty socks,
And when we shit we're afraid to sit
    For fear of getting the pox.
But what do we care – our woes we bear
    Like a lot of yogi saints,
And if our rations were cut by half
    There'd still be No Complaints.

At half-past six the Sergeant Major
    Is shouting 'Show a Leg!'
And if you're late he's very irate
    And he puts you on the peg,
For he's a silly old man, and he don't understand
    That when you've washed your plate,
And made your bed, and said your prayers
    You're bound to be two minutes late.

[145]

Our Sergeant Major's a fearless man
    Of women he's not afraid.
He makes you think of the missing link
    When he's shouting 'On Parade!'
He's got a big crook to bring to book
    The black sheep in the fold,
But he's got a kind face – in the usual place –
    And also a heart of gold.

O we like work and we don't mind
    If everyone does his share
But none of the Corporals seem to work
    I consider it most unfair.
They lounge all day in their elegant way
    Discussing the world at large,
And if some-one reminds 'em that 'corporals work'
    They put him on a charge.

Now Sergeant Moran had had a wife
    He married in Timbuctoo,
He loved her every Friday night
    And then beat her black and blue.
He displayed her once more to Section 4
    While she was still red and raw
And then he dressed her in a sarong
    And sold her to Captain Shaw.

When Sergeant Mackie took ill and he died,
    He thought he'd best go to heaven,
But he stayed in this 'Ship' till closing time
    And didn't get there till eleven.
He'd been locked out, so he turned about
    And went off home to hell,
But there they made him sign the pledge
    And wear the blue ribbon as well.

Now Buckley's not a drinking man,
    Though he certainly likes a few,
And Major Briggs occasionally swigs
    Some Chablis '92.
But it's nice to know that the beer will flow
    And the bottles cheerfully pass;
They'll never be dry in the Officers' Mess
    For they've always got their Bass.

When Worthington is on the beach
    The strongest men turn pale.
If any poor fools lay down their tools
    To pounce he will not fail.
I sometimes fear that inside a year
    He'll be numbered among the slain,
For someone'll lift a 20 foot
    And he'll never rise again.

Alf Lygrove is a popular guy,
    He's got chinas near and far.
When a tart, with a leer, says 'Hullo dear',
    He murmers 'Righto-ta.'
He lays her low in his old chateau
    And then he proceeds to fuck
But when he's given a waggle or two
    She says 'your dog is stuck.'

O the Corporal cook is tower of strength
    And he certainly looks the part.
Among his stews I'd get the blues
    And mightily soon lose heart.
But I'll tell you why in his savoury sty
    He works with never a care.
We'd like to know where our rations go –
    But the Corporal's got them – there!

O we're the heroes of the night
   And we let you know it, too.
There isn't a man in the Pioneers
   Who would rather fight than – woo.
But if flat-arsed boats on enormous floats
   Come over the Channel by night,
There isn't a man in this perishing mob
   Who won't be there to fight.

No, we were not a well-trained lot
   When we came from the old Earl Mill,
But now we're the Wolves of Pevensey Bay,
   The Bulldogs of Bexhill.
We're known from Meads to Wittening
   And from Chi to Selsey Bill,
And when we've arrived in Kingdom Come
   We'll be building these bastards still.

So here's a health to a bloody fine chap
   Whom all of us know by now.
Before Dunkirk he did not shirk
   As even the Guards allow.
And it's on the cards that he'll lick the Guards
   At war or women or beer.
So give a rouse – and it's on the house –
   For the Fighting Pioneer!

         Chorus:
         O we're rusty bums, and jolly good chums,
            We live like Royal Turks,
         And when we're in luck we bum on the chuck
            And pity the guy that works.

Note: This ballad, founded on a well-known bum song, was made up by me while I was, with my mates in the Pioneers, building the scaffolding boom defence on the beaches of south-east England. It became very popular, was sung by everyone and was (in a bowdlerized version) the hit of two concerts. The communal making of it (several of my mates contributed ideas, lines and snatches of stanzas) and the variants which it rapidly developed on the lips of others gave me valuable insight into folk poetry in action.

While in Wittering we lived in 'chalets' (i.e. ramshackle holiday camp huts). Lygrove, whose Cockney speech was as vivid as Synge's Playboy, called his 'The Chateau'. I called mine Rustibums.

The Earl Mill at Oldham had been our training centre and I was there for a fortnight.

[Hamish Henderson Archive and Raymond Ross, ed. *Hamish Henderson: Collected Poems and Songs* (Curly Snake, 2000)]

Nasty little bastard, 'e was. Eyes like piss-'oles in the snow. Cor strike a light, I'd rather 'ave old Goebbels for a china than im for a fuckin pen-pal.

And that bleedin 'ospital. Well, fuck me standin, mother dear. I'd take a blitzed shit-ahse for me billets before that ruddy asylum. No matter if you ad impetigo, syphilis or a broken neck you'd still ave your temperature taken at 6 o'clock. Bastard silly place it is well fuck me – I don't know.

Eighteen bastard stitches they put in me. Every time I look at them I feel all fluty.

But there was a nurse there, lovely little tart, tastiest bit of stuff I've set me eyes on for a long time . . . 'Ow do you feel?' she said. 'With me ands' I said. Lovely girl she was. Cor blimey I could use her shit for tooth-paste.

Coo, what wouldn't I give for a bit of knife. You know, I 'aven't dipped me wick for five months . . . It ain't ealthy.

'If you take any liberties you'll pay for it' she says. 'I'll pay for anything you've got, Miss,' I says. Cor fuck me, that shook 'er.

Blimey when I knew I'd got another stretch in that fuckin mad'ouse me ballocks blew up like a barrage balloons. Well, I applied to see the O.C. 'Orspital, see? When I got there I said 'I'll park my arse on the table if you don't mind, sir!' 'Very well, Sergeant Major,' 'e said, democratic bloke 'e is. 'Y'know sir' I says 'if you want my opinion of this place, sir,' I says, 'I'll give it to you, sir,' I says. 'Its lousy. Lousy as cuckoo' . . . Cor crikey, that shook 'im.

When I was finished, 'Kaput' e says 'I've had it!' You bet 'e 'ad, and all.

[Hamish Henderson Archive]

CLAMAVI (OR, SERENTIS IN REBUS)

Wrest from the strife that dins the stone deaf
wrest from the mamelukes locked in the torments
who cough in the sleet and hail of howitzers
or the whining arquebus death of agonies
        wrest from the wrong smile of snickering mocker
that twists our fingers loose from the rudder
of mind's integrity, that shivers our world
into sick delirium   wrest from the liar
slyly harvesting with lotus of illusion
our norland impulse naked in seawind
and keen in knowledge   wrest from sargassos
of bottomless sloth, of opium nirvanas
of slobbering Caliban mad in the marshes
        wrest from the tumult of others Babels
of drooling and dribbling babble of wave-lengths,
of science hunched on the hurtling nightmare,
wrest from the drone of trolls in the stormwind
lumbering louts on the planks of heaven,
stuttering loons disgorging their vomit
of hell-stuffed thunderbolt, splitting to shivering
splinters the plangent willow of music
        wrest from the sly tod log of betraying
inaction, wrest from the subtle offers
of flattering death   wrest from the sodden
sphagnum bed of tired degradation
from the quivering thin-lipped cajoling of joking
Jesus – in heaven earth's agues shall cease . . .

wrest from this doom of historical nothing
wrest, o wrest, my history, your peace.

[Hamish Henderson Archive]

[151]

DEATH
(after Rainer Maria Rilke)

Death is great.
We are his people
Early or late

In the heart of the life's town
                    when no watch we're keeping
Death is heard weeping
Within the gate.

Note: Written in Egypt not long after I arrived.

[Hamish Henderson Archive and Raymond Ross, ed. *Hamish Henderson: Collected Poems and Songs* (Curly Snake, 2000)]

This is the exile's trouble – the treachery of other grown familiar,
The inevitable erosion of early habit
And the early speech grown halting and clumsy.
And again we are reminded – when other is courteous,
Honeyed and wooing us to shame and betrayal
            The little smile for own foibles
            The smiling excuse for own identity
            The excusing joke of own nationhood and
name.
What are the dangers?
Boldly I number them,
Bitterly name them:
Cunning charity, calculating welcome, courtesan kindness,
All can accuse me
All have cajoled me
To kneeling denial.

But we have much to help us – knowledge and confirming
    friendship
Of own against other, and the protruding hostility
Of our less subtle enemies hearten, uphold us.
Example and tradition maintain our integrity,
We remember the loyal who lived before us.
All underlines our double allegiance,
Allegiance to Scotland and the Scottish people,
Allegiance to our allies in every nation,
To the working world and the waiting people
            Who look to the pitface
            Where you, Johnnie Miner,
            Will hold a red candle.

[Hamish Henderson Archive and Raymond Ross, ed. *Hamish Henderson: Collected Poems and Songs* (Curly Snake, 2000)]

The ocean's pride a winking wanton kimmer
Whose father had no love for barley water.
Ilk evening to the Unicorn he'd saunter
And bash his way to ecstasy. His banter
(Och, blethers! Losh, ye're haverin', auld loon.
How could ye feel the warld a-birlin roon,
How could ye hear the starnies greet, ye fule?
Is't Venus ye've been daein' wi' yer tool?)
His banter filled the heids o' ill-schooled lassies
(The while he fingered ower their sonsie chassis)
Wi' mirligoes, wi' wild and waesome dwams . . .
He lauched, and belted doon his hefty drams.

[Hamish Henderson Archive and Raymond Ross, ed. *Hamish Henderson: Collected Poems and Songs* (Curly Snake, 2000)]

SEASCAPE

Pluck the sea-weed from your sopping hair
And spit the Ionian from your salty lips.
Clear the shingle from between your toes,
And do try and pull yourself together.
In shallow water, without danger,
You daudled too long, morose Dionysus.
Mocker, blubbering flotsam, be reasonable.
Sit down on the sea-spittled concrete.
Listen to me while I talk sense.

I wanted to strike out over glacid waters
Over dove-breasted doldrums to the lonely pharos;
To scare the schools of plopping porpoises
And stand tip-toe on the spires of Atlantis.
But in lazy speech with the slow-tongued breakers
You lolled like kelp on the slimy sea-sand,
And sulking because the tide retreated
You counted the five arms of a starfish.
 – You really are perfectly impossible.

[Hamish Henderson Archive and *Pervigilium Scotiae* (Etruscan Books, 1997)]

DARK STREETS TO GO THROUGH
(16 April 1941)

Evil lurks persistent in craters
lethal for years.
        And the white unsmudged façade
crumbles at touch.

The man said 'God is dead.
Listen, for the news affects you. God is dead.'

The people laughed.

The man again said 'God is dead.
We have ourselves killed him,
        his blood is on *our* hands
The churches are his tomb-stones,
        dotting white the land
Under the east is his head
where the priest says his paters.
God is dead.'

The people laughed.
(Shooting out their lips).

We have still dark streets to go through,
        searching with feeling fingers
for the known contours of a wall, for the familiar
grime in the cracks, for dust in the sockets of the bricks,
for places where beauty is in denial, yet are unspeakably
        dear to us,
and to trace the wrong shape of a razed stump,
no flesh but loathsome ghost.

(This necropolis
Bristles with ugly angels, poised on the dead breasts
                    of children
and lusting for ever in unchallengeable possession).

But poppies in the green corn speak of tomb's supercession
and this river of our inviolable peace.

Dark streets to go through, in nights debauched of quiet;
dark streets blazing like an *auto da fe,* till cease
well after dawn the bombers' roar and riot,
and the city, in daylight's drawn and haggard relief
shifts on its side to sleep for half an hour,
and then goes to work, not bothering to count the dead.
Dopes, morons, mortal cousins, fools, heroes, of heroes flower –
from my heart I say it, not minding what others said.

Yet this 'terrible beauty' must not blind us; men who have lost
    the power
To think without anger are not a pretty sight.
Planes tilting over the quaking black ant-heap of houses
will have much to answer for
(much surely to answer for)
Besides hell through a long-drawn April night.
Making our task less easy.

Still, a task we must carry through.
In spite of murderous men.
                    In the fable
God is murdered, but born again too.

                (Winchester, June 1941)

Note: In the winter of '40 and the spring of '41 I was an NCO in a Pioneer
Corps company building coastal defences in Sussex against the threatened

German invasion. Weekend leaves meant visits to an aunt in London: she had a flat at the top of a tall block directly opposite Westminster Cathedral, and consequently had a grandstand view of the Blitz. When I arrived at Victoria in the evening of 16th April, the sirens were already sounding, and I realised that I had exchanged the comparative calm of the beaches for a somewhat less pleasant night. (That same night saw the second heaviest tonnage of bombs thrown at London during the entire Blitz.)

My aunt disdained to go downstairs to the basement, and we watched London being bombed from the balcony. There was a direct hit on a cellulose factory in the Wandsworth Bridge Rd, and the planes fuelled the flames, till eventually there was an unbroken sheet of flame stretching several hundred yards . . . This spectacular vision remained with me for long afterwards.

Being dog-tired after hard work on the beaches, I had an hour's semi-sleep about 4 a.m. When I woke up in my aunt's spare room, the bombs were still falling.

Later that morning, walking through the smoking streets, I was amazed at the sangfroid of the Londoners, at the complete absence of panic, although rescue work was going on all over the place. 'Dark streets to go through' is a poem I wrote when back on the much quieter beaches with my company. [*Pervigilium Scotiae* (Etruscan Books, 1997)]

['April Night' in Hamish Henderson Archive, also in *Pervigilium Scotiae* (Etruscan Books, 1997)]

SOLDAT BERNHARD PANKAU
(written during his interrogation)

I like little Pancake.
My heart is so warm.
Though he lies like a trooper
I'll do him no harm.

Note: He was a German trooper captured in the desert. He came clean but had no high-level intelligence to offer.

[Hamish Henderson Archive and Raymond Ross, ed. Hamish *Henderson: Collected Poems and Songs* (Curly Snake, 2000)]

MR JIMMY BALGOWRIE TALKING

(in Hyde Park, September 1941)

There's a lot of dumb Nordic dopes, and dumber dopes under that fat slob that call himself the Duce, that go around telling each other – 'this is the historic destiny of our people.'

And maybe there's a few nearer home that'd like tae hand out the same bloody guff to the workers.

Historic destiny of our people!

I'll tell ye what the 'historic destiny of the people' means to the workers –

> in war-time, to be cannon-fodder
> and in peace-time, to be factory-fodder!

We've had enough of this historic destiny business.

Ye won't hear our allies the Russians bletherin about their destiny; they don't blether at all, they've got no bloody time for it. They know they're fightin for a country that's given them a square deal – they know they've got something to fight for, and they'll lick the world to hang on to it. They've got a decent life to fight for, not a damn destiny!

And they're fighting like you never have or will, in this war. *They're* ready to sacrifice everything, and *you're* not, by a helluva long chalk. If you can see our friends the big capitalists carryin the fiery cross for a 'scorched earth' policy you've got better eyes than me. By Christ, we're a fine collection! Men? We're no more men than the nancy boys ye can see any night trippin doon Piccadilly. – What abou the Blitz? Holy Mary, we can take it. We can take it. And I'll tell ye this – we've got to bloomin weel take it, whether we like it or not!

Just work this out on an old bus ticket – 'the test of the dynamic of a nation is its capacity for sacrifice!' – And that's whether ye like it or not, too.

The blowing up of the Dnieperstroy dam! When I heard of that I nearly sat doon and cried. Not because of its strategic value, or its value in cash, nor because it was a wonder of the modern world – but because it represented five years of human endeavour, five years of human planning and toil, five years of human achievement – and ten more years of preparation for the same.

And what's our answer to that? What's *your* answer, you thinking members of the great British public? . . . there's a book our General Staff must be readin just now – *All Quiet on the Western Front.*

What's going to happen in the Eastern wars?

D'ye remember what Jo Stalin said, that he'd never pull the chestnuts out of the fire for the Western democracies? Well, now he's doing it, very nicely . . . I'm no a military expert, so naturally, I don't know how the hell the Russian war's going to turn out, but know one thing: Jo isn't going to die to make the world safe for the Western democracies, to make the world safe for Mr Churchill's Utopia, or Roosevelt's either. We didn't lift a damn finger to help the Spanish people when *it* was struggling to keep its freedom and make Spain safe from Fascism, so we can't expect Jo to put on shining armour and act like St George, for England's bloody benefit.

And we'll only have ourselves to thank if Hitler makes another deal with Stalin – and Jo accepts. Hitler knows by now that the Red Army's no picnic, and Jo wants to salvage something of what he's built in 20 years of socialism. And then – well, wouldn't that be just too lovely for ye! By God, after tackling a real army the Germans would go through you like melted butter. Use what you've got for brains, for God's sake. I say – we'd have no one to thank but our bloody selves!

Still – perhaps you'd rather leave it all to Mr Churchill. *Great* Mr Churchill!

Great! . . . The myth of that man's greatness is a greater illusion than anything Maskelyne and Devant ever put on. What's he done, I'm askin ye – what's the man *done*?

Norway, Dunkirk, Greece, Crete – that's what he's done. There's a series of disasters for ye, that's unique in the history of this punch-drunk isle. And there'll be more too, before the play's played.

Great Mr Churchill! That man has got the mind of a child. We must have our sailor suit and our vanity head-gear – we're never photographed without a cigar in our mouth. I grew out of that stage years ago. – God knows I like a fag, but I can do without it when I'm having my photo taken.

Did ye read that wretched hotch-potch of political slops, the so-called Atlantic charter? I did, but I wasn't so interested in that as something else I noticed on the same page. D'ye know who was on the *Prince of Wales* too? Our old working-class friend, Monty Norman. And what was *he* doing aboard, I wonder? Brother, I wouldn't know. I just wouldn't know.

There's a stink arisin from somewhere.

By God – if I find that they've sold Scotland, there's going to be just one hell of a shindy! . . .

What I don't like about this war is that it's neither flesh nor fowl nor good baked herrin. – I should have been in a concentration camp long ago, but instead I'm here bletherin – yes, bletherin . . .

What's to happen now?

Well – *strictly speaking* – we should have a revolution.

God knows we're ripe for it, rotten ripe for it.

My horror is that it won't happen.

Anyway, there's no fear of their calling me up for the Army. They don't like intelligence in the Army, and as my face simply radiates intelligence I'd get no further than the first medical inspection.

But what's the use of joining it? I shite myself enough in the Blitz as it is.

I suggested, with an eye to business, that he hould offer his services to the Intelligence Corps.

[Hamish Henderson Archive]

THE SALAMANDER
(A Dream in the Great Freeze)

So through the hard grey rind of the world I dig
Away from cold into the flaming centre.
The ice and iron spark. O false supplanter,
I find my own, which cunningly you hid.

Hephaestus was my father. In my flesh
Smoking and whimpering, fire with livid symbols
Had burnt a path-way. Fire makes clean and humbles,
Fire is the healing finger and the lash.

Kneeling by frozen waters, my fingers numb
And nipped in the whilring winds, I scent the furnace
And tear at the snow. I sniff the reek of fire.

Fire snaps the hobbling chain, the haggling pander,
And cuts down winter, stiff in rusty harness.
From fire to fire I leap, quick Salamander.

[As 'A (Wet) Dream in the Great Freeze' in Hamish Henderson Archive,
also in Raymond Ross, ed. *Hamish Henderson: Collected Poems and Songs*
(Curly Snake, 2000)]

WHEN THE TEASED IDIOT TURNS

When the teased idiot turns
And in his little eye, before so patient,
The quickened anger burns
      I think with faith
Of all the uncouth, humped, hooped, malformed,
          wry-fashioned
In the traitor's gate of death.

They to their cramped ledge cling
Death's hostages from among the living people
      And in the torments sing.
          They give me power
To hammer our verse, who am learner yet,
          time's pupil
And spurn this unheeding hour.

Unheeding, because the sky
Draws eyes into its dark, and spikes their sockets
And drowns the blindbuff cry
      In silence. Yet
The blind man twists his poppies, clasps his lockets
And splits the enfolding net.

[Hamish Henderson Archive and Raymond Ross, ed. *Hamish Henderson: Collected Poems and Songs* (Curly Snake, 2000)]

HATE POEM

I hate him. Shuffling round the room,
A faded bloodless vampire bat
Feeding on worms in a dry tomb.
Most genteel harbinger of doom,
A withered hook-nosed diplomat.

Easy to see that he knows all
The right people – that in Berlin
Or Rome he's only got to call
And whisper three words in the hall
For every door to bow him in.

The world was all right in his day
 – All right for him – but now the sky
Is overcast, the sky is grey
And working men 'get much more pay',
'Do much less work.' (A Tartuffe sigh.)

He'd call himself a realist,
By which he means the status quo
Is real and hard inside his fist.
And sickly conscience won't be missed
If, indisposed, he has to go.

I think he once was Thyssen's guest,
Talked 'cordially' with Ribbentrop;
By Carinhall was much impressed
And with the bonzes had the best –
Yes, Uncle Herman was the top.

The legionaries from Baldur's bed,
The bankers of the Holy Ghost
Would soon defeat the bloody Red.
To sots who with Horst Wessel bled
He'd pledge his gentlemanly toast.

And now? – The tale is different.
Five wars in eighty years begun
With brutal and depraved intent:
To serve the wargod's flourishment
He lams the bloody Hun!

By 18 B his heart is warmed,
The Home Guard, too, is sound, but he
Admits that he's 'a shade alarmed'
To see the workers may be armed.
It makes one nervous, certainly.

He reads that change is in the air,
Want will no more the land defile,
Masters and men the profits share.
He reads this all with thoughtful care,
Permits himself a little smile.

Mistake to underestimate
This fly beggar. The coppers' narks
Steer clear of his sort. *He's no blate.*
Unlike our boys, he's slow to hate
And unlike Bevin, knows his Marx.

But long enough he's had his fun,
This dodo of a die-hard race.
When Seumas finds a tommy-gun
He'll find, or his vile course is run
That liquidation meets his case.

[Hamish Henderson Archive and Raymond Ross, ed. *Hamish Henderson: Collected Poems and Songs* (Curly Snake, 2000)]

HOSPITAL AFTERNOON

In the hand projecting from the blue pyjamas
The nerves dart like a pond of minnows,
Betraying a brief agitation in the brain,
Timid deer start in the parkland spinneys:
Through our shutters the fine sand blows like rain.
The waves of heat loll lazy aggression
Against our feverish island of illness,
The bumble buzz of an electric fan
Makes a weakly wind in a covey of coolness.
Whispering starts behind the crimson screen.
We lie out of sheets in defeatist languor.
The wardrobe mirror takes up my attention.
After lunch feelings grow fat in the head.
My nihilist brain nods its own suspension,
On a tide of treacle drifts off towards sleep.

(Helwan, Egypt, 1942)

[*Oasis* (Cairo, 1943)]

POEM FOR SILVANO

(written in the gardens of the Maadi Club, Cairo, 12 May 1942)

Here I have wandered off the raw
And rutty track of history.
This garden flouts the arid law,
Tropic and arctic irony
        The panther's avid paw.

And all that I expected here
Is rather subtly re-arranged.
The shapes are not what they appear
The scene directions have been changed.
        Still this instinctive fear!

It's odd. Why should I want to call
(This pathway never seems to end)
And on the level fear to fall?
I think there's something round the bend . . .
        I don't like this at all.

[*Lines Review*, No. 5, June 1954]

BALLAD OF THE STUBBY GUNS

Another secret weapon's here
To fill us with despair and fear.
The latest things to please the Huns
Are bulgy tanks with stubby guns.

The musulmans, indifferent, look
From minarets in fenced Tobruk
At havoc caused within our ranks
By stubby guns on bulgy tanks!

Old Rommel's cup of joy is full
Now Cruewell's sitting in the cool.
He loves them like so many sons,
His bulgy tanks with stubby guns.

'The time's at hand' he crows with pride
'When Cairo will be occupied
And Groppi's stuffed with squareheads – thanks
To stubby guns on bulgy tanks.

'What's more' he cries in boisterous mood,
'The petrol problem's solved for good.
They run on gyppo beer and buns,
Mein bulgy tanks mit stubby guns'.

The Nordic youth in days gone by
For Gretchen or for Max would sigh.
They now prefer the rounded flanks
Of stubby guns on bulgy tanks.

I can't be free of them, it seems,
For rudely ripping up my dreams
Come rumbling tanks of ninety tons –
Great bulgy tanks with stubby guns!

And isn't it a bloody shame
The Bosch can never play the game.
The ball is on the roof-top – thanks
To stubby guns on bulgy tanks.

Of normal tanks we knew they'd heaps,
But now our fate is sealed for keeps.
Who'll blame the swaddy if he runs
From bulgy tanks with stubby guns?

(19 June 1942)

Note: Written the day before Tobruk fell.

In the hectic days of Rommel's offensive an extraordinary report was current (it emanated from the heated brain of an intelligence officer) that the Germans were using on their new tanks hollow armour of such abnormal thickness that it gave the gun mounted on the tanks a 'stubby' appearance.

Cruewell – a German general and rival to Rommel.

Groppi's – a Cairo restaurant.

[Hamish Henderson Archive and Raymond Ross, ed. *Hamish Henderson: Collected Poems and Songs* (Curly Snake, 2000)]

WE SHOW YOU THAT DEATH AS A DANCER
(for Captain Ian McLeod)

Death the dancer poked his skull
Into our drawing-room furtively
Before a bullet cracked the lull
and stripped jack-bare the rowan tree.
Now flesh drops off from every part
and in his dance he shows his art.

The fundamental now appears,
the ultimate stockade of bone.
He'll neutralize the coward years
and all poor flesh's ills condone.
When we lie stickit in the sand,
He'll dance into his promised land.

(Alamein, 1942)

[Nicholas Moore, ed., *Atlantic Anthology* (1945)]

HONEST GEORDIE

(Tune: 'Monymusk')

When honest Geordie said good-bye
Tae truth, and a' the diddle o't –
The cherry tree? *Some other guy* . . .
   Och deil tak the riddle o't.

Ye cuidnae hear frae awfy near
Ye cuidnae hear the piddle o't,
When auld Mahoun poured oot his beer –
   Och deil tak the riddle o't.

> *Sae doddle the drum wi' bibbery bum*
> *The glamourie o' the fiddle o't.*
> *The dominie tweaks the minister's breeks*
>   *Och deil tak the riddle o't.*

There wisnae hope for Deil or Pope
Nor a' the heathen squiddle o't.

[Hamish Henderson Archive and *Poetry Broadsheet* (Cambridge), No. 1, 1951, as cited in Timothy Neat, *Hamish Henderson: A Biography*, Vol. 1, p. 292.]

STRATHSPEY

There's nae lass can haud the laddie
Nae lass but's up and ready
Nae lass cuid let him pass
   When Johnnie gaes doon the High Street.

Frae Brighton tae Clachnaharry
He's left horns for a' tae carry
There's *ae* loon will wear 'em soon
   When Johnnie gangs doon the High Street . . .

[Hamish Henderson Archive and *Poetry Broadsheet* (Cambridge), No. 1, 1951, as cited in Timothy Neat, *Hamish Henderson: A Biography*, Vol. 1, p. 292.]

LEAVING BRANDENBURG 1939

A last word to the guardsmen
stalking *stramm* among the pines,
and to them that tread the Markish sand:
there are hands with wood
and hands with iron
that shall yet be torn
with triumph,

under the eagle.

[As 'Bye Bye Brandenburg' in Hamish Henderson Archive, and in
Raymond Ross, ed. *Hamish Henderson: Collected Poems and Songs* (Curly
Snake, 2000)]

BALLAD OF THE CREEPING JESUS

Boots trample the boards.
Take that moan off your face my lad
                    Says the Great I Am
What's your bleeding name?
Sycophant sniggers
Drive gash of eating gall through the heart of Gormless
On a skewer of pain

And weasel-keen
The eyes of the creeping jesus
With a face as long as the rain.

Moonslime on fields.
Behind our hust the peep of a crookshank shadow
Spawn of batsbane.
Queerfellow shivers.
Like poison pools the washy eyes of the bleeders
Sneer at his brain

But they're gummed in sleep
The eyes of the creeping jesus
With a face as long as the rain.

Thumb-nail in groove
Of jagged jack-knife.
                    He kens where the bastard dosses
– Hi, what's your game?
From noo till doomsday
Ye yellow-belly, ye snivellin' pregnant nun
Ye'll creep in vain

Bemused in death
The eyes of the creeping jesus
With a face as long as the rain.

Note: This poem, one of a series of grotesques, is a revenge tragedy of the Army underworld.

A 'queerfellow' is betrayed by his mate, the sneak, called a 'Creeping Jesus'. The halfwit, after doing a course of punishment called 'jankers', pursues his friend with a vendetta and makes an attempt on his life with a jack-knife.

The first verse is company orders, where the queerfellow is convicted on his friend's evidence for a crime which the latter committed.

The second is the desire for vengeance, in a cold landscape of moonlight.

The third is the resolve taken, and the deed done.

[Hamish Henderson Archive and Raymond Ross, ed. *Hamish Henderson: Collected Poems and Songs* (Curly Snake, 2000)]

BALLAD OF THE TWELVE STATIONS
OF MY YOUTH

'Ladyis, this is the legend of my life, though Latin it be nane.'

(Here is the legend of the youth of Seumas
*   Who flunked the role some half-god cast him for;*
Was born like Platen in an evil decade
*   And in one still more evil grew for war.)*

I climb with Neil the whinny braes of Lornty,
    Or walk my lane by drumlie Ericht side.
Under Glasclune we play the death of Comyn,
    And fear, wee boys, the Auld Kirk's sin of pride.

Spring quickens. In the Shee Water I'm fishing.
    High on whaup's mountain time heaps stone on stone.
The speech and silence of Christ's word is Gaelic,
    And youth on age, the tree climbs from the bone.

We squabble through the shapeless Devon village,
    A tribe of schoolboys, bound for dens we know,
And act Tod Slaughter in the ferns of Haldon
    Where cloven hoofs of Horny singed the snow.

Brighton. Last night to the flicks. And now I'm sitting
    In a dressing gown on the rumpled unmade bed.
There's a trunk in the room, and plates, and morning sunshine,
    And Mrs O'Byrne saying my mother's dead.

Cramming ourselves with fish and chips we saunter
    Myself and Paddy, down the Wandsworth Road.
'Good beds for men' the shabby chapel offers:
    Sup of salvation in the Lord's abode.

So I stroll on, and cry, and make for Clichy,
   Old gossip Clichy with your bawdy joys.
I hear the workers' speeches, and I see them
   Your pretty girls and pretty painted boys.

From Acre Lane I catch a bus to Dulwich
   And read *Le Misanthrope* (an act a day)
Then stroll next door, and say hallo to Michael
   And quiz the Hogarth in our gallery.

With Frau Popo I tour baroque museums
   And throw largesse – *mit Meisterhand gemalt* –
Then leave behind the puffy Prussian statues
   And stroll with Gies-chen through the Grunewald.

I hitch-hike north from foolish virgin Cambridge,
   And in a lorry sleep by Berwick sea
Till shivering dawn – a day more and I'm thonder,
   A wolf in Badenoch among rock and scree.

It's tarzan work till sundown in the saw-mill
   But Billy, me and Cameron slog along;
Foregather in the Balavil for our ceilidh
   And drink malt whisky, swapping song for song.

From Spain return the Clyde-red brave Brigaders.
   I clench my fist to greet the red flag furled.
Our hold has slipped – now Hitler's voice is rasping
   From small square boxes over all the world.

There's fog. I climb the cobbled streets of Oldham
    With other conscripts, and report to one
Who writes with labour, and no satisfaction
    That I've turned up. – From now, my boyhood's done.

Note: Graf Platen, a German poet mocked by Heine. 'Where cloven hooves
of Horny singed the snow' refers to a local legend of the Devon village of
Haldon. '*mit Meisterhand gemalt*' – painted with a Master's hand.

[Hamish Henderson Archive and Raymond Ross, ed. *Hamish Henderson:
Collected Poems and Songs* (Curly Snake, 2000)]

BACK FROM THE ISLAND OF SULLOON
(for M.C. who fared better)

The dark impetuous hussar
That kinged the track with imperious pennant,
He who was known for himself from far
(The dark impetuous hussar)
Has had a come down – he slips from the ward,
Scuffing along in home-made slippers.
He skids
And flips like a ghost in a werewolf's track;
He flattens himself in the wardrobe's shadow
And holds his breath like a Gold Coast diver
For fear nurse sees him and sends him back.

Note: This was written in Helwan General Hospital just south of Cairo in 1942. I was in hospital with some kind of dysentery thing. This chap was an officer in the 8th Army, in a tank regiment. He was badly damaged physically.

[Hamish Henderson Archive and Raymond Ross, ed. *Hamish Henderson: Collected Poems and Songs* (Curly Snake, 2000)]

BALLAD OF SNOW-WHITE SANDSTROKE
(20 August 1942)

The multiple sands on the round world's seashores
*   are a grain of sand in the Great Sand Sea.*

By mobile columns of bone dry doom
I've been cut off from the streams of home.
I'm living here off my sagging hump
On Egypt's sand-caked wrinkled rump.

The wind skelps up the sand that flies
(The vrithy sand) in your mouth and eyes,
And malice of limestone, grated fine
Whirls dust like mad when you drink or dine.

With coloured glass my eyes I fend
From the snowy Jungfrau glare of sand,
And froth-wet words of songs I've sung
Are frizzling to death on my furnace tongue.

I scratch the itch on my arms and feet
Of the blood-rose rash and prickly heat,
And desert sores on the mind and brain
Leave you far from matey, and not quite sane.

When Yahweh saw that the sand was vile
A plague of flies he sent to the Nile.
Though old King Pharoah yelled and swore
He couldn't get rid of the flies no more.

And Rameses' sins you've got to rue;
Flies sit on your mouth, and your corned beef stew.
You may stagger through sand to get away
But they'll follow your flight like beasts of prey.

If scourged by heat I pound through drifts
Of shuddered sand that the Khamsin shifts,
The scorpions leer, and a demon knows
There are gobbets of sand between my toes.

O that is the sand, the little sand
That smacks round the brain an elastic band –
That puzzles the eyes, and twitches the lips,
And worries the sun to a mind's eclipse.

Good drams I had from a kitchen cup:
The billows of sands have gulfed them up.
A curse of sandy hell's on me
From Culbin Sands to the Great Sand Sea.

Note: After the fall of Tobruk – which the previous year had remained in our hands, an unconquered fortress – on 20 June 1942, Rommel's Afrika Korps invaded Egypt, and it had reached to within 60 miles of Alexandria, before it was brought to a halt by the 2nd New Zealand Division, in the first battle of Alamein. On 13 August Montgomery arrived in the desert to take command of the 8th Army, and at once began to prepare for a defensive battle against the renewed German offensive which was bound to come. Rommel's order of the day on 30 August called on his men to advance and capture Alex, Cairo and the Delta; instead he was decisively beaten by the tanks and anti-tank guns dug in on the height of Alam Halfa, and was obliged to withdraw, leaving behind 49 tanks, 55 guns, 395 vehicles and 2,910 dead.

After the enemy's retreat I was given the job of taking a jeep through the minefields and counting the still smoking and smouldering armoured fighting vehicles and guns lying around on the now empty desert battlefield; because of the uncertain distances and directions I ticked them off with a piece of chalk, in order to make sure I was not counting the same ones twice!

In his book *Panzer Battles*, von Mellenthin described Alam Halfa as 'the turning point of the desert war, and the first of a long series of defeats on every front which foreshadowed the defeat of Germany'.

[Hamish Henderson Archives and *Pervigilium Scotiae* (Etruscan Books, 1997)]

THE BALLAD OF GIBSON PASHA

(Tune: 'Solomon Levi' – more or less)

My name is Gibson Pasha. I'm a wily PMC.
You bet I know a thing or two, there are no flies on me.
A fellow who could do me down has never yet been born
For I go to bed at 4 a.m. and rise before the dawn.

> Chorus:
> *O Gibson Pasha*
>   *Tra la la la la la la*
> *O Gibson pasha*
>   *Tra la la LA la laa.*

I bought a very old gamous, it died upon its feet.
I cut it up and gave it to the other blokes to eat.
I pocketed their akkers – then I quickly left the scene
For when they cough the brute up they're a most unpleasant green.

I like the Duty Officer. I put him at his ease.
He has six eggs for breakfast, cooked in any way he please.
But at dinner he's less lucky, for the food I give the fool
Is rissoles made from Wally's arse and Adam's gnarly tool.

I treated Courtney Smith to Scotch, I knew he'd understand.
Between us we arranged the thing, as easy's kiss your hand.
He audited the mess accounts and gave them his okay
Then I kicked off with family prayers by saying 'Let Us Pray'.

I come from bonny Paisley, where to gamble is a sin,
Though its sons have no objections to the bawbees rolling in.
But now I prey beside the Nile, I keep the Sabbath day
And rob all simple Musulmans the Presbyterian way.

By now I've got young King Faruk quite helpless in my net
And Nahas Pasha – keep it dark – is deeply in my debt.
When Marschall Rommel felt the wind he did not hesitate
But came and popped his Bastico for LE 28.

If ever you've been naughty (for example, thieved and raped)
You'd better pay hush money, for I've got your dossier taped.
And a warning in conclusion – if you try and queer my pitch
I'll bleed you till you're just as poor as Gibson Pasha's rich.

Note: Written in 1942, Gibson Pasha is a fictitious character who acts as a symbol of the kind of predatory small mind not unknown in times of war.

[Hamish Henderson Archive and Raymond Ross, ed. *Hamish Henderson: Collected Poems and Songs* (Curly Snake, 2000)]

LINES TO A FOOL

(who called a contemplative man 'dead')

You snigger at him, a walking corpse that gropes
For 'barren leaves' on learning's desert slopes.
Yet never to art (*or* life) you gave your praise,
Nor risked a fall, all your efficient days.

That man with inward eyes and laggard tongue
Can sit tonight the living trees among,
While you from truth under your boards are hid
And weary me, scratching on your coffin lid.

[Hamish Henderson Archive and Raymond Ross, ed. *Hamish Henderson: Collected Poems and Songs* (Curly Snake, 2000)]

YOU, MY POEMS, ARE MY WEAPONS
[Louis Fürnberg]

You, my poems, were not created
like beautiful flowers in expensive vases
to charm cultivated men of leisure.
You, my poems, were not created
to be like blown soap bubbles,
coloured glistening lies against life.
You, my poems, are my weapons!

You, my poems, were not created
to pander to gentle nostalgias,
poetic play-acting, languishing mummery.
You my, poems, were not created
to help humanity escape from the jaws
of the famished wolves of their misery.
You, my poems, are my weapons!

When I still let the rooms sing with you
in my homeland, in the Sudeten,
my comrades the workers heard.
By you they were thrilled to rebellion
and they seized you like rifles
and you became their battle song.

I still see the broad rooms before me –
The lights blurred blue with tobacco smoke
over the sea of loved faces – how
it seemed to surge hot towards me! –
And I was your brother, the poet,
and, comrades, you were my brothers too.

O those that call themselves pure poets,
if only they knew how impoverished they are!
They fumble through life solitary and blind

because their eyes can't see its face,
and so they go squealing and whining
and piping their rhymes into the wind.

God, for squealing and whining
I've never yet had time in my life.
And these days there's less time than ever
now the gangsters are looting and burning.
My gun is ready for action. I'll use it
against those we know of. – And you, my poems,
are my weapons dedicated to that.

Note: In the original this poem is in rhymed verse. I have not attempted
the rhyme, because of having to wrench the meaning. It's direct enough as
it is. Also – so great a harm have our Neo-Romantics done us – a rhymed
translation would sound too artificial.

[*Our Time*, Vol. 4, No. 3, October 1944]

REQUIEM FOR THE MEN THE NAZIS MURDERED

[Louis Fürnberg]

The hour of the dead is coming,
The dead, they don't stay dumb.

I

Fetters and rope won't choke the song
that wakens our dead. They'll not sleep long.
WE CONDEMN YOU: the voices drum!
The dead are speaking! They don't stay dumb.
You carted them off to their graves by night
but *we* were watching. We heard all right.
We saw the wounds on our comrades plain
and you can trust us! They'll rise again!
Him with the broken limbs! Him with the smashed-in face!
On our judgement day they'll rise from their resting place!

II

Before us still the unstruck blow.
The dead who have not ceased from hating
are watching us, and mutely waiting.
Over them the flag we throw.

For when their eyes were shut for ever
that was the last thing that they saw.
They could not reach (by history's law)
the desired land across the river.

And yet they saw that promised place.
The flag was peace in thick of battle.
In dying passion, in death-rattle
a smile made whole the breaking face.

III

O when our dead awaken,
    that you condemned to death,
the cause that seemed forsaken
    will breathe their living breath.

Then you who gave the order,
    you who at once obeyed,
will reach no friendly border.
    The reckoning will be paid.

The hour of the dead is coming
    The dead they don't stay dumb,
they hear the death's-head drumming
    and drown in blood the drum.

When weals from Dachau beaters
    begin to bleed again,
your jackboots, daggers, fetters
    and whips won't save you then,

and you who sowed the horror
    and made the earth unclean
will sweat your blood in terror.
    The sickle's edge is keen.

IV

The reaping starts tomorrow,
    the sowers cut down like weed,
the sowers who in the furrow
    once sowed the bloody seed.

The crop of death we'll level.
    The field of harvest bleeds!
The sickle shears from evil
    with one quick shave its heads.

The hangman and the flayer
　　the flogger and the slave,
for them we'll say no prayer,
　　for them we'll dig no grave.

If all lay swollen rotten
　　Black on the German plain
The pure sky they've forgotten
　　Its tears of joy would rain.

Never was harvest richer!
　　The stubbled fields are red!
Death has cut down his creature,
　　the earth drinks where it bled.

– So for victory the forbidden
　　red flags of love we'll raise.
The hour of the dead was hidden.
　　Now welcome the living days!

Though once from mutilated
　　fingers the weapon fell,
the desire of the dead is sated,
　　the killers hurled to hell.

Note: Requiem is irony.

　　The thrilling violence of this poem in German is hard to recapture in English. We are not used to such strong stuff. The anti-Castlereagh broadsheet technique has not been much in evidence in England during the broad-bottomed era of Baldwin and Chamberlain: instead we have had the unvirile political badinage of the thirties. The blitz however seems to have made it plausible even to bourgeois Communists that English civilization cannot remain protected for ever, and Alamein should have done the same for their counterparts in Cairo.

　　This *is* the sort of period when ('The Song of Roland' puts it succinctly):

Païens ont tort et Chrétiens ont droit.

A young Sudeten German poet who calls a gun a gun and vengeance vengeance should not have difficulty now finding hearers.

[*Our Time*, Vol. 4, No. 3, October 1944]

THE SERBIAN SPRING, 1941
[Louis Fürnberg]

(for Marko Ristić)

The sun was cold still
but already it was melting the snow.
Earliest green of spring
was frozen in the brushwood: silver grey
of sky floated over the avenue
like a cupola canopy. The rain came
and there came the spring wind.
The trees set up
a snapping and creaking. The wind
sprang at their throats and let them
loose from their rigor, tore the dead matter from them
like a dry scab: and drove
the idol of winter off before his swinging
whip with whistle and yell.
He ripped
the cloth of cloud to rags: the swaddled sky
was suddenly bright and blue.
He drove the snow from Goč, drove it down dale,
the sleeping brook became a wild spring flood
and roared and raged, in riot with swollen head
high as the embankment – despising its narrow bed.

Silent and frightened we walked on, you pushing
the pram in front of us. Our hearts beat dull
and heavy through this real seeming spring
which was no spring, for all the tender glistening
green of the grass, green of the bush and tree.
He'd walked abroad in the land. This Serbia
was wet with Satan's spittle . . .

His gentlemen were travelling to Berlin,
treason in bags, death in portfolios. Glossy
on special train a royal coat of arms.
The hangman's noose was waiting to receive them.

Silent and frightened we walked on. Our eyes
were fixed on the hills. It seemed as though already
we saw the slow-winged messengers of death
hovering over them. Yes. Yes. It was spring
and sunshine.

That season spring was singing all his measures.
That season death in special train was skimming
along the railroad track towards Berlin.

Our child was laughing in the pram
and playing at hide and seek with the sunshine.
The spring wind was blowing a bloom
into his little cheeks from its lusty
lungs. How fine you travel
when you're pushed by mother-power!
                What heavenly joggling
just from being pushed along a road!
                And if
the spring-wind made the coloured pram-hood flap
our baby laughed!

And we – today were saddened by his laughter.
We couldn't laugh back, although we wanted to.
For it was spring, and it was spring with terror
and troubled all the trees in the avenue.

[*Our Time*, Vol. 4, No. 3, October 1944]

4 SEPTEMBER 1939

Bonjour, misère

We had twenty years – twenty years for building and learning.
   Those twenty years come back no more.
An incendiary dawn is prelude to this soft morning
   First morning of the new war.

Note: This quatrain was written about 6 a.m. in Kensington Gardens. I had
spent the night under a tree there, having almost no money, and no place
to stay in London – the previous day I had hitch-hiked from Ledbury in
Herefordshire, the HQ of a Quaker organisation for which I worked for
several weeks in Nazi Germany that summer. I heard of the declaration of
war while en route to London.

[As 'First Morning' in Hamish Henderson Archive and *Pervigilium Scotiae*
(Etruscan Books, 1997)]

THE HIGHLANDERS AT ALAMEIN
(Rejected Opening)

The enemies of freedom are here in Africa
and have got to within sixty miles of Alexandria.
Therefore, seeing that we want to ensure
and enlarge and supplement our valued freedom
it is clear that to down a blatant tyranny
seems necessary to the logical Gaels.
And that is why there will be a battle
for five acres of desert that is featureless
                              and cracked and stony,
for a ridge the height of a man.

I remember a ceilidh
I had in Badenoch with the forestry boys
when the talk was of nothing but the killed
and the laming casualties from France.
Cruel to hear
in the savaged Highlands, of War's depopulation.
This decimation more thorough, though less
                              familiar the way.
The questions put formerly remain unanswered
and still trouble us: but this more
                              pressing question
(superceding even the others)
we intend now shall receive our reply.

A moon to do us proud
enters into alliance –
it waits cannily for action
behind bluffs of mottled
conspirational cloud.

[...]

Feu d'artifice!
Coloured tracer swerves over deadly illumination.
We watch it
this *auto da fe*, this show for lusty arch-angels.
End to end
of the western horizon it crackles, crepitates and lightens:
four hundred and eighty guns on a front of twelve kilometres
between Ruweisat ridge and the sea.
Our ears become indifferent
to the faceless din of ejaculation. Only our eyes
our eyes watch with eager elation
the jittering St Vitus dance
jabbing, jerking and quivering
from the middle distance into shivering jerryland;
bringing to the children of Wotan
wild blood-letting of witches sabbath
rough riotous road to Valhalla
Walpurgisnacht with a vengeance.

[...]

Flowers of the forest: Alamein: this is what it means.
A boy of twenty, married nine months,
who died tonight among the first on Mitereiya.
The lament is for him, who will have
no more kisses for his pretty Jeannie
(and no more 'beeze' in the Cameron barracks)
After nine hours
of deaths like his, the ridge is ours.

[Hamish Henderson Archive]

ALAMEIN, OCTOBER 23, 1942
(Rejected lines from 'Opening of an Offensive')

On this moon surface
of cracks, craters and depressions
the ant-hill stirs. The spring is compressed for the blow.
As we jib and jolt
in a shiver-shaken Dodge down the Springbok
road, the clouds muffle
the vast mobility: the clouds cloak
the continuous whirr and clatter of our
advancing armour, mustering for the thrust.

Only the pipes this night will match
the music of revving Shermans: with this name
we'll bring jubilee to the whiggish desert!
The hardy Highlanders
have trained hard: ten times over they
      have stormed and taken
the trial sangars, have sworn and sweated
by order of the laconic self-confident General.
And now the real thing. The Jocks greet it
for they know they are in good company:
the Aussies are here,
surest-footed in the desert, who captured
Tel el Eisa: there are Afrikaners,
the burly Jaapies, the Saray Marays,
now longest in the line: and the cool New Zealanders
well-acquainted with action –
together, the hard spear-head.
              And a moon to do us proud
enters into alliance.

Note: 'Jaapies' a nickname for the South Africans, also known as 'Saray Marays' from the title of the Afrikaans song 'Sarie Marais' they sang. 'Beeze' is 'spit and polish'.

[Hamish Henderson Archive and Victor Selwyn, ed., *From Oasis Into Italy* (Shepheard-Walwyn, 1983)]

THE GUILLOTINE
For Ian Hamilton Finlay

In 1847 Heinrich Heine, who had been living in exile in Paris,
was able – during the 'softening up' period before the year of
revolutions – to travel to Hamburg to see his mother. In his poem
Deutschland: Ein Wintermärchen (Germany: a Winter's Tale), which
is a mixture of fact and fantasy, he chronicles his progress, and
describes various legendary characters met on the way. These
include Father Rhine, Hammonia (the Goddess of Hamburg)
and the Emperor Frederick Barbarossa. This last, waiting in his
mountain fastness for the trumpet summons to sally forth and
free the Fatherland, is portrayed as a bumbling old buffer, wearing
a dressing gown and carpet slippers. He's naturally eager to hear
news of the outside world from his newly arrived guest, and Heine
willingly obliges . . .

   . . . We chatted away. Our echoing words
     Through the musty halls resounded.
The Emperor asked about this and that,
     And dutifully I expounded.

About all events since the Seven Years War
     He asked for information;
No morsel of news had reached him here
     In his splendid isolation.

The French Court gossip intrigued him much,
     So many choice items affording:
About the Dubarry he first enquired,
     And I answered him according.

'The Dubarry had a gorgeous life
     Just as long as her beau was reigning,
But when they guillotined her, she
     Had not one charm remaining.

King Louis the Fifteenth died in his bed
 – An end decidedly better!
King Louis the Sixteenth was guillotined,
 Like Marie Antoinette.

The Queen was very proud and stiff
 As her royal breeding taught her,
But poor Dubarry blubbered when
 To the guillotine they brought her.'

The Emperor stopped in his tracks, and said
 'I don't quite catch your meaning,
I haven't heard that expression before,
 What is this . . . guillotining?'

'The guillotine', I explained to him,
 'Is a novel apparatus
Which polishes off the upper class
 Because of their social status.

They tie you down on a sizeable plank,
 And then with address they shove you
Between two posts – you've already observed
 A triangular blade above you.

A rope is pulled. The knife descends.
 It gaily performs the task it
Has been assigned. Your head now falls
 Into a wicker basket.'

'Be silent, Sir!' The Emperor roared.
 'Not another word of this knife, Sir!
Of more subversive goings-on
 I've never heard in my life, Sir!

Their Majesties! The King and the Queen!
  Bound down! Upon a plank, Sir!
Why, that's against all etiquette,
  And every respect for their rank, Sir!

You'll give an account for these monstrous crimes,
  Or else I'll know the reason!
Your every word's lèse-magesté –
  Your very breath's high treason.'

[Pamphlet from the Hamish Henderson Archive]

LAMENT FOR THE SON
[Corrado Govoni]

He was the most beautiful son on earth,
braver than a hero of antiquity,
gentler than an angel of God:
tall and dark, his hair like a forest,
or like that intoxicating canopy
which spreads over the Po valley;
   and you, without pity for me, killed him
– there, in a cave full of dull red sandstone.

He was the whole treasure
of war, of sanctuary and of crown,
of my accepted human poverty,
of my discounted poetry –
You, once his hiding place was discovered
(after which no angel could sleep) –
You, with your thieving hands
that were strangers to no sacrilege,
you carried him away at the run
into the darkness
to destroy him without being seen –
before I had time to cry out:
'Stop!
'Put him down!
'*That is my son!*'

He was my new sun, he was the triumph
of my betrayed boyhood;
and you changed him, in front of my praying hands
into a heap of worms and ashes.
   Mutilated, hurt, blinded,
only I know the tragic weight I am carrying.
I am the living cross of my dead son.

And that tremendous and precious weight
of such great suffering, of such unbearable glory
becomes daily harder and more heavy:
it breaks my skin,
it fractures every joint

it tears my soul;
and yet I shall have to carry it
as my sole good –
as long as I have one beat
of love in my old veins for him.
I shall carry him, sinking on to my knees, if I have to,
until the day of my own burial.
Only then will we be down there together,
a perfect and obscure cross.

[*Our Time*, Vol. 5, No. 5, December 1945]

Note: 'Lament for the Son' is part of a long prose poem written by Govoni after the death of his son Aladino, a partisan of Italy, who was one of 335 hostages shot by the SS under Kappler in the Ardeatine caves, 24 March 1944.

DIALOGUE OF THE ANGEL AND THE DEAD BOY

[Corrado Govoni]

To my poor Aladino,
Barbarously put to death by Nazi-fascists
24 March 1944.

The Angel.

Let us go, come! Fly! Remain motionless!
It is early, it is late, it is the hour.
Not yet, and now for ever.
All alone with you; you alone with me! . . .

The Dead Boy.

Help me then
in the first drunken paces
of my poor stiffened limbs
because I am like a blind man.
You must tell me where there are hedges and rocks,
bridges and fords, ascents and abysses:
you do not know what weight I am carrying
of senses not yet burnt out to ashes.

The Angel.

Follow me, hurry, don't be frightened!
There are no longer the obstacles you imagine.
Don't you hear my voice – don't you see me?

The Dead Boy.

How can I comprehend you, angel,
like this, all of a sudden, when the warmth
still flowers redly in the garden of my severed
veins, and such sweet fetters
still bind me closely to my senses?
I am too confused and absorbed
in my sleep of dead childhood,

and the insistent rumour of being
has not stopped yet: it is still filling
my brain with syllables and visions:
there are 'mother' and 'sun' . . . and 'brother' . . .
After the avalanche
of onrushing blood that was opened
in my neck by a thunderbolt of murder . . .
In my clairvoyant blindness
is it you then, new angel,
who are this breath of light
I find here on my first steps of darkness?

The Angel.
In the black kingdom
of sun, ice and the dead, with one single
face, these syllables, country, mother and brother
have no longer any meaning:
one with
the rapt cloud,
and the fixed tree.
If life on earth was no more than
a tiring and troublesome learning
to say 'flower' and 'tree,' to say 'sun' and 'mother,'
there will be no more here than an easy
and a quick forgetting.
Only then will you comprehend me
in my form of perfect angel.

The Dead Boy.
The crown of glass of my mother
and no longer the thin cord of torment
binds over my breast the little bones
of hacked-off hands.
You tell me to walk forward quickly
and me not knowing how to fumble in this dark!
How can I if my head is still . . .

you know, angel, how it exploded
and was full of the detonation of the mine
which at one blow brought down on me in ruin
the whole weight of blood
of the Ardeatine caves, the shambles?

The Angel.
Mother, blood, birthplace,
laborious words
soaked in sunlight
that you learnt slowly on the earth –
they have no longer any sense here.
It is as if someone among the living should say
cemetery of the wind.
Less than nothing, of that nothing
(floating mildews, proliferations
of will o' the wisps) which for your human
was the stellar silence above them.

The Dead Boy.
But to abandon like this for always
the sweet memory of life, with its sweet
pain . . . to be deaf even to the sweet dreams
for always, and to those sweet
voices of the earth . . .
sweet life, sweet earthly . . .

The Angel.
Did you think then *that* was paradise
where even the pure coruscating fire
must leave its ugly ashes?
Where the more the bright flower of legend
glows, dreams and is fragrant, the more hateful
and foul is its tiny canker?
Are you still regretting that life of men, condemned
to wander about like prisoners in a compound

between the earth and the rain: with their weary
mask, with the shafts of sun, moon and starlight?
And your own life, made up
of inert and deluded yesterdays
which was from and almost the patient
suffering of mnemonic coral
of which the dead and submerged tree is
the entire future?

The Dead Boy.
– Help me, angel, do you not see
how inexpert I am at dying?
No-one had given me any warning
to prepare myself for learning this eternal
death, which was always
a word in my head without face or echo.
I thought of it only as a free-moving shadow,
in flight from men like a shame or scandal
or kept quiet like some tremendous guilt
already expiated at birth's climax.

The Angel.
Do not fear!   Fly!   Walk forward!
And remain motionless for ever.
Soon you will learn me,
when seeing without eyes will turn into
a vaster seeing
and your stone deafness will be infinite hearing.
You will know very soon
what sweet labour it is to learn
the illiterate language of silence.

The Dead Boy.
I feel a light around me, and a heat
still moist and human
which persists and will not leave go of me.

It brushes against my cheek like a kiss
and it fills my hand with sunlight;
it is she, carrying her poor candle of suffering,
it is my dear mother: she searching for me, and groping
through the frozen darkness.
I will come with you then, my angel,
but if you do not want me to linger
let me cry out once more, so loudly
that the whole earth will hear it, the sweetest
name: mother
which on earth is all – is country, love, Jesus.

The Angel.
You know that I cannot weep any more . . . come!

The Dead Boy.
Blind, deaf and unknown angel
why do you answer no longer?
Now at last I feel and know, I cold and in darkness,
that you have already entered into me for ever:
indifferent angel of emptiness,
angel nothing but wall.

[*Poetry Scotland*, No. 3, July 1946]

HERE'S TO THE MAIDEN

(In 1331 the heads of 50 executed 'misdoaris' decorated the castle of Eilean Donan)

When Moray rade intil Wester Ross
    tae further the rule o' law
he was 'richt blythe' tae see the heids
    that 'flooered sae weel that waa'.

Noo, efter Sasunn has felt the win'
    and lowsed her grup o' wer lugs
I wadnae mind providin' for show
    juist twa-three elegant mugs.

A when Lavals got leid i' the guts
    or danced their wey tae the rope –
but *oor* Scots Quislings hae aa been spared
    tae gie us the same auld soap.

Ye'll see them shinin' the Southron's buits
    or kissin' his weel-faured seat.
They'd be mair use adornin' the waas
    o' yon tour whaur the three lochs meet.

The heids o' a score o' *Vichy Scots*
    wad suit these partisan days,
and mak mair sense as an ornament
    than dizzens o' wild MacRaes!

[*Voice of Scotland*, March 1947]

EPITAPH FOR A BARN-STORMER

Under the gibbet's scarecrow canopy
contorted iron rasps an execration,
                curled in red claw.
By deathly Sweeny's razor I'm clean-shaven,
and topple backwards into howling pit.

Boys, show your wit!
Fetch Doctor Fell to mouth my obsequy
and grip the raven, caw your Titus caw!

Under the gibbet's scarecrow canopy
A poor deid many swing who once were braw
and boozed away their full clear day's daw
Is now withouten any company.
Yet even death can suffer a scene-change.

[Hamish Henderson Archive]

ON TWO CAMBRIDGE PROFESSIONAL
ATHLETES

(Tune: 'Daddy Wouldn't Buy Me a Bow-Wow')

Geoffrey wouldn't buy me a Bawa, Bawa,
Geoffrey wouldn't buy me a Bawa, Bawa.
　　　　　I've got a little Craig
　　　　　But his value's rather vague
and I *do* want a Bawa, too.

[Hamish Henderson Archive]

THEY'VE GOT 'ESS!

I was in my Wittering chalet (Rustybums) when Alf Meyrick came
rushing up and announced:
    'They've got ESS! They've got ESS!'
    I asked 'They've got *what?*'
But all he could do was haver away that
'they'd got ESS.'
    'Listen, Alf.' I said 'sit down and take it easy . . . Now just try and
tell me this – who's they and what's ess?'
    'ESS, Corp' he said, '*ESS* – Rudolf Ess.'
    'Oy Sarge' I called, 'come over here and talk kindly to Alf
Meyrick – he's gone crackers.'

[Hamish Henderson Archive]

THIS ISLAND A FORTRESS

It is ill living now in doomed Troy.
Mothers hide now in cellars of anxiety
to be orphaned children. Fatherless,
                              each girl and boy.

. . .

Man's misery is little to his fellow.
Blood's river is water to the safely sailing.
No Swift need tell us that the oak's heart's hollow.

Hollow and rotten like grey-crumbling apple.
Hollow as a skull. Hollow as history
On God's blackboard –
                              Hollow as death's mystery.

Note: Elsewhere titled 'Poem from 1939'.

[Hamish Henderson Archive]

'IN THE MIDST OF THINGS':
MORE FROM THE
ANTI-FASCIST STRUGGLE

MYSELF ANSWERS

Though death be glowerin' in the woods
    He wullnae fricht nor fray.
When ye're singin' on the Malvern Hills
    At the dawin' of the day.

[Hamish Henderson Archive]

POEM

When we were children
time ran errands for us. Later we tried
to launch our craft on it; it was a grown-up
counting ten while the children ran to hide.
Or lay isolated, a ship in a bottle,
straining in stillness
against the stone pull of an immeasurable tide.

Through wash of rubble
this Time defeats me. And the headland's spike
is crumbling stump. I turn to
a burnt-out croft behind a ragged dyke.
From time past a whisper of battle.
O child, child, hurry.
For life our mortal blow quickly we'll strike.

[*Lines Review*, No. 4, January 1954]

The Fa' o' the Year.

This is the fa' o' the year, that – braks yer hairt in twa.
Flee awa, Flee awa.
The sin creeps tae the hull
An' climbs an' climbs
An' rests at ilka step.

Och, but the warld's wede!
On wearit strings the wund
Plays his auld sang.
Hope is awa'. For her
He maks his mane.

This is the fa' o' the year, that – braks yer hairt in twa'.
Flee awa. Flee awa.
O fruit o' the tree,
Dae ye tremble and fa'?
Whit secret is it then
Ye hae lairnt frae the night
That an icy grue
Covers yer gowden cheek?
Ye're deif – ye winnae speak?
Whae's speakin' noo? . . .

This is the fa' o' the year, that – braks yer hairt in twa.
Flee awa, Flee awa.
'I amnae bonny' –
Sae says the gillyflower.

Note: This seems to be translated freely from across an early draft of
Nietzsche's poem 'Im deutschen November' [In the German November]

and its final published version. My thanks to Alan Riach for this reference.
[Editor]

[Hamish Henderson Archive]

FRANCY

Francy yes and Francy no
Francy is my only jo.

Francy doesn't like the Reds
Hates and *hates* their wily heads.
Francy felt that they had got
The Labour leaders on the spot.
Francy said: 'Ay, there's the rub' –
Brought to birth the Labour Club.

Francy yes and Francy no
Francy is my only jo.

Francy's place is in the House,
Francy's quite the country mouse.
Francy's rally just a kid,
Is sure to do what she is bid.
Francy likes the tune I make
Francy need not be afraid.

Francy yes and Francy no
Francy is my only jo.

[Hamish Henderson Archive]

SIR ORIFLAMME CHAMMLINTON

Sir Oriflamme Chammlinton walks in the park
His boiler's a beaver, his copper's a nark.
They apply for permission to enter the Ark.

Sir Oriflamme Chammlinton strolls in the palace
While Engels confers with the Duchess and Alice.
We'll claw him with inwit and maul him with with malice.

Sir Oriflamme Chammlinton died on the eve of All-Hallows.

(Cambridge, 1939)

[Hamish Henderson Archive]

GOETTINGEN NICHT

On Nikolaus Hill
the wund blaws will:
whiles it's blaffy
an' whiles it's still.
In Goettingen toun
Its fechtin's dune.
Lik an auld Pharoah
it shauchles roun.

Och, gleg I'll be
whan I'm out o ye.
This was aye a fremmit
place tae me.
But tae clear out nou
whan the wund's blinfou –
by Christ in Heivin
it gars me grue.

Hirplin feet
on their week-kent beat.
Nae livin craitur
comes doun the street.
Juist toom waas, bricht
i the lantern's licht.
By Adam's curse
it's an oorie nicht!

[Hamish Henderson Archive and Raymond Ross, ed. *Hamish Henderson: Collected Poems and Songs* (Curly Snake, 2000)]

UNTITLED

I have dyed my hair
with grey logic
I the young magic
lover of her
Thus I am forgiven
for being myself
the serious wealth
of my great sin forgiven

I that had once
the young magic
Have dyed my hair
with grey logic
the serious wealth
of one sin shriven?
for being myself
Am thus forgiven.

[Hamish Henderson Archive]

EN MARCHE

This nicht the glamourie o the wuids is daith
this nicht the mune is breengin west wi me
though clogs o ice maun smite my clangin path.

O mune, I canna hear their raucle singin
I'm hearin nocht ava but *yuir* frore music –
the mime of *eine kleine Nachtmusik*

Yestreen our barrack cradle brawly rocked,
but wakie's bashed us wi a douche o doom.
The cairts are scattert, an' the aumrie's toom.

The cranreuch maks a snell incisive physic
 – an me stravaigin ower these darkling brilliant
uplands, unsiccar o the foe I seek.

[Raymond Ross, ed. *Hamish Henderson: Collected Poems and Songs* (Curly Snake, 2000)]

THE GUID SODGER SCHWEIK

(after the novel by Jaroslav Hašek)

The guid sodger Schweik was a guid sodger.
He kenned how to get his liquor.
'He's gey an' daft' they were a' sayin',
But he tuik the beer and they did the payin!
   Christ, whit fules!

The guid sodger Schweik was a guid sodger,
And I ken a lad that's sic anither.
Whaurever there's extras or lassies goin'
He taks whit he wants and they're never knowin'.
   Christ, whit fules!

The guid sodger Schweik was a guid sodger,
But this laddie's as guid a dodger.
'Whit'll ye hae?' – and he gies ye whisky
Pinched frae the tent of Colonel McClusky!
   Christ, whit fules!

The guid sodger Schweik was a guid sodger.
If they found him oot he'd haver and haver
And blither awa' wi' his balls and blethers
Till they said 'Och, ye're daft' like a' th ithers.
   Christ, whit fules!

Ay, the guid sodger Schweik was a guid sodger.
There's a lot ye can lairn frae the auld bugger.
He can teach ye a twa-three things in tactics
That ye winna find in your dialectics.
   Christ, whit fules!

[Hamish Henderson Archive]

... The Lazarett
Has apple-green shutters to hide the rot.
Paint is wet
Over rice-mould and sickly leech-blood clot.
The slick surgeon
Lancets the lust from out goat's genitals.
Fat cancers burgeon
Making our sex run sore in the urinals.
So give me salt
And sprinkle it along my wound's red ribbon.
Eat out the fault –
Give me pain's ecstasy. Prick me.
For I am bidden
To this lascivious lazar-house ...

[Hamish Henderson Archive]

HATE SONG AGAINST A SERGEANT

I don't like Moran
   And he's no friend of mine,
And in my opinion
   He's a filthy old swine.

Hallelujah! He's a bastard!
   Hallelujah! He's a cunt.
Hallelujah! He's a red-faced
   Short-arsed little runt.

[Hamish Henderson Archive]

BRUTALITY BEGINS AT HOME

Misshapen mortals who snuffle in slums
Behold! For I bring of cold comfort the crumbs.
Your bug-bitten dwellings were ruins before
You were born, yet alone this particular war.
Your moth-eaten sticks and sweat-mouldy clothes
(both items which ev'ry good Christian loathes)
Are not worth the bother you're taking to rescue 'em
Now that the Peabody Building is only a vacuum.

Still, as 'mid the wreck of Grandma you search
Shed a tear for the vanishing rents of the Church
And reflect that the Archbishop, safe in his smuggery
Is very much grieved that you've been bombed to buggery . . .

[as cited in Timothy Neat, *Hamish Henderson: A Biography*, Vol. 1, p. 58]

BAWDY SCRAWLED ON A POSTCARD FROM EGYPT

The sexual urge of the camel
Is greater than anyone thinks
Away out there in the Desert
So he tires himself out on the Sphynx.
Now the intimate parts of that lady
Have been blocked by the Sands of the Nile
Hence the hump on the back of the camel
And the Sphynx's inscrutable smile.

[Hamish Henderson Archive]

Note: This is written in Henderson's hand. It is difficult to establish authorship, though Henderson is confirmed to have had a hand in circulating the piece (in both more and less explicit versions). [Editor]

TWA BLADS FRAE AFRICA AS TAE A WHEEN ANGLO-CAIRENES

When I hear ye airily bummin your chat
and bandying 'wog' aroun
I'd like tae fog ye in Sodger's claes
an' whisk ye aff tae Khartoum.

Ay, an conjure a clood frae Dongola
– lik yon peerie clood that was seen
When Mohammed Ahmed cam oot of the west
Wi the black flags an' the green.

[Hamish Henderson Archive]

One night we walked upon our feet
The poor old P.B.I.
We walked across the desert sands.
The moon was in the sky.

Old Rommel he was waiting there
Behind his mines and wire
And all we wanted was to sit
And brew up by a fire.

But on again we had to go
The Scottish Fifty-First.
We'd sooner booze in Cairo but
We had to shit or burst.

The way was long, the night was dark
The bloody sand was soft
And all that we could see ahead
Were shells that burst aloft.

And when we got near to Zem-Zem
Our feet were bloody sore
Our tongues were hanging out all right.
Of miles we'd walked a score.

We didn't want to go and fight
We'd sooner go to town.
We'd sooner go and have a drink
With a bint to lay me down.

Zem-Zem now had come in sight
But Rommel wasn't there.
He'd seen that we were coming and
He bolted like a hare.

And there we sat upon the sand
We didn't have a fight.
We didn't even have a pint
To sleep with us that night.

Note: Though this piece is unattributed in the Archive, given its position there, and the other works it appears among, I believe it is likely a Henderson original. [Editor]

[Hamish Henderson Archive]

THE GODS IN EXILE

(part of a long poem titled 'The God from Greece')

On the whaup's mountain
Rain, and the estuaris
Dim with the whipping rain. Today
The Sidhe will keep abed. Come near
(Never wore green, lad) and behold
And look on the ancient wonder of the Sidhe
Who are dead. For all gods die. But sure
Their ghosts live, and their power endures
For the seeing soul. They give
Graciousness to the race of the Gael,
And unfastened eyes. My heart
O child heart, they took in their hand
Under the whaup's mountain.
Here had they ruled endlessly,
The Men of Peace in the blessed glens,
Had not,
Latterly.
From Shiel and Moidart
And the confines of the western sea
A giant come, and asked for the king's
House. Strike ye sons of Brude!
But, ah, he makes
Enchanter the sign of a
Cross – and the great sleep
Of the Picts sink
Powerless. He strides
Onward. He knocks. They fall
Backward, the mighty doors
Before him. Unto the King he strides
Onward, the terrible one.
Columba.

After him
The culdees came. – These
Came, Jesus, from thine Iona
And died for thee in waste palaces,
Thou Son of the Living God.

[Hamish Henderson Archive]

At rest,
Yet knowing well
That the beckoning of the woods is
Death and that sleep sifts
In the caressing snow
I lie and remember many things
In foul age
After the Fèinne.

In my ears a murmur
Of wind-borne battle
Now, or in time past.
The herons stalk
Over the blood-stained flats; screaming cranes
Come to my mind. Splintering shields,
And Conall with hair like gold
Is conqueror. His spear
He washes in rushing waters. They flee
Before him, howling, the dark
Fomors flee, now they fear him
Their eye made night. They tread
Seething the blood-red surf and fathom,
Shrieking, the godless, sun-hating deeps.
But around us
They tower, the dispassionate ones.
That high thing's guardians
The impenetrable, famous keeps.
So shall we mount her, the
Grind-toothed monster where lay
The Sons of Fionn, and feel
For her breasts. We have sought
Her heart. Then stumbling
In the wilderness of thy white corries,
Kithairon,

We shall find consummation flesh to flesh.
Smoke belches. Life turns white,
And nothingness among the invisible snow.

Of the beauty of Aonghas
My shame and my pride to sing
Over a storm on the little hill.
For he has gone from me, ochone,
Into the insatiate Earth.
Down into the silence where I cannot
In place of thy cheek
See what is left to me,
A little stone among withered heath;
Yet they comest of a noble house,
Lion of winged Skye,
And thy name brought peace to the islands
Swift hawk of Mull of the white walls,
Now is thy dwelling place
With the Trinity, the King of yonder sun.

*

It comes upon me to listen.
The cry is far from Loch Awe
And help from the Clan of O'Duibhae.

Who now, in that man's wise,
Will succour Gael from Saxons,
In our time, as once Lugh
Aided his race against reproach?

Our distress
Thou knowest, therefore make
No tardy coming; the islands
Are dark to this day. With Aonghas
Their house if he cometh not.

For the highlands
A cold house, mhanuri. Come, come
In the name of Fionn's race!
Save us from the honourless,
Know thine own children,
As in old time – with thy sword
Deliver us,
Δεξοσειρος.
Then reign,
Thou that art King of Ithaca and King of Islay,
From Arran to where, in the tombed waves
Sky-cleaving Cuillin fall sheer,
Older than Agamemnon.

Note: My thanks to Nikolas Stamatopoulos for his help with the Greek.
[Editor]

[Hamish Henderson Archive]

POEM FROM THE DIARY OF CORPORAL
HEINRICH MATTENS

(Heinrich Mattens, 225 Shultz regiment)

'Some sort of form is inevitable. It is the surface crust of the
internal harmony.'
                                        – E.M. Forster

Today the swallows have come here, far over the mountains and
    seas – we took
It as a happy omen, for they came from the north.

They came their way to us when war had sent us southwards; now
    they find us by
roads where palms wave on the beaches.

They saw the fields of home, and the villages occupied with
    harvest, they saw the
forests in the brown blossom of autumn, and in the twitter of their
song they tell it.

And one of the dead men in the platoon goes back restlessly to his
    rest in the song.
The twittering flight is around us. My listening ear has caught its
    meaning . . .
Now we go forward on the road to Tripoli, to Tobruk and Sollum
– 14th October 1941.

[as cited in Timothy Neat, *Hamish Henderson: A Biography*, Vol. 1, pp. 70–1]

NEARLY XMAS 1941

Impatience is a virtue
like restlessness in sand;
Heads holding, hand folding,
Recalling to old land . . .
What will? Better far
To stand by science,
To break new land
With sureness, or even
With little certainty
Of life or death:
There must be believing,
There must be foundation
If our bodies be the rocks
. . . But they are soft
And oddly full of love.

(Tobruk, December 1941)

[Hamish Henderson Archive]

LOVE SONG
(to a Highland air)

I'll always be waiting
Where streams are afore me.
A silly sun is lighting
The clock that ticks surely
And others desire me.
But seven streams with leaping
To one love will keep me,
For loneliness arm me.

I'll always be waiting
Where Linnhe lies under
And mountains are beating
The long loch with thunder
Its waters rain-fleeting.
But thoughts can never fley me.
There's killing and fighting
But soon ye'll be near me.

And I'll aye be waiting
Where streams are afore me.

(1942)

[Raymond Ross, ed. *Hamish Henderson: Collected Poems and Songs* (Curly Snake, 2000)]

Remembered from a childhood
Continental journey:
           His Schokolade melts;
And always a part of him
In adolescence:
           The Flat Fifty Players:
But did the scalp in the sand
And the blood
Look as good
As the original man?
No, but the other things there
And a bunch of hair
Made much better subjects for the Art Surreal:
           A modern art, they say . . .

[Hamish Henderson Archive]

BALLAD OF THE FAMOUS TWENTY-THIRD
(Alamein, 23 October 1942)

(Tune: 'The Galloway Tinker's Song')

Whatever history is made, in this old world of strife El Alamein will still remain and follow us through life.

Who would not praise the glory there that our 8th Army won:
Invincibly their unity put Rommel on the run.
Like lions at bay the guns roared, on that famous Twenty-third.
Living death the barrage it gave that Jerry herd.

RE's there, clearing minefields, showing courage brave and rare –
Each track marked out, lamps coolly lit, by CMPs placed there.
And signals working constantly, they kept the troops in touch
The debt we owe the Signallers, we'll never know how much!

To send the lads no ammo, sure it would have been a crime
But the Royal Army Service Corps had seen to that in time.
We'll ne'er forget the sacrifice of those brave boys who died
While bringing up the ammo for to keep the front supplied.

Still, the toughest job's the infantry's as you will all allow
And 50 Div, as hard as nails, was there to show them how.
And honour to the Springboks too, who sing *Saraie Marais*;
They gained all their objectives long before the dawn of day.

Fourth Indian fought like heroes when the word came to attack;
The Ghurkas are the lads for me, they'll always have a crack.
And we'll recall the Kilties too, the boys that Rommel cursed –
Praise to the gallant Highlanders, the famous Fifty-first!

It was the bold New Zealanders that earned undying fame
With cracking Rommel's battle-line, and putting him to shame.
While anyone will tell you that the Aussies know no fears
For they won the Hill of Jesus from the Panzer Grenadiers.

The Tank Corps boys they waited long, till Monty told them when.
Their orders came, and in they went – resolved to die like men.
They tackled Jerry's Armoured Divs without a simple fear
And they brewed up plenty panzers in the fight at Aqqaqir.

. . . Now if you've no objections, lads, I'm finishing my song.
To sing some other verses would detain you far too long.
But when you're back in Blighty, and you're all as right as rain
Spare a thought for those who bought it, in the fight at Alamein.

Note: Henderson's annotations suggest that he collected this song
in several variants through the War and afterward and produced this
composite version himself. The choice of tune is Henderson's. [Editor]

[Hamish Henderson Archive]

MY WAY HOME

A path through the black-cored moorland
Is my way home, where no voice calls my name.
Only the weasel
Running a nimble courier
Starts from my stride and flees.
Now the west knows
I have come. Now night has lowered its barrier

I can take my rest.

[Raymond Ross, ed. *Hamish Henderson: Collected Poems and Songs* (Curly Snake, 2000)]

TRANSLATIONS OF ITALIAN ARMY SONGS

ARMY LIFE

In the morning there is coffee,
But no sugar.
Oh yes, they give us coffee
But no sugar,
spoken (Because there ain't none).

> I get thinner, thinner, thinner,
> For there's bugger all to eat,
> And I'm tired, tired, tired,
> Oh, my feet, feet, feet!

Well, at midday there is soup,
But it's water.
Oh yes, they give us soup,
But it's water,
> (To wash your feet in).

> I get thinner, thinner, thinner,
> For there's bugger all to eat,
> And I'm tired, tired, tired,
> Oh, my feet, feet, feet!

Well, at night you get a bed.
It's a trick one.
Oh yes, you get a bed.
It's a trick one.
> (It won't stand up).

I get thinner, thinner, thinner,
For there's bugger all to eat,
And I'm tired, tired, tired,
Oh, my feet, feet, feet!

LA SEMANA NERA

Monday I'm on guard,
Tuesday I'm booked.
Wednesday I do fatigues,
Thursday I cook.

Friday, holy Friday
It's gunnery drill.
Cursed be Saturday,
March till we're ill.

Next it comes Sunday.
I think myself free.
I read the fatigue-list,
My own name I see.

I go to the captain
And lay down the law.
The captain gets up and
Hits me in the jaw.

In the gaolhouse so gloomy,
No soul do I see
But the men from the guardroom
Who bring food to me.

They bring me some water,
A small bit of bread,
Leave it in the doorway.
I might be stone dead.

My friends, my dear comrades,
By the very next mail,
Write a note to my sweetheart
That I am in gaol.

Done fifteen long days.
Got thirty to come.
I'd not been a soldier
If I wasn't so dumb.

CAPTAIN, CAPTAIN OF THE GUARD

Captain, captain of the guard,
Muster the buglers all,
Make them stand in the barrack square
And sound the demob call.

Driver, driver of the train,
Start your engine off.
We're in a hurry to get back home.
Of war we've had enough.

At home, at home in the countryside
So sweetly blows the breeze.
We'll walk up the street, our friends we'll greet
In different hats to these.

At home, at home in the countryside,
We'll pick up a piece of goods,
And all the route march we shall do
Is trot her to the woods.

At home, at home no bugle call
To wake us from our sleep;

But my little duck with coffee and a roll
Into my room will creep.

Just one more signature to make
Upon the back-pay claim.
Turn in my kit and go straight home,
And never leave home again.

Driver, driver of the bus,
Run through the streets of Rome.
Make her go like a racing car.
We're hurrying to get home.

No more, no more shall we mount guard,
And no more wars we'll see.
All we'll mount is some little girl
On the edge of the old settee.

THE ALPINE RECRUITS

Early in the morning they have us out of bed.
They send us on the barrack-square to drill.
They march us up and down, and they march us round and round,
Till the poor alpineer feels ill.

> O-o-o-oh, we don't know why,
> But our feet they make us cry.
> It's no joke marching on the cobbles!

We cheer up on the day when they dish us out our pay,
For it means that at last we'll get a smoke.
But with our few lousy lire and *toscanis* getting dearer,
The poor alpineer is soon dead broke.

O-o-o-oh, we don't know why,
But our feet they make us cry.
It's no joke marching on the cobbles!

Every general's visit, we get a special feed.
There's sausages that make us stink like hell.
There's pasta and there's cheese that's like a latrine breeze,
No wonder the alpineer is never well.

O-o-o-oh, we don't know why,
But our feet they make us cry.
It's no joke marching on the cobbles!

[Hamish Henderson Archive]

THE HIGHLANDERS OF SICILY – A PIPE TUNE

Ti hey durry ha durry hum da
    Ti hee durram durry dum dumda.
Ti hey durry ha durry hum da
    Ta hurry dum da durm deeree.
        Ti hey durum hee
        Ti hi durum ha
Ti hi durum hurry dum deer
    – Tate hidurum hurry dum deeree –
        Te hie hiderum dee
        Te hie diderum da.

[as cited in Timothy Neat, *Hamish Henderson: A Biography*, Vol. 1, p. 107]

Headlines at home. The gangrel season varies,
And Spring has gained a beach-head with our blood.
I've half a mind to kiss the blooming Jerries
And then just beat it while the going's good.
I'll bed down where deserters live on berries . . .
I'll play at possum in yon cork-oak wood . . .
    Machine-guns prate, but dannert flowers, this Spring.
    Over the grave all creatures dance and sing.

Phil shows the latest snap of his bambino.
The new mail's brought a great big box of tricks
For Donny, lucky bastard, – but for me no
Reminders: not a sausage – naethin – nix!
We hear of 'heavy fighting by Cassino'
But still no sign of jeeps on Highway Six . . .
    In Rome the fascists lie between soft sheets
    And numbskull death his little tabor beats.

The watching Jerries sight a convoy's funnels:
It's coming into range now, Anzio-bound.
The railway gun emerges from a tunnel's
Commodious depth, and plonks a single round
A hundred yards beyond one mucker's gunwales.
I bet they'd feel much safer underground!
    This fight one's better off inside the ring.
    Over the grave all creatures dance and sing.

Last night we got a bash from Fritz's 'arty'
And then his mucking jabos gave us hell.
Our mediums up and joined the mucking party.
At last our mucking planes appeared as well.
Now thirteen Jocks are dead as Bonaparty.
(Yon Heinie in the tank's begun to smell).
    Lilac in bloom: the cold's White Guard retreats
    And numskull death his little tabor beats.

[252]

Kenny's bomb-happy: I a ruddy poet.
By Christ, my case is worse and that's a fact.
Maybe I'm nuts. Maybe I'll start to show it.
Sometimes I think that all the rest are cracked.
They're on the spot, and hell they hardly know it
. . . Or so you'd think, the damfool way they act.
    Spud's writing home, and Eddie thinks he's Bing.
    Over the grave all creatures dance and sing.

Snap out of that. Brigades of battered swaddies
Have got to stay and shoot – or lose their pants;
While strange to say our Jocks (the muckle cuddies)
Have still an inclination to advance.
Down Dead-end Road, and west among the wadis
They'll pipe and make the Jerries do the dance.
    Next month the race. Today we run the heats,
    And numskull death his little tabor beats.

Red Neil, whom last I saw at lifting tatties
Pulls-through his rifle, whistles *Tulach Gorm*.
. . . Two drops of rain. We know whose warning *that* is.
A plum-hued cloud presents in proper form
(The old court-holy-water diplomat) his
Most courteous declaration of the storm.
    The dance is on. Strike up a Highland fling!
    Over the grave all creatures dance and sing
    (And numskull death his little tabor beats).

Note: 'Jabos' are German fighter bombers

[Lines No. 3, Summer 1953]

THE BALLAD O CORBARA

Come listen tae me
partisans o the Romagna
an' I'se tell ye the tale
o yon wuddifu callant

that connached the pride
o the ramstam tedeschi
in his haun a Biretta
in his cap the Reid Star.

Corbara rade south
owre ford, by pineta
tae mak contack wi 'Bob'
in his Apennine eyrie

and tae gie him the gen
about black gaird detachments
that were our for a dander
frae the toun o Forli.

Corbara rade south:
he passed bothy and fairmyaird;
he skirted the wuidlands
o heich Sassonero

and lang or the glenside
was smoort i the gloamin
he'd maistered the pass
and was clear o its broo.

Drummelin torrent
rimbombed tae the valley.
A wee clachan cooried
amang the gray olives.

An auld wife ran out
frae the bield o her hoosie:
'May God an' his mither
an' Jesus Christ sain ye

ye champioun o aa
partisans o the Romagna
i yer haun the Biretta
i yer cap the Reid Star.

Turn ye yer ways
tae the wynds of Faenza –
turn ye an' flee
tae your ain yins, Corbara.

The Jerries are ragin
thro tounland and clachan.
They've haangit puir Bob
wi his taes ower a fire.'

Thunner's black tawse
cracked the still o the forenicht.
Bluid o the sun
sweeled the track o Corbara.

'And hae they killed Bob
my ain fere o the Prato?
Hae they killed him, auld Bob,
that was gleg i the tulzies!

Gif they think that I'll turn
and I'll rin frae tedeschi –
I'm tellin ye, mither,
ye ken na Corbara!

Satan himsell
can fecht for the limmers.
I'll libb an' I'll gralloch him
For Inez and Stalin.'

Killin and clearin's
the wark for tedeschi.
(Richt ploy for *die lustigen
Hanoveraner!*)

Rastrellamento
an' bestial brandmord.
Slauchter's fell reik
smoored the wuidlands and vineyards.

Black Gairds an' Jerries
were rapin and burnin:
they'd made thon paese
a kirkyairdy tooroch

an' left ilka wean
i his bluid on the heathstane
– when intil the clachan
rade gallant Corbara.

Twa shots he fired
and twa bastards were skirlin:
anither he fired
an' their Hauptmann had had it

and aince mair he fired
i the reekin piazza
and ower the brig
and awa tae the mountain.

They were gawpin dumbfoonert
for he'd left them aa staunin.
Then a skinny Feldwebel
sterted skreichin his orders

Du faehrst nach Faenza
ich bleibe hier unten.
Ja! Wir schnappen sofort
den Banditen Corbara.

Slap intae third
the Volkswagen lurches:
out on the road
five switherin Kraeder.

Twal seconds: they've left
the paese ahint them.
A meenit: they're climbin
thro wuids o Kastanien.

God, whit a lick!
They maun aa be blinfou
tae be breengin tae hell
i sic boneheid bravado.

Swerve tae the left
(whaur the brig isnae blawn yet)
an' swerve tae the richt
(swirlin dust on Our Leddy)

. . . Lik bogles they zoom
roun the muckle Deil's Elbuck –
and arise ower tits
twa crash tae the valley.

Mantrap o raip
hings lose frae a boulder.
Heich on the hill
the lauch of Corbara.

Dorst ist er! The Jerries
fire wild at the mockin
loud lauch – and they scramble
ower branches an' bracken.

Senta! Sei matto?
A Dolmetscher wheezes.
Rendati ... porco ...
Widerstand ... nutzlos ...

Cursin and blindin
they fire at the corries –
bairns playin tig
tak mair tent o their cover!

Trippin an' staucherin
hirplin an' stummlin
they near whaur their quarry
lies mum in a fox-hole,

an' think that they hae him
their prize Sau-Itacher
 – safe i the bag
a garrotted Kaninchen.

... Corbara caresses
his bonnie Biretta
'Cawa nou' he whispers
'ma wee tedescacci!

Yer're slaw on your pins
yé elite o Valhalla!
I canna be waitin
aa day on your comin.'

The first o the batch
is a saxfit Berliner;
aye, nou he's sae near
ye cuid mak out the gowd bits

that gleam in his mou
when he bawls out an order.
 – Ae denty slug
an' he's stretched on the bruthach

'Deckung.'   'Voran.'
'Ist der Luemmel des Teufels?'
'Was ist mit Euch los?'
'Soll der Schweinhund entkommen?'

Karlheinz and Rolf
mak a rush for the summit.
A Yankee grenade
blaws their shanks tae Auld Hornie.

'Schnapp ihn!' screams Rolf
but the rest are no carin.
The fechtin *they* ken
is wi weemin an' hauflins.

Whud doun the brae
an' splishsplash thro a lochan:
lik fower drookit rats
they vamoose ower the sky-line.

Corbara walked doun
to whaur Karlheinz lay bleedin
an' he luiked on the face
o a puir moribondo:

syne he bandaged the wounds
o the ither S.S. man
an' sat on his hunkers
a whilie aside him.

'I'm thinkin' he said
'that ye'll no be sae keen
tae be sherrickin bhoyos
lik Bob an' Corbara!

'But if ye're no wearit
o me and ma mainners
the ither compagni
sall shaw ye their paces.

'We'll tear ye an' bluid ye
wi Sangue an' Lupo.
We'll blaw ye aa doun
wi our fierce Uragano.

'Luik out for your hurdies
if Fulmine spots ye –
And nou I'm awa so,
And nou I'm awa so.
Guid nicht tae ye, maisters.'

Corbara lauched loud
an' he spat i the lochan:
syne he lifted his heid
lik a true Romagnolo

and turned on his ways
tae the wynds o Faenza
in his haun the Biretta
in his cap the Reid Star.

Note:

tedeschi:	plural of tedesco, the Italian word for German. It also means 'boorish', 'mis-shapen' and 'uncouth'
Biretta:	make of revolver
pineta:	pine wood
die lustigen Hanoveraner:	'The merry Hanoverians' (German folk song)
rastrellamento:	anti-partisan operation
Du faehrst etc:	'You make for Faenza, I'll stay down here. We'll put the bandit Corbara in the bag right away'
Kraeder:	motor-bikes
Kastanien:	chestnut trees
Dorst ist er:	There he is
Senta, etc:	'Listen! Are you mad? . . . Surrender . . . Resistance is useless'
Dolmetscher:	interpreter
Sau-Itacher:	Sow Italian
Kaninchen:	Rabbit
tedescacci:	*Accio* in Italian is an ending signifying repulsion or hatred
Deckung, etc:	'Cover!' 'On you go!' 'Is the bitch in league with Satan?' 'What's up with you?' 'Are you going to let the bastard escape?'
Schnapp ihn:	'Catch him!'
moribondo:	dying man
Sangue – Lupo – Uragano – Fulmine:	(Blood, Wolf, Hurricane, Thunderbolt) Battle names of partisans

My intention in writing this poem has been largely to achieve the effect that several notable Italian films have to their credit, namely, the recreation of the atmosphere of the campaign by re-producing fragments of all the many languages spoken in that extraordinary period. The ballad will be found to be packed with technical expressions relating to anti-partisan warfare in both Italian and German and there are two whole stanzas in Landser's colloquial speech.

However, just as the *fondo* of *Vivere in Pace* is Italian so the foundation of this ballad is Lallans: a flexible modern Lallans based on the language of the Perthshire uplands, an area where for three generations at least it co-existed with Gaelic.

Corbara was one of the great partisans of Emilia. The legend of his prowess is related over the whole province, and into the Tuscan Apennines. The Germans eventually captured and shot him: they then hung up his body in the piazza of Forli. The bodies of his woman Inez (who was pregnant) and of his principal Lieutenant were exhibited along with his own. (1944).

If the episode on which this poem is based seems larger than life, so in fact are most of the stories told about Corbara between Faentina and the Futa Pass.

[*The Voice of Scotland*, Vol. 5, No. 1, September 1948]

VICTORY HEY-DOWN

(6th (Banffshire) batallion of the Gordon Highlanders, celebrating the
German surrender in Italy, dancing a reel to the tune 'Kate Dalrymple')

Hey for the tall
horned shadows on the wall
and the beer-cans bouncing in the crazy Corso.
Hey for a hoor
for a meenit or an 'oor
and a tanner for a taigle wi' her sonsy torso.
Banffies hustle
through the randy reel-rawl;
lowpin' like a mawkin see oor dames frae Hell go.
Bang!
through the steer
they advance
tae the rear,
and the ankles jiggin' like a fiddler's elbow.

Slash o' a dirk
bleeds the guts o' the mirk
wi' the glentin' cramassies, the greens and the yellows.
Wind crack the cheeks
o' the dudelsack's breeks
like twa damn poltergeists at wark wi' the bellows.
Tae Hell wi' your oboes
and your douce violas –
your flutes and your cellos and your concertinas!
Oor pipes
and oor reeds
they supply
a' the needs
o' oor dear wee silly little signorinas.

Schlapp in the pan

    frae a billy tae a dan –

o we'll pound aul' Musso tae a weel-tanned tyke's hide.

      We'll beery soon

    yon melancholy loon

an' we'll ding doon Kesselring tae dee in the dykeside.

      Plums we'll pree 'em

          wi' the *partigiani* –

they bluid-reid billyboys, the rantin'-rory.

      Ye mean

          crood o' bams

              gie's anither

                    twal drams

an' we'll reel aul Hornie an' his gang tae glory.

(Italy, April 1945)

Note: A similar piece under the title 'Eightsome Reel' appears in Raymond Ross, ed. *Hamish Henderson: Collected Poems and Songs* (Curly Snake, 2000). [Editor]

Well, actually this was very fresh in my mind because it was written just at the time of the cave-in of Italy. And it's Gordons Battalion celebrating in the streets on an unknown Italian town, which is actually Perugia . . . or it could be any place . . . but I thought of it as Perugia . . . for that's where it was (Laughter).

Anyway! It's to the tune of 'Kate Dalrymple', 'cause I always felt that the song that's sometimes sung to the tune of 'Kate Dalrymple' is an ugly song. It's about a wrinkled old crone, you know. And the real Kate Dalrymple was apparently a beautiful girl! And to adapt a tune made in honour of a beautiful girl and sort of have these ugly words! I mean, Burns got away with it with 'Willie Wastle Dwalt on Tweed' because it's a good thing, although any song like that is a bit displeasing to me, but anyway it's a funny song although it's a grotesque song. It's a kind of 'Kempy Kay' song, as you might say, whereas the one to 'Kate Dalrymple' is just a puir bloody sort of – well, it's not a good song in my opinion. So I thought I would write better words to 'Kate Dalrymple', and this is 'Victory Hoedown' [sic]. [Henderson]

[Victor Selwyn, ed., *From Oasis Into Italy* (Shepheard-Walwyn, 1983) and *Tocher* No. 43, 1991]

EPITAPH

We biggit here
        thir twa cairns,
Bane on bane.
To keep yoursels
        and your bairns' bairns
Frae makin mane.

[Hamish Henderson Archive]

UNTITLED

Be the depth that awaits
The hour that sends the wave bright
Up to the summit of life – bright like a singing light
From the blaze that for seven years
    has raged on these parts,
Spring the Salamander,
    the spirit of fire,

From the dire conflagration that has reddened the earth
    sprang up in my heart the blood of my song;
A song that with lofty notes will crown
    the summits of time like a dawn.

A poetry directly connected to reality, a poetry transformed into
a weapon of struggle against the exploiter, its revolutionary
élan opening up large and just prospects for the future, not only
remaining true to every cause espoused by the working class (from
the General Strike to the Fight for Peace) but risking unpopularity
by fighting continuously for a Marxist view of the National
Question as it affects Scotland.

Lie alongside me, put your ear to the ground
    and listen: the earth rocks with fruitful adventures
And listen: the sap rises – sweet springs of song
    like hymns of belief to the buds that will blossom.

My brother, no wails and no sterile revolt!
    Tell the words from the depth,
        tell the fragrance above us
For soon, very soon, we shall harvesters be.

A lark in the skies shall arouse us from darkness
In happy embrace we shall hear in the dawn
You sowers of dreams, the crops have now ripened.

[as cited in Timothy Neat, *Hamish Henderson: A Biography*, Vol. 1, pp. 175–6]

PRODUCTS OF THE FOLK REVIVAL

THE JOHN MACLEAN MARCH

(First sung by William Noble at the John Maclean Memorial Meeting in the Saint Andrew's Hall, 9 November 1948)

Hey Mac, did ye se him as ye cam' doon by Gorgie,
    Awa ower the Lammerlaw or north o' the Tay?
Yon man is comin', and the haill toon is turnin' oot:
    We're a' shair he'll win back to Glesgie the day.
The jiners and hauders-on are marching frae Clydebank;
    Come on noo an hear him – he'll be ower thrang tae bide.
Turn oot, Jock and Jimmie: leave your crans and your muckle
    gantries.

        Great John Maclean's comin' back tae the Clyde.
        Great John Maclean's comin' back tae the Clyde.

Argyle Street and London Road's the route that we're marchin' –
    The lads frae the Broomielaw are here – tae a man!
Hi Neil, whar's your hadarums, ye big Heilan teuchter?
    Get your pipes, mate, an' march at the heid o' the clan.
Hullo Pat Malone: sure I knew ye'd be here so:
    The red and the green lad we'll wear side by side.
Gorbals is his the day, and Glesgie belongs to him.

        Ay, great John Maclean's comin' hame tae the Clyde.
        Great John Maclean's comin' hame tae the Clyde.

Forward tae Glasgie Green we'll march in guid order:
    Wull grips his banner weel (that boy isnae blate).
Ay there, man that's Johnnie noo – that's him there, the bonnie
    fechter.
    Lenin's his fiere, lad, an' Liebknecht's his mate.
Tak tent when he's spaekin', for they'll mind whit he said here
    In Glesgie, oor city – an' the haill warld beside.
Och hey, lad, the scarlet's bonnie: here's tae ye, Hielan Shony!

Oor John Maclean has come hame tae the Clyde.
Oor John Maclean has come hame tae the Clyde.

Aweel, when it's feenished, I'm away back tae Springburn
    (Come hame tae your tea John, we'll sune hae ye fed).
It's hard work the speakin': och, I'm shair he'll be tired the nicht
    I'll sleep on the flair, Mac, and gie John the bed.
The haill city's quiet noo: it kens he's restin'
    At hame wi' his Glesgie freens, their fame and their pride!
The red will be worn, my lads, an' Scotland will march again.

Noo great John Maclean has come hame tae the Clyde.
Great John Maclean has come hame tae the Clyde.

(Repeat 1st verse, starting very softly and working up to crescendo)

Note: William Noble's performance on 9 November 1948 was later described by Morris Blytheman (Thurso Berwick) as 'the first swallow of the Folk revival'.

[*The Rebels Ceilidh Song Book*, 1953]

THE CROWNED HEADS OF EUROPE

1.

In us you see the remnants
        blue of blood but broken-hearted
Of families from which the ancient
        glory has departed.
We used to drive through cheering crowds
        in open horse-drawn carriages,
Whilst making Europe's history with
        our births, our deaths, our marriages.
But now our sway's restricted
        to the Royal Suite at Claridges!
In all the countries where we reigned
        the masses that we spit upon
Have rudely moved the throne
        from underneath the Royal sit-upon.

1st Refrain

The crowned heads of Europe are vanishing one by one
        Their aces are trumped
        divine right has slumped
        and Royalty's on the run.
We're shaken –
        forsaken –
                we've not been the same since the Bastille was
    taken –
        Alas for the dead days
        The 'off with his head' days
        When thrones were abundant
And a King was a King and not merely – redundant.

2.

In old Vienna at the Ball
        where royalty charaded
The archest Duchess of them all

I gaily promenaded.
Though it was said I was in-bred
     and mentally retarded
I don't suppose a Hapsburg nose
     was ever so regarded.
With blood so blue I hope to woo
     a King like my mama did.
To think that I who aimed so high
     who once shone like a star did
Now sip my gin in White Horse Inn –
     disconsolate, discarded.

3.

Before the Iron curtain fell
     with bolshevik brutality
I ruled (and on the whole, quite well)
     a Balkan principality.
Was I to blame if Adolf came
     demanding hospitality?
Ah well! He lost and mine the cost
     I should have backed neutrality.
Since it's my fate to abdicate
     and cast off all regality,
I give my thanks to foreign banks
     that saved me from frugality
Some millions I had salted by
     for this eventuality.

4.

When Stalin was a name unknown
     and Europe feared Rasputin,
My bedroom was a Russian Zone
     the Tsar was absolute in.
There was no Red beneath the bed
     that we were dissolute in.
I loved to doff for Romanoff

those gowns I looked so cute in.
Time marches on; those days are gone
        that fact there's no disputin'
But yet they may return some day
        When cold way ends in shootin'
And I'll be there *en vivandière*
        to do my share of looting.

5.

Before the last great war but one
        I reigned in the Palatinate
but when the fighting had been done –
        they staged a tit-for-tat in it.
They turned me, if there's no doubt
        they knew what they were at in it.
I lost a throne, though Kings alone
        for centuries had sat in it.
(A president's in residence
        and wears a bowler hat in it.)
My palace? A museum now
        I have a tiny flat in it.
A dingy attic, so democratic
        I couldn't swing a cat in it.

2nd Refrain
The crowned heads of Europe
            are part of the expat drive,
        our people still thwart us,
        they won't re-import us
        no matter how hard we strive.
Depressed so distressed o
           we've not been the same since that damned
manifesto,
        Alas for the past days
           the 'too good to last' days
        When life could not vex Kings
And a King was a King and not one of the ex-Kings.

3rd Refrain

The crowned heads of Europe want history to reverse,

for the rate for the job

        was a crown for his nob

             and a plentiful privy purse,

The nation's orations displayed the respect that was

            due to our stations

      Alas for the failure

          to keep the regalia

      That splendidly decks one

When a King is a King and merely an ex-one!

(Xmas 1950)

[Hamish Henderson Archive]

BALLAD OF THE MEN OF KNOYDART

(Tune: 'Johnston's Motor Car')

'Twas down by the farm of Scottas,
　　Lord Brocket walked one day,
And he saw a sight that worried him
　　Far more than he could say,
For the 'Seven Men of Knoydart'
　　Were doing what they'd planned –
They had staked their claims and were digging their drains
　　On Brocket's Private Land.

'You bloody Reds,' Lord Brocket yelled,
　　'Wot's this you're doing 'ere?
It doesn't pay as you'll find today,
　　To insult an English peer.
You're only Scottish half-wits,
　　But I'll make you understand.
You Highland swine, these hills are mine!
　　This is all Lord Brocket's Land.

'I'll write to Arthur Woodburn, boys,
　　And they'll soon let you know,
That the "Sacred Rights of Property"
　　Will never be laid low.
With your stakes and tapes, I'll make you traipse
　　From Knoydart to the Rand;
You can dig for gold till you're stiff and cold –
　　But not on this e're Land.'

Then up spoke the Men of Knoydart:
　　'Away and shut your trap,
For threats from a Saxon brewer's boy,
　　We just won't give a rap.

O we are all ex-servicemen,
    We fought against the Hun.
We can tell our enemies by now,
    And Brocket, you are one!'

When he heard these words that noble peer
    Turned purple in the face.
He said: 'These Scottish savages
    Are Britain's black disgrace.
It may be true that I've let some few
    Thousand acres go to pot,
But each one I'd give to a London spiv,
    Before any Goddam Scot!

'You're a crowd of tartan bolshies,
    But I'll soon have you licked.
I'll write to the Court of Session,
    For an Interim Interdict.
I'll write to my London lawyers,
    And they will understand.'
'Och, to hell wi' your London lawyers,
    We want our Highland Land.'

When Brocket heard these fightin' words,
    He fell down in a swoon,
But they slapped his jowl with uisge,
    And he woke up mighty soon,
And he moaned: 'Those Dukes of Sutherland
    Were right about the Scot.
If I had my way I'd start today,
    And clear the whole damn lot!'

Then up spoke the Men of Knoydart:
    'You have no earthly right,
For this is the land of Scotland,

And not the Isle of Wight.
When Scotland's proud Fianna,
    With ten thousand lads is manned,
We will show the world that Highlanders
    Have a right to Scottish Land.'

'You may scream and yell, Lord Brocket –
    You may rave and stamp and shout,
But the lamp we've lit in Knoydart
    Will never now go out.
For Scotland's on the march, my boys –
    We think it won't be long.
Roll on the day when The Knoydart Way
    Is Scotland's battle song.'

[*The Rebels Ceilidh Song Book*, 1953]

SONG OF THE GILLIE MORE

   O horo the Gillie More
Whit's the ploy ye're on sae early?
Braw news, sae tell it rarely
   O horo the Gillie More
News o' him, yon muckly callant
    Whistlin' at the smiddy door.
Tak your bow, for here's your ballant
    O horo the Gillie More

   O horo the Gillie More
Come awa an' gie's your blether.
Here's a dram'll droon the weather
   O horo the Gillie More
Sons o' birk an' pine an' rowan
    Jocks an' Ivans by the score
Swappin' yarns tae cowe the gowan
    O horo the Gillie More

   O horo the Gillie More
Noo's the time, the haimmer's ready.
Haud the tangs – ay, haud them steady
   O horo the Gillie More
Gar the iron ring, avallich!
    Gar it ring frae shore tae shore.
Leith tae Kiev – Don tae Gairloch
    O horo the Gillie More

   O horo the Gillie More
Here's a weld'll wear for ever.
Oor grup they canna sever
   O horo the Gillie More.
Ane's the wish yokes us thegither –

Ane's the darg that lies afore
You an' me: the man, the brither!
   Me an' you: the Gillie More.

Note:

Gillie More, (Gaelic, Gille Mor):	'big lad'
ploy:	affair, job
'tae cowe the gowan':	to beat all
rowan:	mountain ash
gar:	make
avallich (Gaelic, a bhalaich):	my lad
darg:	work, toil

Among messages of fraternal good wishes exchanged during Scottish-
Soviet Friendship Week, at the height of the Cold War, was one

'FROM THE BLACKSMITHS OF LEITH
TO THE BLACKSMITHS OF KIEV'

This song was published by the Associated Blacksmiths' Forge and Smithy
Workers' Society to commemorate that event.

[*Song of the Gillie More* (Associated Blacksmiths' Forge and Smithy Workers'
Society, 1951)]

THE BELLES O' MARCHMONT

In Marchmont we are awfu nice
        Tanteery orum
We've never heard o' bugs or lice
        Deedle um de orum.
Damn the common damn them a' –
We wouldnae gie them floor-room.

In Marchmont we are a' genteel –
The price we pey wad mak ye reel.

We'll pey a wife tae wash the stair
For washin' stairs is common here.

A new piano wad be graund
We'll talk tae work tae pey the bond.

We'll pey the school-fees for the nippers
Although we have tae leeve on kippers.

We like tae ape the upper cless
Although we hae tae dae wi' less.

Of course we hae the television –
On may mair, and we'll gang tae preeson.

We'll let Sir Alec hae a go
For he'll maintain the status quo.

Private enterprise we like tae see –
Although nae enterprise hae we.

And when oor peys are cutten doon,
We'll bear it a' without a froon.

But never mind, we'll hae a cheer
Thank God, this is Election year.

                    – Diarmid MacHugh

Note: Though this piece is not directly attributed to Henderson, the context of the archive suggests that it is his. [Editor]

[Hamish Henderson Archive]

MAINS O' RHYNIE
(a modern folk-song now going the rounds in various parts of Scotland)

Collected in Aberdeenshire by Seumas Mór.

(Tune: 'The Barnyards o' Delgaty')

As I cam in by Mains o' Rhynie
   Early on a summer's day,
I met in wi' lang Jock Scott,
   Wha spier'd gin I'd join the SRA.

> Chorus:
> *Liltin adie toorin adie*
>   *Liltin adie toorin ee*
> *Liltin adie toorin adie*
>   *EIIR is no for me.*

Says I, man Jock, I wish ye weel
   Although your numbers are but sma'.
The maist that talk o' Scotland's wrongs
   They havenae got a clue ava.

Says he, my lad, we'll try wer strength.
   A guid strong blow 'ull ring the bell!
I need twa chaps to dae a job –
   Come on an gie's a hand yersel'.

A hundred men was a' wer portion –
   Noo we hae a puckle mair.
When we fight for Scotland's honour,
   Ilka Scot will dae his share.

Will ye join your home batallion?
   Will ye fight in Scotland's wars?
Or will ye crawl on your bended knees
   To lick auld England's EIIRs?

EIIR was ne'er my fancy,
    EIIR is no for me.
I had aye a better notion –
    SRA, and Scotland free.

I am but a prentice laddie
    Workin' for auld Rhynie's fee,
But I wad leave my job and hame
    To see puir Scotland rightly free.

The youth o' Scotland's on oor side, man.
    Ay, and half the polis tae!
The sodger on the castle wa'
    In secret backs the SRA.

Douce folks ca' us wild and lawless
    But they'd best just bide a wee.
When the Scots hae got their freedom
    Better bairnies will we be.

We can drink and nae be drunk.
    We can fight and nae be slain.
We can gie auld England's loons
    A bonnie Bannockburn again.

        Liltin adie toorin adie
            Liltin adie toorin ee
        Liltin adie toorin adie
            EIIR is no for me.

[TS Broadsheet in Hamish Henderson Archive]

THE FREEDOM COME-ALL-YE
For the Glasgow Peace Marchers, May 1960

(Tune: 'The Bloody Fields o Flanders')

Roch the wind in the clear day's dawin
    Blaws the cloods heelster-gowdie ow'r the bay,
But there's mair nor a roch wind blawin
    Through the great glen o the world the day.
It's a thocht that will gar oor rottans,
    Aa they rogues that gang gallus, fresh an gay,
Tak the road and seek ither loanins
    For their ill ploys, tae sport an play.

Nae mair will the bonnie callants
    March tae war, when oor braggarts crousely craw,
Nor wee weans frae pit-heid and clachan
    Mourn the ships sailin doon the Broomielaw;
Broken families, in lands we herriet
    Will curse Scotland the Brave nae mair, nae mair;
Black and white, ane til ither mairriet
    Mak the vile barracks o their maisters bare.

So come all ye at hame wi freedom,
    Never heed whit the hoodies croak for doom;
In your hoose aa the bairns o Adam
    Can find breid, barley bree and painted room.
When Maclean meets wi's freens in Springburn
    Aa the roses an geans will turn tae bloom,
An a black boy frae yont Nyanga
    Dings the fell gallows o the burghers doon.

Note: Non-workshop, much richer language. The Scots has been wedded, after the Gaelic fashion, to the pipe-tune. Style: rebel-bardic.

[*Ding Dong Dollar*, 1962]

ANTI-POLARIS

(Tune: 'The Captain and His Whiskers')

There's a high road tae Gourock
    and a ferry tae Dunoon,
And the world will be watchin
    When we're mairchin through the toon.

Ban the Bomb and biff the base
    till it's sunk without a trace.
Pit the Yanks intae orbit, for
    there's plenty room in space.   *Repeat*

You may come frae Odessa, mate,
    frae Baltimore or Perth,
But the threat o Polaris
    Maks ae country o the Earth.

Ban the Bomb, an blaw the base
    far awa tae Outer Space,
It's tae Hell wi Polaris – or
    The puir aul human race.   *Repeat*

O, K. stands for Kennedy
    Wha maks us aa sae blue,
An H. stands for Holy Loch
    An Hiroshima, too.

Ban the Bomb and blaw the base
    Tae some ither hotter place,
It's tae hell wi Polaris or
    The puir human race.   *Repeat*

*

(Tune: 'The Keel Row')

As I cam by Sandbank,
By Sandbank, by Sandbank;
As I cam by Sandbank,
   I heard a Yankee cuss –

O deil tak the mairchers,
The mairchers, the mairchers,
'O deil tak the mairchers,
   They've got it in for us.'   *Repeat*

We'll hae tae shift Polaris,
   Polaris, Polaris.
We'll hae tae shift Polaris,
   Proteus an aa.

For if we dinna shift them,
Shift them, ay, shift them,
For if we dinna shift them,
   We'll get nae peace at aa.   *Repeat*

*

(Tune: 'Ho ro mo nighean donn bhoidheach')

Oor een are on the target
Oor een are on the target
Oor een are on the target
   We'll blaw the base awa.

We'll hae tae shift that target,
We'll hae tae shift that target,
An no juist doon tae Margate!
   We'll blaw the base awa.
O I can see a captain,

A cocky Yankee captain,
O I can see a captain,
   Wi ribbons up an aa.

We'll pit him intae orbit,
We'll pit him intae orbit,
The shock he'll juist absorb it,
   He'll sook as weel as blaw.

Note: A clanjamfrie of Highland Division, international brotherhood, mouth-music and Presbyterian psalm-singing.

The third tune is known in English as 'Ho-ro My Nut-brown Maiden' and parodied in the Scottish regiments as 'Ah canny see the target'. Style: rebel-medley.

[*Ding Dong Dollar*, 1962]

IF YOU SIT CLOSE TAE ME, I WINNA WEARY

(Tune: Traditional)
(Communal creation credit: Raymond Grant, Cults)

'I saw Macmillan through the toon
Wha's that, my dearie?
That's aul Blundermac
Hey, Jimmy Tyrie
Blundermac, Scabbytash
That's a', my dearie
If you sit close tae me, I winna weary.

'I saw a Tory doon the toon
Wha's that, my dearie?
That's a boneheid
Hey, Jimmy Tyrie
Boneheid, Blundermac, Scabbytash
That's a', my dearie
If you sit close tae me, I winna weary.

'I saw Profumo doon the toon.
Wha's that, my dearie?
That's a Poodlefaker
Hey, Jimmy Tyrie
Poodlefaker, Boneheid, Blundermac,
    Scabbytash
That's a', my dearie.
If you sit close tae me, I winna weary.

'I saw a Yankee by the Loch.
Wha's that, my dearie?
That's a Bullyboy
Hey, Jimmy Tyrie
Bullyboy, Poodlefaker, Boneheid,
    Blundermac, Scabbytash

That's a', my dearie
If you sit close tae me, I winna weary.

'I saw a polis by the Loch.
Wha's that, my dearie?
That's a Croakerjack
Hey, Jimmy Tyrie
Croakerjack, Bullyboy, Poodlefaker,
    Boneheid, Blundermac, Scabbytash
That's a', my dearie.
If you sit close tae me, I winna weary.

'I saw a nark abuin the brae.
Wha's that, my dearie?
That's a Hornygolloch
Hey, Jimmy Tyrie
Hornygolloch, Croakerjack, Bullyboy,
    Poodlefaker, Boneheid, Blundermac,
    Scabbytash
That's a', my dearie.
If you sit close tae me, I winna weary.

'I saw a blubbin' Buchmanite.
Wha's that, my dearie?
That's a Bamstick
Hey, Jimmy Tyrie
Bamstick, Hornygolloch, Croakerjack,
    Bullyboy, Poodlefaker, Boneheid,
    Blundermac, Scabbytash
That's a', my dearie.
If you sit close tae me, I winna weary.

'I saw a banker on his knees.
Wha's that, my dearie?
That's a Buttonpusher
Hey, Jimmy Tyrie

Buttonpusher, Bamstick, Hornygolloch,
    Croakerjack, Bullyboy, Poodlefaker,
    Boneheid, Blundermac, Scabbytash
That's a', my dearie.
If you sit close tae me, I winna weary.

'I saw Jack a-tellin' his beads
Wha's that, my dearie?
That's a Coonter-doon
Hey, Jimmy Tyrie
Coonter-doon, Buttonpusher, Bamstick,
    Hornygolloch, Croakerjack, Bullyboy,
    Poodlefaker, Boneheid, Blundermac,
    Scabbytash
That's a', my dearie.
If you sit close tae me, I winna weary.

'I saw the Hunley on the Loch
Whit's that, my dearie?
That's a Daith Wish
Hey, Jimmy Tyrie
Daith Wish (nae mine!), Coonter-doon,
    Buttonpusher, Bamstick, Hornygolloch,
    Croakerjack, Bullyboy, Poodlefaker,
    Boneheid, Blundermac, Scabbytash
That's a', my dearie.
If you sit close tae me, I winna weary.'

Note: From amidst (and manifestly *for*) the demonstrators who march
and sit down in close companionship and protest by the Holy Loch,
Hamish Henderson has written this boisterous 'tour de force'. It lambasts
in inexhaustible extravaganza the specious, the domineering, the
slimy. From verse to mounting verse it cumulatively pours upon pluto-
politico-religiosity and upon all that is meretricious and hypocritical,
and upon all that is anti-life a pejorative avalanche worthy of Thomas

Urquhart in its massive inventiveness and reminiscent of Joyce in its fresh and brilliant use of symbolical analogy. Its climactic glimpse of the sinister Polaris depot-ship as a 'daith-wish' (reversing as it does so tellingly the accepted poetical process of rendering concrete what is abstract) is particularly powerful.

(Hamish Henderson has asked us to explain two other words in the text of his song:- 'Bamstick': a painted hoax; a joke; the painted horse-head on a jester's stick. The word symbolizes both the Moral Rearmament crusader and the thin and painted hobby-horse on which he rides. 'Nark': an informer. 'Croakerjack': bull frog. 'Hornygolloch': centipede. cf. Shelley's simile equally full of loathing – 'two scorpions under one wet stone'.)

[*Scottish Broadsheet*, No. 2, June 1963. Also published as 'Jimmy Tyrie' in Farquhar McLay, ed., *Workers' City* (Clydeside Press, 1988)]

THE FLYTING O' LIFE AND DAITH

Quo life, the warld is mine
The floo'ers an' trees, they're a' my ain
I am the day, an' the sunshine
Quo life, the warld is mine.

Quo daith, the warld is mine
Your lugs are deef, your een are blin'
Your floo'ers maun dwine in my bitter win'
Quo daith, the warld is mine.

Quo life, the warld is mine
I hae saft win's, an' healin' rain
Aipples I hae, an' breid an' wine
Quo life, the warld is mine.

Quo daith, the warld is mine
Whit sterts in dreid, gangs doon in pain
Bairns wi'oot breid are makin' mane
Quo daith, the warld is mine.

Quo life, the warld is mine
Your deidly wark, I ken it fine
There's maet on earth for ilka wean
Quo life, the warld is mine.

Quo daith, the warld is mine
Your silly sheaves crine in my fire
My worm keeks in your barn and byre
Quo daith, the warld is mine.

Quo life, the warld is mine
Dule on your een! Ae galliard hert
Can ban tae hell your blackest airt
Quo life, the warld is mine.

Quo daith, the warld is mine
Your rantin' hert, in duddies braw,
He winna lowp my preeson wa'
Quo daith, the warld is mine.

Quo life, the warld is mine
Though ye bigg preesons o' marble stane,
Hert's luve ye cannae preeson in
Quo life, the warld is mine.

Quo daith, the warld is mine
I hae dug a grave, I hae dug it deep,
For war an' the pest will gar ye sleep
Quo daith, the warld is mine.

Quo life, the warld is mine
An open grave is a furrow syne
Ye'll no keep my seed frae fa'in in!
Quo life, the warld is mine.

Note: The motif of a flyting, or argument, between Life and Death, appears
in Mediaeval German folksong, but this is the first use of it in Scots, as far
as I know. The tune, which is not unlike the urlar (or 'ground') of a pibroch,
is my own. 'Quo Life' (for says life) is good ballad-Scots, but there's no
reason why folk shouldn't sing 'says life' etc., if they prefer it. Three words
in the song had perhaps better be defined –

dwine:	dwindle or be consumed
crine:	shrivel
galliard:	gaily courageous

The writer asks that we do not publish the music for his song. The tune is of
the musical nature of the urlar or ground work of pibroch: it is best learned
aurally, for from verse to verse it can be subtly varied to the interpretation
of the singer, allowing as it does of considerable grace-noting and shift of

mood and emphasis. Hamish Henderson himself, Archie Fisher and other singers (in the Scottish Folk Clubs for a beginning) will soon orally have established this magnificent song as one of the deservedly great favourites of the modern folk-song movement.

[*Scottish Broadsheet*, No. 1, May 1963]

MAY'S MOU FOR JAMIE

in honour of James and May Macdonald married in April.

(Tune: 'Whistle O'er the Lave O't')

Lord, the year is a' agley!
May's in April, Jamie's wey.
Jamie's simmer's here tae stay –
   It's May's mou for Jamie.
Lily May gars a' kind smell,
Flings them intae bed herself.
Mair o' May I maunna tell
   But May's mou for Jamie.
Strip the willow, ding the deil!
And roset up your fiddles weel.
I'll set the pace for Stumpie's reel
   Wi' May's mou for Jamie.
Let it rip, a gallus splore,
For May has richt til springs galore.
Frae Crammond Brig tae Berwick shore
   It's May's mou for Jamie.

Wae your pairtners – mak the ring –
Let randie hurdies hae their fling.
An' aye the owrecome o' the Spring
   Is May's mou for Jamie.
Springs for May will ne'er be few.
My spring is auld, sweet May is new.
Sae dinnae dauner – here's your cue –
   It's May's mou for Jamie.

[*Scottish Broadsheet*, No. 3, Jan 1964]

RIVONIA

(Tune: 'Viva la Quince Brigada')

They have sentenced the men of Rivonia
 Rumbala rumbala rumba la
The comrades of Nelson Mandela
 Rumbala rumbala rumba la
He is buried alive on an island
 Free Mandela free Mandela
He is buried alive on an island
 Free Mandela free Mandela.

Verwoerd feared the mind of Mandela
 Rumbala rumbala rumba la
He was stifling the voice of Mandela
 Rumbala rumbala rumba la
Free Mbeki, Goldberg, Sisulu
 Free Mandela free Mandela
Free Mbeki, Goldberg, Sisulu
 Free Mandela free Mandela.

The crime of the men of Rivonia
 Rumbala rumbala rumba la
Was to organise farmer and miner
 Rumbala rumbala rumba la
Against baaskap and sjambok and Kierie
 Free Mandela free Mandela
Against baaskap and sjambok and Kierie
 Free Mandela free Mandela

Set free the men of Rivonia
 Rumbala rumbala rumba la
Break down the walls of their prison
 Rumbala rumbala rumba la
Freedom and justice, Uhuru

Free Mandela free Mandela
Freedom and justice, Uhuru
Free Mandela free Mandela

Power to the heirs of Lutuli
Rumbala rumbala rumba la
The comrades of Nelson Mandela
Rumbala rumbala rumba la
Spear of the nation unbroken
Free Mandela free Mandela
Amandla Umkhonto we Sizwe
Free Mandela free Mandela.

Note: It was at a party in the South London flat of my old friends Douggie and Queenie Moncrieff that first thought of fitting anti-apartheid words to the well-known Spanish Republican tune 'Long Live the 15th Brigade' ('Viva la Quince Brigata' alias 'El Ejecito del Ebro' – the Army of the Ebro). The refrain of the Spanish song includes the girl's name Manuela – which suggested Mandela – and the Rumbala chorus suggested African drums. (This was not long after the end of the Rivonia trial). The song was sung by me a little later in Athens at a folktale conference and began to circulate internationally.

In September 1964 I sent a copy of the song to the ANC office in London and received a reply from Raymond Kunene dated 13 October 1964. I then asked Roy Williamson and Ronnie Brown of the folk duo 'The Corries' to record the song for me; this they did and I sent several copies to Raymond Kunene who sent one on to Dar-es-Salaam. Some months later I heard from several sources – including (if I remember rightly) Abdul Minty – that the song had been carried across to Robben Island by prisoners who had heard it while awaiting trial. I was naturally very proud to think that it may have been heard by Nelson himself.

[Note from *End of a Regime?* (1991)]

[Hayden Murphy, ed. *Broadsheet* 22 (Dublin)]

THE BALLAD OF THE SPEAKING HEART

A puir lad yince and a lad sae trim
   (Hey the haw, the gillieflour,
      Hey the thyme)
A puir lad yince and a lad sae trim,
He lo'ed a lassie that lo'ed na him.

Says she, gae fetch tae me, ye rogue,
   (Hey the haw, the gillieflour,
      Hey the thyme)
Says she, gae fetch tae me, ye rogue,
Your mither's hert tae feed my dog.

Tae his mither's hoose gaed that young man
   (Hey the haw, the gillieflour,
      Hey the thyme)
Tae his mither's hoose gaed that young man,
He cut oot her hert, and awa he ran.

And as he ran, he trippit and fell
   (Hey the haw, the gillieflour,
      Hey the thyme)
And as he ran, he trippit and fell,
And the hert rolled on the grun as well.

Noo the hert it stotted against a stane
   (Hey the haw, the gillieflour,
      Hey the thyme)
Noo the hert it stotted against a stane,
And the laddie heard it makin' its mane.

The hert was greetin' and cryin' fu sma'
   (Hey the haw, the gillieflour,
      Hey the thyme)
The hert was greetin' and cryin' fu sma',
'Are ye hurt, my bairn, are ye hurt at a'?'

Note: The power of the heart, and the heart's blood (aboriginal folklore magic) is discussed by Lowry C. Wimberly, *Folklore in the English and Scottish Ballads*, pp 73–82 and 391–394. There is a Norse ballad 'Nattergalen' in which a youth is changed into a wolf by his stepmother, but regains his original shape when he tears out her heart and drinks her blood.

'The Ballad of the Speaking Heart' is a genuine 'folk product' in that it owes a great deal to previous handlings of the theme. One of these is a 19th-century 'chanson populaire' by Jean Richepin, who was a buccaneering Villonesque bohemian figure in the Paris of Verlain and Rimbaud (indeed, he was about the only literary friend that couple eventually possessed). His own name was notorious, because he had written a book of poems about the Parisian underworld scene of his day which created a furore similar to that stirred up more recently by *The Naked Lunch*, *Cain's Book*, and *Last Exit to Brooklyn*.

A contemporary translation of this particular song was made by the Anglo-Irish poet Herbert Trench, who was born in Co. Cork about the middle of the last century. In the '90s, Trench was a member of Yeat's circle at the 'Cheshire Cheese' pub in Fleet Street – the circle which included Ernest Dowson ('I have been faithful to thee, Cynara, in my fashion') and Lionel Johnson, and this translation became popular with these poets. Like many literary folk-products of the day, it is easier to read than to sing. What I did, in order to turn it into a song, was to re-sing it in ballad-Scots, and give it a tune of my own. Here, for example, is Trench's fifth verse ('Noo the hert is stotted against a stane'):

> 'And the lad, as the heart was
>   a-rolling, heard
> That the heart was speaking, and
>   this was the word ... '

Trench's version of the French song has a rollicking refrain (Fol de rol de raly o! Fol de rol!) which counterpoints the stark narrative with bluff devil-may-care. If singers prefer, they could retain it, as I did originally. My flower-refrain harks back to those mysterious refrains found in some of the classic ballads, and in the love-laments which grew out of them. Some of these refrains may have had sexual significance (cf. James Reeves, *The Everlasting Circle*, Introduction, pp. 21–33); elsewhere, the sexual significance, if it existed, has become muted or obliterated.

I usually sing the final 'at a" staccato or in monotone, in the style often employed by our older ballad-singers when ending a song. This coda can be a highly effective artistic device, especially when the last line detonates the explosive charge which the narrative has planted.

[*Chapbook*, Vol. 4, No. 2, 1967]

PADDY'S HOGMANAY
(or, 'The Shamrock and the Thistle')

O come all ye true-born Glasgow boys, and listen to my song;
I'm going to speak of Hogmanay, it won't detain you long.
I've made this little tune for youse, I played it on my whistle,
And I think the name I'll give to it is the Shamrock and the Thistle.

Aboard the 'Royal Ulsterman' we had a dram or twa.
When daylight broke, we all awoke, and saw the Broomielaw.
The journey o'er, we went ashore, our friends they raised a cheer,
And soon the word was going round 'the Irishmen are here.'

We were not rash, we wore no sash, we sang no party lay,
For we had come to join the fun, a real Scotch Hogmanay.
We marched up to Argyle Street, we bought whisky, stout and
    rum,
And the songs we sang were 'Sweet Strabane' and 'Brigton, here
    we come.'

A welcome rare we soon got there, it was a glorious spread.
Bill Thomson cried, 'Get that inside! I see ye're needin' fed.'
So when we'd had a tightener, we were feelin' in good trim.
Bob said 'Come on, I'm for the Tron,' so we went along with him.

Now many's the hooly we've been at, at home across the sea,
And at New Year, with stout and beer, we go upon the spree.
But you Scots don't just make whoopee, or have drinks with Mum
    and Dad,
On the 31st of December, boys, you all go roaring mad!

Forgive me friends for being rude, I'm not, you will agree.
The Irish too are a crazy crew – just look at Bob and me!
But a Scotsman seeing the New Year in is a sight for gods and men,
And it takes an Irish Paddy to be equal with him then!

For the Scotsmen have their thistle, and the Welshmen have their
    leek,
The English have the rose, my boys, and lots of flamin' cheek.
The Irish have their shamrock, and they hold it very dear,
But you'll find it with the thistle in old Glasgow at New Year.

Now my little song is ended, boys, I made it just for you.
There is a moral to it, and I'm telling you it's true.
The Scots folk and the Irish are as one, you will agree,
And the only thing between them is the dear old Irish Sea.

Note: On several trips from Belfast (where I was working) to Glasgow on
board the Burns-Laird steamers in the late '40s, I collected from fellow
steerage passengers a number of fragments of a song with the theme of
'Paddy's Hogmanay'. It seemed to be about a party of Ulster Orangemen
who crossed the water to enjoy the festive season a good few years ago, but
the song – like the party itself, maybe – had become a bit chaotic. Although
the fragments could clearly be sung to a number of 'come-all-ye' tunes,
they were always given as spoken rhymes. One of these contained the Scots
expression 'a dram or twa', and this started me off on a reconstruction of
the song.

    In the process of re-singing it into shape, most of the already existing
fragments fell away, and the song, as it stands, is nearly all my own work.
The only collected stanza which I was able to work in unchanged was the
penultimate one ('For the Scotsmen have their thistle . . .') The tune I chose
for it is one of the more attractive of the familiar 'come-all-ye' tunes, but it
goes quite well to a number of others. The Corries have recorded it, and it
appears on their forthcoming Fontana LP 'Kishmael's Galley'.

    P.S. There is no song called 'Brigton, here we come.' Maybe the reader
might care to have a shot writing one . . .

[*Chapbook*, Vol. 4, No. 5, 1968]

A VOICE FRAE YONT THE GRAVE

Look roon the bar whaur auld freens meet,
An' listen fur the sigh:
The cri de coeur o' a' they ghaists
Wha greet fur days gone by.

The days o' talk an' fiddle strings,
Baith music on the air;
Tho' now, alas, a jukebox 'sings' –
There is nae music there!

Nae music o' the kind folk mak
Or they can ca' their ain:
Sangs sweet tae them o'er a' the clack
O' the bandit's bleak refrain.

The TV's on fur ither folk
Wha watch it without carin';
Fur thaim that sit an' cannae talk
Abuin the tele's blarin'.

Whit happen'd tae the pub that was –
A pub like naewhere else?
We hannie focht near hard enough
Fur the memory o' Bell's.

A memory, 'Is that a'', ye say,
An' wonder why ah girn.
'We a' maun move wi the times', ye say:
'We a' maun live an' learn'.

But memory's mair than sentiment,
Tho' mixed wi myth or dream.
It counsels a' wad gan forrit
Tae ken whaur they hae been.

It needna act like fetters
Tae tie ye tae the past,
Fur whit was guid is ayeways guid,
An' ayeways shair tae last.

Tho' folks buin a' are different
But wad speak as if yin voice,
There's some wad hae vain profit
An' submit they hae nae choice.

Sic folk, ah say, hae sellt their soul
An' nae man may ken pain worse:
Tae furgo the swellin' o' the hert
For the swellin' o' the purse!

Whit happen'd tae auld Sandy Bell's
That it maun suffer sic a fate?
Sae symptomatic o' the times
Whaur truth maun lie prostrate.

A truth that yince fired a' folk's herts
Is draped wi blackest soot:
But we maun blaw upon the flame
Afore the fire gans oot.

Fur a' we girn in Sandy Bell's
We each maun tak oor share,
Fur wha bit us is there tae blame
Fur things that are nae mair?

– The Ghaist o' Sandy Bell's

Note: This poem from a 'ghaist' – indeed the principal ghaist of the season
– is a response to what the writer considers a rather euphoric article in
the *Broadsheet* about the present state of Sandy Bell's, and a poem by Will

Martin – almost equally euphoric – which has appeared on its walls. [Note in Henderson's hand]

[Hamish Henderson Archives]

THE OBSCURE VOICE
AND
'OH, THE FADED CHURCHES'

WIND ON THE CRESCENT
[Eugenio Montale]

The great bridge did not lead to you.
I would have reached you even at the cost of sailing
along the sewers, if at your command.
But already my energy, like the sun on the glass
of the verandas, was gradually weakening.

The man preaching on the Crescent
asked me 'Do you know where God is?'
I knew where, and told him. He shook his head.
Then he vanished in the whirlwind that caught up men
and houses
And lifted them on high, on a colour of pitch.

(Edinburgh, 1948)

[Alec Finlay, ed., *The Obscure Voice* (Morning Star, 1994)]

COLOUR OF RAIN AND IRON
[Salvatore Quasimodo]

You said: death, silence, solitude;
and like love, life. Being the words
of our provisory images.
A soft wind rose gently every morning,
and time the colour of rain and iron
passed over the stones,
and over us, the damned, and our low murmurous babble.
The truth is still far away.

And tell me, man split asunder on the cross,
and you whose hands are thick with blood,
how shall I answer those who ask?
Now, now: before another silence
invades our eyes, before another wind rises
and before rust flowers again.

[Alec Finlay, ed., *The Obscure Voice* (Morning Star, 1994)]

THE SLEEP OF THE VIRGIN
[Vincenzo Cardarelli]

One evening, having crossed
the threshold of your room, with your mother,
I saw you asleep,
contrary little virgin.
There you were, lying on your bed,
motionless, without breathing
tamed at long last.
There was nothing angelic about you sleeping
dreamless – soulless –
like a rose sleeping;
and a little colour
had left your cheeks.
Your face closed, enveloped
in a distant sleep
you were great with secret ferment –
while you slept you were rising like yeast
as once in the womb of your mother.

And, child, I witnessed
Your stupendous sleep.

[Alec Finlay, ed., *The Obscure Voice* (Morning Star, 1994)]

IN UN MOMENTO

[Dino Campana]

(from four poems for Sibilla Aleramo)

In a moment
The roses have faded
Their petals fallen
Because I could not forget the roses
We searched for them together
We found some roses
They were her roses they were my roses
This journey we called love
With our blood and with our tears we made the roses
That shone for a moment in the morning sun
We let them wither under the sun among the brambles
The roses that were not our roses
My roses her roses

P.S. And so we forgot the roses.

[Alec Finlay, ed., *The Obscure Voice* (Morning Star, 1994)]

LETTING GO OF A DOVE
[Eugenio Montale]

A white dove has flown from me
among stelae, under vaults where the sky nests.
Dawns and light suspended; I have loved the sun,
the colour of honey – now I crave the dark.
I desire the broody fire, and this immobile tomb.
And I want to see your gaze downfacing it.

(Ely Cathedral, 1948)

[Alec Finlay, ed., *The Obscure Voice* (Morning Star, 1994)]

OH, THE FADED CHURCHES
[Alfonso Gatto]

Oh, the faded churches in the fields,
the channels of the grass where the wind
climbs the steps, carrying its silences
and the wooden doors, and the tinkling
of a bell, up to the iron gates . . .
But the country will go down into the sea
to find its dead, the bare ironworks
of the world and in the houses the vast
silence of the crosses. Like marble
that love will be cold which burns more fiercely
with the remaining lights and the shouting –
deep down, deep down in our black blood.
Naked that day it will break through
into the thick of the thighs of snow.
The coral on the red mouth will drown
in darkness, and the lights extinguish
its songs against a background
of rainwet night . . .
the sea the sea will hurl on to the long
dreams the rains and the hovels, carrying the vast
odour of the earth and the tombs.

[L.R. Lind, ed., *Twentieth-Century Italian Poetry* (1974)]

UNSORTED WORKS

TAE GEORDIE FRASER ON HIS WADDIN DAY

The Gordon pipes play up like mad
   – by Christ, they flaunt their pride.
Nou, Geordie, listen – tear up your pad
   An' sling your pen aside.
If ye feel to-night the urge to write
   think: 'Whit the deil is it worth
tae be caad the Swan o Dee Don
   nou I'm th Cock o the North?'

If Tambi peddles his dirty cracks
   Juist crown him wi a plate.
When aince ye're safely ahint oor backs,
   by Gode, ye'll no be blate!
We hope ye keep the stars frae sleep
   till Thames reels into the Forth.
When the piers blaw ye'll up and craw
   nou ye're the Cock o the North!

[Hamish Henderson Archive]

COMRIE PORT A BEUL

Cowden linn by Comrie
   by Comrie, by Comrie
Cowden linn by Comrie
   yon's whaur her hame is.
An' Cathie Rae o Comrie
   O Comrie, o Comrie
Cathie Rae of Comrie
   that's whit her name is.

Cathie Rae o hee oro
   – o hee oro
   o hee oro
Cathie Rae o hee oro
   that's wha ma dame is
Cathie Rae o hee oro
   o hee oro o hee oro
Cathie Rae, o hee oro
   That's whit her name is.

Gowpin roun in Glasgae
   in Glasgae in Glasgae
Gowpin roun in Glasgae
   – Tryan ma luck nou.
An' Risk Street in Glasgae
   In Glasgae in Glasgae
Risk Street in Glasgae
   Here's whaur I'm stuck nou.

Risk Street o hee oro
   o hee oro o hee oro
Risk Street o hee oro
   Wantan a pluck nou,
Risk Street o hee o oro
   o hee oro o hee oro
Risk Street o hee oro
   Here's whaur I'm stuck nou.

But Cowden linn by Comrie
   by Comrie by Comrie
Cowden linn by Comrie
   yon's whaur her hame is.

An' Cathie Rae o Comrie
   o Comrie o Comrie
Cathy Rae o Comrie
   that's whit her name is!

[Hamish Henderson Archive]

LIMERICKS

(written to please Rev. Alan Armstrong)

It was the old Bishop of Birmingham
Who wrote 'Legends, and my views concerning 'em.'
      He's dispensed with the need
      For an Anglican creed,
And as for the Gospels – he's burning 'em!
Bishop Barnes, who's remaining in Birmingham
said 'Damn the Archbishops: I'm spurning 'em.'
      And he added 'Till they
      make me Vicar of Bray
I'll still be the Bishop of Birmingham.'

It was an old Bishop called Barnes
Who said 'Who could believe in those yarns
      Told by Matthew and Luke?
      I believe in the Book
Of the Gospel according to Barnes.'

[Hamish Henderson Archive]

SONG

(adapted from Horace)

Vivamus mea Lesbia atque amemus

Nou Jeannie dear, ye mauna fear
   the rants o dour auld bodies O.
Ye're daft to miss a single kiss
   to please sic muckle cuddies O.

We havenae land for 'luve's sweet sang' –
   It's shair the morn's the deil's O.
He'll douse the licht, an' leave in nicht
   the waltzes an' quadrilles O!

Sae kiss me mair, ma carrot-hair,
   a thousand kisses gie me O.
(But dinna count the hale amount
   lest Dick an' Denny see me O).

[cf. 'As Burns Might Have Translated Catullus's Ode' and 'Vivamus Mea Lesbia atque Amemus']

[*Conflict*, May 1949]

BILLET DOUX

A word tae the go-by-the-wa's – aye, *you* I mean
that cannae thole these black dirk words o mine –
wha yelp my claw o satire gars ye bleed,
and tear yuir fingers on this thorny leid.

Ye vent yuir sickly venom timorously
on 'bletherin bolshie tinks' the like o me:
yet back afore my filibusterin lash
and close yuir lugs tae *slancio* and *panache*.

I dinna ken whit bluidy flaw dryrots
the hairts an' minds an' guts o some damn Scots!
Cheatin the tomb yous gash cadavers are.
There's mair like I the daithsheid O Dunbar.

Passion ye've nane. A slaw revenge to pree
Wi falset's bodkin, sarcasm's snickersnee . . .
But whit is ours, and smeddum, and delyte.
Ae pleasure yet we hae, ye coons – tae flyte!

[*Voice of Scotland*, Vol. 5, No. 3, June 1949]

PROLOGUE TO A BOOK OF BALLADS

A braw new song, a bonnie new song
   My freans I randilie sing ye.
– An' manger chiel, ye can listen tae,
   For bonnilie doon we'll ding ye!

Aye, these are the words o' the raucle tune
   We'll sing like lads o' spirit –
We want nae truck wi' Heaven or Hell
   Wha this bra earth inherit . . .

[as cited in Timothy Neat, *Hamish Henderson: A Biography*, Vol. 1, p. 235]

SCOTTISH CHILDHOOD

I climb with Neil the whinny braes of Lornty
    or walk my lane by drumlie Ericht side.
Under Glasclune we play the death of Comyn,
    and fear, wee boys, the Auld Kirk's sin of pride.

Spring quickens. In the Shee Water I'm fishing.
    High on whaup's mountain time heaps stone on stone.
The speech and silence of Christ's word is Gaelic
    and youth on age, the tree climbs from the bone.

[*Poetry Scotland*, No. 4, 1949]

The theme of lyric perfection in exchange for the sacrifice of the
   creator
Recur here once again denuded of myth and addressed
In direct and clear words to those who seek to enclose
The struggle of life in the crystal of the verse flames.

[as cited in Timothy Neat, *Hamish Henderson: A Biography*, Vol. 1, p. 248]

DEATH OR THE BED OF CONTENTION –
MACDIARMID OR ME?

Wheesht, wheesht, Grieve I dinna care
    Whether you're richt and I'm wrang –
Gin dark is the price o' licht
    And silence the price o' sang

[as cited in Timothy Neat, *Hamish Henderson: A Biography*, Vol. 1, p. 299.]

AFTER CHURCHILL

We will fight them on the Lochside
And in the sheiling –
We will fight them in the corrie
And in the glen.
We will fight them in the gloaming
And in the moonlight
And we will never give in.

[Hamish Henderson Archive and as cited in Timothy Neat, *Hamish Henderson: A Biography*, Vol. 1, p. 326]

UNPUBLISHED HAIKU

Viet Cong: peak of valour,
This name becomes them,
 – Now, what name becomes us?

[as cited in Timothy Neat, *Hamish Henderson: A Biography*, Vol. 2, p. 103]

UNPUBLISHED QUATRAIN

The crowd hailed Jesus
That soon howled for his blood –
How glad they must have been
To get back to normal.

[Hamish Henderson Archive and as cited in Timothy Neat, *Hamish Henderson: A Biography*, Vol. 2, p. 104]

UNPUBLISHED POEM FRAGMENT

There is the crowning in thorns
   Our heids under
      Our whole lives long
         Or the faces of bronze
            Who gave to the workers
         A ragged pottage of red banner – chairborne tartuffes.

[Hamish Henderson Archive and as cited in Timothy Neat, *Hamish Henderson: A Biography*, Vol. 2, p. 107]

There is one sin,
　　To call a green leaf, grey,
Whereat the sun in heaven, shuddereth.

There is one blasphemy,
　　For death to pray,
For God alone knoweth the praise of death.

There is one creed:
　　Neath world terror
Apples forget to grow on apple trees.

There is one thing needful –
　　Everything
The rest is vanities of vanity.

[Hamish Henderson Archive and as cited in Timothy Neat, *Hamish Henderson: A Biography*, Vol. 2, pp. 138–9]

Folksong belongs to the body
    As if in some mystic way
        Folksong had been implanted
            Like the soul in everybody.

Folksong runs unofficial and anti-cultural
    It is the bawdy in the bothy
        The thried o' blue
            The Horseman's Word.

The rebel song, and army songs.
    Folksong belongs to everybody –
        A mystic Rousseauesque idea
        And true.

[Hamish Henderson Archive and as cited in Timothy Neat, *Hamish Henderson: A Biography*, Vol. 2, pp. 139–40]

Tempus originates
   Tempus coagulates
      Tempus conflagrates.

        Underdog
           Underground:
              And we in drams
                Behold the Hebrides.

[Hamish Henderson Archive and as cited in Timothy Neat, *Hamish Henderson: A Biography*, Vol. 2, p. 343]

UNPUBLISHED POEM FRAGMENT #5

The piper is still on the parapet
But like the indomitable old whore of Nantucket
Who went to hell in a bucket
He won't be blate when the moment comes
To offer a soldier's farewell.

[Hamish Henderson Archive and as cited in Timothy Neat, *Hamish Henderson: A Biography*, Vol. 2, pp. 344–5]

VERSE OF GOOD WISHES, COLLECTED FROM CATHERINE DIX OF BERNERAY

(translated from the Gaelic)

Gweed luck, this seely day o' Yule
And a' the days that come ahint.
May love and joy be yours for aye,
And naething may ye ever wint.
May fortune guide ye as ye gang,
Nae slippery stane e'er gar ye fa'.
An ashet fu', a cosie bield,
And routh o' joy be wi ye a'!

[as cited in Timothy Neat, *Hamish Henderson: A Biography*, Vol. 2, p. 346]

THE DRUID AND HIS DISCIPLE

an ancient, Breton Song/Dialogue collected in the early nineteenth century by Vicomte De La Villemarque – translated into English, for the first time, by Hamish Henderson 31 March 1989

Druid –
: Handsome boy, beautiful Druid's son,
Tell me, my handsome one;
What do you want me to sing to you?

Disciple –
: Sing me the series of number one,
So that I can learn it.

Druid –
: There is no series of number one:
There is Single Necessity;
There is Sin, father of Sorrow:
Nothing before, nothing after.

Handsome boy, beautiful Druid's son,
Tell me, my handsome one,
What do you want me to sing to you?

Disciple –
: Sing me the series of number two,
So that I can learn it today.

Druid –
: Two oxen harnessed to a shell:
They're pulling it; they breathe, they die.
There's a marvel for you!

There is no series of number one:
There is Single Necessity;
There is Sin, father of Sorrow:
Nothing before, nothing after.

Handsome boy etc.

Disciple –	Sing me the series of number three:
	So that I can learn it today.
Druid –	There are three parts of the world:
	Three beginnings and three ends,
	For man as for the oak.
	Three Kingdoms of Merlin,
	Full of golden fruit, brilliant flowers
	Little children laughing.
	Two oxen harnessed to a shell:
	They're pulling it; they breath and die.
	There's a marvel for you!
	Handsome boy etc.
Disciple –	Sing me the series of number four,
	So that I may learn it today.
Druid –	Four stones to sharpen,
	Stones to be sharpened by Merlin,
	Who sharpens the swords of the valiant.
	There are three parts of the world etc.
Druid –	Six little children of wax,
	Given life by the energy of the Moon.
	If you don't know, I do!
	Six medicinal plants in the little cauldron;
	The little dwarf mixes the brew,
	His little finger in his mouth . . .
Druid –	Seven Suns and seven Moons,
	Seven planets, the Hen included.
	Seven elements in the stour of the Air . . .

Druid – Eight winds which blow;
Eight fires with the Great Fire,
Lit in the month of May, on the mountain of
  the Earth.

Eight young calves white as foam,
Eating the grass of the Deep Isle:
The eight white calves of the Lady . . .

Druid – Nine little white hands on the threshing
  floor,
Near the tower of Lezarmeur,
And nine mothers grieving bitterly.

Nine sacred virgins who dance
With flowers in their hair,
And in robes of white linen,
Around the fountain,
In the light of the full Moon.

The great sow and her nine piglets,
At the door of their sty,
Snorting and snuffling.

Little one, little one, little one,
Run to the apple tree.
The old boar will teach you a lesson . . .

Druid – Ten enemy vessels seen coming from Nantes.
Bad luck to you! Bad luck to you!
Men of Vannes! . . .

Druid – Eleven armed priests coming from Vannes,
With broken swords;
And their robes all bloody;
And on crutches;
And three hundred more than these eleven . . .

Druid –   Twelve months and twelve signs;
              The penultimate, the Sagittarius,
              Lifts his bow with an arrow ready.

              The twelve signs are at war.
              The beautiful Cow, the Black Cow with a
                  white star
              on her forehead, comes out of the forest.

              In her breast is the head of the arrow;
              Her blood flows in floods;
              She slumps forward, her head lifted.

              The trumpet sounds; fire and thunder;
              Rain and wind; thunder and fire.
              Nothing! Nothing more! No more of a series
                  of numbers.

              Eleven armed priests etc.

              Ten enemy vessels etc.

              Nine little white hands etc.

              Eight winds which blow etc.

              Seven suns and seven moons etc.

              Six little children of wax etc.

              Five terrestrial zones etc.

              Four stones to sharpen etc.

              There are three parts of the world etc.

              Two oxen harnessed to a shell etc.

There is no series of number one:
There is Single necessity;
There is Sin, father of Sorrow:
Nothing before, nothing after.

[Hamish Henderson Archive]

UNDER THE EARTH I GO

Under the earth I go
On the oak-leaf I stand
I ride on the filly that never was foaled
And I carry the dead in my hand

     There's method in my magic!

Seeing I have passed my sell-by date
And will no doubt be hanging up my clogs quite soon
I have come back to Padstow to dance – to dance!

Doddle of drums on a May morning
Slashes of sunlight on hill and harbour
High-jacked greenwood looping along the quay

To hell with Aunt Ursula Birdhood
And her auld yowe deid in the park.
While my love lives, I'll dance with the Mayers
Teasing the Old Oss till there's new life in him
Chasing sweet lusty Spring with pipes, goatskin and bones.

Sunshowers over the estuary
Cormorant black on the pale sands yonder
Taste of dank earth on my tongue
Trembling oak-leaves coortin' the Sun,
And the twin dragons, Life and Death,
Jousting thegither under the Maypole.

Change elegy into hymn, remake it –
Don't fail again. Like the potent
Sap in these branches, once bare, and now brimming
With routh of green leavery,
Remake it, and renew.

Makar, ye maun sing them –
Cantos of exploit and dream,
Dàin of desire and fulfilment,
Ballants of fire and red flambeaux . . .

Tomorrow, songs
Will flow free again, and new voices
Be borne on the carrying stream

Asleep in Spring sunshine
Cornish riverbanks
Flower again!

Back in Fyvie's lands
I'll say fareweel wi' the plooman's week:

Soor Monday

Cauld Tysday

Cruel Wednesday

Everlasting Thursday

On Friday – will ye ne'er get duin.

Sweet Setterday, and the efternuin

Glorious Sunday – rest forever.

Amen.

Note: In 'Under the Earth I Go' Hamish's trains of thought run north and south of the Scottish border. In a letter to me he writes: 'The opening lines are a trickster-riddle reputedly made up by a lad who escaped hanging by thinking up a riddle the judges couldn't unravel. He put earth in his hat, oak-leaves in his shoes, rode to the court on a filly, which – like Macduff – was ... 'from his mother's womb untimely ripped', and the whip he carried was made from the hide of a dead mare.'

The scene then shifts to Padstow in Cornwall where on May Day the mysterious black-aproned Obby 'Oss swirls and dances to music and singing from dawn to dusk. Hamish attends this custom frequently and was among the crowds again this year. The poem ends with a traditional 'plooman's week' from North East Scotland. This poem is most emphatically not a valediction but a paean to the continuity of life which Hamish, like Joyce, has celebrated frequently in his work.
[Note by song-collector Tom Munnelly]

[*Chapman*, 69–70, Autumn 1992]

PECCADILLO

Because, because the mystery
Is all, and the apparent tangible
Trash delights us, I go
Walking with a companion alone.

The familiar horrors greet me
Among the outskirts of the trees. They saunter
With their raw bones and razor-edged whistling
Tempting my fingers to tear out my tongue.

My tongue trembles to a frivolous wooing
And flutters among images. They taunt me
With encouragement, those blackamoor eyes.
The trolls are nesting in the rowan branches.

By the bottomless loch is a summer-house
On a white egg-shell of island.
To the chunking of oars we murmur
'Ich kenn Dich nicht und liebe Dich.'

Grime is grey on the floor-boards.
The smell is of a mouldering dodo.
We do it. Because, because the mystery
Is all, I beg, do not repeat this.

Note: 'Ich kenn Dich nicht und liebe Dich' – I don't know you and I
love you.

[*Pervigilium Scotiae* (Etruscan Books, 1997)]

CLANRANALD'S SONG TO HIS WIFE

When I saw you in our spring-time
Sweet the season, sweet our heart-beats:
By a word made poor and trembling,
By a look raised up to heaven

>   Chorus:
>   *As the star high o'er the darkness,*
>   *As the white swan on the waters,*
>   *As the full rose spreading fragrance*
>   *I remember my beloved.*

When I saw you in your paleness
Smile and look upon our first-born,
I remembered who at Beth'lem
Suffered pain for our Redeemer.

>   [Chorus]

Like the raven, like the blood-drop,
Like the white rose shining clearly
Was the lovely face of Deirdre
Was the cheek of my beloved.

>   [Chorus]

You are Deirdre in the spring-woods
You are Mary in the stable.
You are Marie in the stillness
You are light that shines in darkness.

Note: This song is unattributed but appears in a notebook in Henderson's
hand alongside other originals and translations.

[Hamish Henderson Archive]

WRITTEN AT A CONFERENCE

Show me the way to
the company I wish for
of saints and drunkards
of madmen and angels.
And the quickest way out of
this synod of sane men,
luthers and cromwells
and next door strangers.

Now a curt monosyllable
curse of derision
for bosses and bonzes
and holy delilahs.
Please send to my cell
twelve motherly harlots
and a weak sodomitical
man of perception.

[Hamish Henderson Archive and Raymond Ross, ed. *Hamish Henderson: Collected Poems and Songs* (Curly Snake, 2000)]

VIVAMUS MEA LESBIA ATQUE AMEMUS
(after Catullus, for Gayle, on her birthday)

Noo Gayle, my dear, ye maunna fear
    The clash o' dour auld bodies O.
It's daft to miss a single kiss
    Tae please sic muckle cuddies O.

Live while ye may, and lo'e, the day –
    In life there's naething certain O.
Oor peerie licht sune ends in nicht,
    When Fate rings doon the curtain O.

Sae kiss me mair – and mair – and mair
    A thoosan kisses gie me O.
– But dinna count the haill amount
    Lest a' my senses lea me O.

[cf. 'Song' and 'As Burns Might Have Translated Catullus's Ode']

[Hamish Henderson Archive]

HEINE'S DOKTRIN
(Heinrich Heine)

Beat the drum, and don't be afraid – and
Kiss the vivandière. That is the whole of
Knowledge, that is the deepest meaning of the books.

Wake people up out of their sleep: beat
reveille with youthful strength; march with your
drum at the head of the van: that is the whole of Knowledge.

That is the philosophy of Hegel, that is the
deepest meaning of the books. I have
understood it because I am clever, and
because I am a good drummer-boy.

[Hamish Henderson Archive]

Since you are with me always, your footstep and your firm-staff are giving me comfort and release from my necessity. You prepared a table for me in the face of my foes: you anointed my head with oil. Moreover my cup is brimming over with the size of the fullness that is in it.

That goodness and mercy shall follow me as long as I am alive; and I shall dwell in the house of God for as long as my time and my day endures.

*

It is God himself that is a shepherd to me; I shall not be in want. He will observe that I lie down on green meadows with peace. Moreover, he is guiding me by the side of the rivers which wander past slowly (downwards) – he leads me gently and peacefully in every place.

He restores my soul back to me, and guides my step on the pure paths of righteousness, for the sake of his own good name. And indeed, although I should move through the glens of the shadow of death, I shall not be afraid nor be reduced to extremity any evil or misfortune that comes on me.

Note: On the back of the first of these pieces Henderson has drawn a picture of a devil, and a man with a heavy chin and an earring smoking a cigarette. [Editor]

[Hamish Henderson Archive]

AULD REEKIE'S ROSES

That hoor the dawn is rouging
    The Portobello Road.
A clapper over cobbles
    The lorries bum their load.

        Lay the lily O
        O lay the lily O

Through Jessie's wanton window
    A single bulb still burns.
The tall chain-smoking chimney
    Stands by while Jessie earns.

At stair and close and vennel
    The grimy day keeks in.
The wayside pulpit calls us
    To keep it free from sin.

Wake up wake up Alanna
    The room is full of light
You've got to earn my loving
    It can't be always night.

Alonie and alonie
    You'll have to bide your lane.
There's Woodbines in the dresser
    And a lolly for the wean.

He walks down by the fun-fair
    A cold forsaken den.
Tarpaulin drapes the gee-gees
    Till Destry rides again.

A breeze from Incholm swithers,
    Flakes out among the groins.
The bells of doom come jangling
    From Calvin's stony loins.

Day empty day advances:
    A siren skreichs its pain.
Up vennel, close and stairheid
    The wifies mak their mane.

O would you be a sodger
    And list with Sergeant Death –
Queen's shillings in his sporran
    And whisky on his breath.

Or would you be a charmer
    Aloft where angels sing?
The monumental mason
    Will clip that angel's wing.

          Lay the lily O
          O lay the lily O

Day empty day advances
    Gives lightsome dawn the lie.
The wayside pulpit calls us
    To seek for joys on high.

The brothel-banks are open –
    They cater for all needs.
The fozy voyeurs gather
    To watch how money breeds.

But when the fun-fair opens
    And bairnies ride the range,
The Oriental Gambler
    Will snitch their smallest change.

Lay the lily O
O lay the lily O

Wake up then Camerados
   It's time to make a move.
You can't be aye beach-combing
   On lucky shores of love.

The brothel-bank's for busting,
   The inmates all set free.
The Kirk, that dour dissembler,
   We'll brak its back in three.

This seely Earth's our Salem,
   To hell with Kingdom Come.
If Sergeant Death struts near us,
   We'll slash his painted drum.

The wayside pulpit's dredgy
   Can soond for ither lugs.
The joys o' Heaven we'll leave til
   The angels – and the speugs.

Lay the lily O
O lay the lily O
Lay the lily O
O lay the lily O

Note:

fozy:	fat, flabby, bloated
seely:	lucky, blessed
dredgy:	office for the dead
speugs (pron. 'spyugs'):	sparrows

Substantially composed in the 1940s, a shorter version of this poem was first published as 'Ballad' in Alan Riddell's *Lines*, in 1952. [Editor]

[Hayden Murphy, ed., *Broadsheet* 24 (Dublin)]

AULD REEKIE'S ROSES II
(Floret Silva Undique)

Floret silva undique
The lily, the rose, the rose I lay.

Tell-tale leaves on the elm-tree bole:
Reekie's oot for a Sabbath stroll.

Tim and Eck from their pad in Sciennes –
Cowboy T-shirts and Brutus jeans.

Gobstopper Gib and Jakie Tar,
Billies oot the Victoria Bar

And Davie Bowie plyin' his trade
The sweetest minstrel was ever laid.

Floret silva undique
The rocker, the ring and the gowans gay.

The bonniest pair ye iver seen
Play chasie on the Meedies green.

Undressed to the nines, frae tit tae toe,
The kimmers o' Coogate are a' on show.

Ripper o' flies, lord o' the tools,
Yon mental boot boy Eros rules.

Floret silva undique
We'll hae a ball, though the Deil's to pay.

The quick and the slaw are game for a tear;
Sma'back snooves from his Greyfriars lair.

Out of the darkmans the queer coves come,
Janus guisers from bield and tomb.

Scrunchit hurdies and raw-bone heid
Junkies mell wi' the livin deid.

Get stuck in, Hornie, and show's the way.
The lily, the rose, the rose I lay.

Floret silva undique
The rockin righteous are makin hay.

Oot from their dens, as shair's your life,
Come Knox the poxy and Mac the Knife;

Major Weir o' the twa-faced faith,
And Deacon Brodie in gude braid claith.

Seely sunshine and randy mirk
Like Auld Nick's wing ow'r a pairish kirk.

Whae's yon chattin' up Jess MacKay?
It's Bailie Burke, wi' his weet wall-eye.

The kinchin's bara, so clinch the deal:
Gie her note, son, and hae a feel.

Edina – Reekie – mon amour.
Dae't, or I'll skelp your airse, ye hoor.

The flesh is bruckle, the fiend is slee
Susanna's elders are on the spree.

The bailie beareth the belle away.
The lily, the rose, the rose I lay.

Floret silva undique
Sweet on the air till dark of day.

Sma'back pipes and they dance a spring.
Over the grave all creatures sing.

The sun gangs doon under yon hill
Jenny and Jake are at it still.

To the greenwood must I go alas
Could you gie me a loan o Balaam's ass?

Alano I dig you the most
The lily I laid, the rose I lost.

Whit dae ye hear amang the broom?
Spreid your thies, lass, and gie me room.

Twa gaed tae the woods, and three cam hame
Reekie, tell me my true love's name.

Edinburgh castle, toun and tour
The gowans gay and the gilliefloor.

Luvers daffin' aneath the slae
Floret silva undique.

The bonniest pair ye iver seen
Fuckin' aneath the flooerin' gean.

Bairnies wankin' abuin the clay
Floret silva undique

Flora is queen of lusty May.
The lily, the rose, the rose I lay.

Note:

Floret silva undique:	The wood is flowering all about
billies:	chums
gowans:	daisies; yellow wildflowers
kimmers:	girls
Sma'back:	Death
darkmans:	night (travellers' cant)
bield:	shelter
scrunchit hurdies:	thin wizened buttocks
mell:	mingle
seely:	blessed, lucky
The kinchin's bara:	the child is good (i.e. willing) (travellers' cant)
gean:	cherry tree

One of my chief loves has always been the anonymous song-poetry of Scotland, in both Scots and Gaelic. While in the army I composed several songs for the troops, one of which ('Banks of Sicily') really caught on, and turned into a kind of folksong.

Another permanent interest of mine has been the various lingos of the 'underworld', and of minority cultures generally; slang can often by its very nature get more ingeniously under the skin of a group or community than can a literary language of 'respectable' antecedent. The cant of the Scots travelling folk, which in some areas has invaded the local Doric, is the one I have drawn on in 'Floret Silva Undique'.

This line occurs in a medieval goliardic poem, and I have interwoven throughout lines from the marvellous English anonymn 'The bailey beareth the bell away', a superb example of the magical effect which can sometimes be engendered by the free flow of oral transmission.

Folksong can often treat the comedy of sex with a much surer touch than 'literary' poetry, and the eloquent tender rumbustious bawdry of the Scots anonymns is second to none in this respect. Fusing these various elements together, I have done my best to create a unified poem in celebration of 'Sexy May in Auld Reekie'.

[Note: from Robin Bell, ed., *The Best of Scottish Poetry* (Chambers, 1989)]

[Hayden Murphy, ed. *Broadsheet* 26–30 (Dublin)]

TÀLADH DHOMNAILL GHUIRM – BLUE DONALD'S LULLABY

(after a traditional Gaelic song)

The sun rising
And it without a spot on it,
Nor on the stars.
When the son of my King
Comes fully armed,
The strength of the universe with you,
The strength of the sun
And the strength of the bull
That leaps highest.

That woman asked
Another woman,
What ship is that
Close to the shoreline?
It's Donald's ship,
Three masts of willow on it,
A rudder of gold on it,
A well of wine in it,
A well of pure water in it.

[Tim Neat and John MacInnes, *The Voice of the Bard* (Polygon, 1999)]

JUVENILIA

AFTER THE BATTLE OF TRAFALGAR –
A THANKS GIVING SERVICE

Ye Hypocrites
Mon be yer pranks
Tae murder men
And then give thanks.

Stop!
Go no further
God won't accept your thanks
For murder.

[Hamish Henderson Archive and as cited in Timothy Neat, *Hamish Henderson: A Biography*, Vol. 1, p. 4]

TWO POEMS
[as Agrippa]

TO LEDBURY

Tonight the beckoning of the woods is death.
Tonight the moon is striding west with me,
Though clogs of ice must smite for me my path.

But I will keep no close account of death,
Listening as I am to the cold music.
The mime of *eine kleine Nachtmusik*.

The frost will make a sharp, incisive physic –
And I walking the darkling brilliant uplands
Remembering the Saxon boy I seek.

FOR COLIN ROY

Down by the green-roof pool he found the line
And with his spittle daubed it on his eyes
I thought it was his keen desire to please
        And now this leaping shame.

Over the low hills gropes a muffled hate
With slouch hat over brow and eyes – dark
Sightlessly cruel in the intricate ways
        No lightening soon or late.

[cf. 'Inverey']

[Hamish Henderson Archive]

GREEK DRINKING SONG

Come drink and love with me my lad
Come sport with garland o'er your eyes
With me be mad when I am mad
With me be wise when I am wise.

[*Alleynian*, October 1935]

EPIGRAM – Z. MARCAS

Fashioned against those arrogant classicals who deride Moderns because they cannot read the glories of Greek literature in the originals.

> Scorners of Goethe, is your laughter meet,
> Boasting monopoly of this wealth untold?
> Remember that the wine of Greece is sweet
> Though sipped from bowls of silver, not of gold.

[*Alleynain*, Vol. 64, No. 453, March 1936]

AS BURNS MIGHT HAVE TRANSLATED
CATULLUS'S ODE

[as Z. Marcas]

Vivamus mea Lesbia atque amemus.

Noo, Jeannie, dear, ye mauna fear
The rants o' dour auld bodies oh!
A' cares ye miss whene'er ye kiss
Despite sic muckle cuddies, Oh!

Live while ye may and lov', the day –
Ye ken the morn's the deil's Oh!
Awa's the licht, and endless nicht
For a' puir mortal cheils, Oh!

Sae kiss me mair, my lassie fair
A thousand kisses gie me, Oh!
– But dinna count the hail amount
Lest jealous ladies see me, Oh!

[cf. 'Song' and 'Vivamus mea Lesbia atque Amemus']

[*Alleynain*, Vol. 64, No. 453, March 1936]

MERRIE INGLETON

A Fragment of an Epic Poem in 'vers très libre' by H. Henderson

1. Introductory

Good gentlemen all, ye know full well
(For every wise man you meet doth tell)
That to drown your sorrows in laughter free
And mock complaints with irony
Is a recipe sure for mutual joy
Which ne'er through luckless days may cloy –
Therefore I sing in laughing vein
Of things which have my fancy ta'en;
While though I have of others treated
And to them tardy judgement meted,
All prithee mark in levity
Here is no animosity!

2.

Oh Ingleton House is a manor gay,
Its rulers smile while its subjects play
A home of mirth and jollity
A tiny kingdom it seems to be;
All have plenty, no want is there
Now time has banished every care
From the bounds of this realm so rich and fair –
Yet, think not, pray, that all was so
Adown the depths of history dim
Little enough historians know
Of truth among the legends grim,
Yet do I strive to pierce the haze
That rests antiquity upon
And chronicle the ancient days
Of mighty Merry Ingleton . . .

3.

See, see, the wisps of mist to part in twain!
Mark well before the vision fades again!
A new-built castle rears its majesty
With turrets – chimneys – haughtily on high
Outlined against the bright blue of the sky;
An older, higher mansion stands nearby
Whose square, white form adjoins the brighter brown
Of this, the finest manor in the town –
Within, rays beam on oaken panelling;
From chapel, decked with flowers, young voices sing;
And all resplendent with a first fine glory
Which has not faded through this varied story.

4.

Wherefore these marks of great magnificence?
Surely some mighty overlord has deigned
To grace the whole of Clapham with his presence
And so this peaceful, older house obtained;
See now how beautiful, enlarged it is
Extensive grounds, with lawn so smooth
And beds of daffodils, all meant to sooth
The fellows stricken with adversities
Who here their haven found and gratefully
Thanked 'Sir' for his great generosity –
Lo, there he comes, and walking by his side,
Smiling to see the happy boys around,
His sister walks, a steadfast comrade tried
When weaker colleagues other interests found.
A pleasant scene by high intent illumed –
But readers, ye're deceived if ye've assumed
The course of life was ever light and free
In Ingletonian halls; more must you see!

5.

The main point you must know
And which I'll try to show
Is the constitution of Ingleton
And the laws for high and low.

Up at the top of the tree
Of omnipotent royalty
Is the overlord of whom you've heard
Whose rule is equity.

It pleases him to ordain
To a lower vassal reign
And elevates to potentates
The trustiest of his train.

Of these subordinates
The highest always rates
As judge and jury to wreak with fury
Revenge on cheeky pates.

He draws up all our laws
And often he has cause
To be maligned (though when he's kind
He merits our applause).

The fellows who have erred
All tremble at his word
As he seldom tries to sermonise
(For some 'twould be absurd) –

But keeps strict order well,
To mischief rings the knell
By judgement sharp and to the mark
(And painful so they tell) –

Now the history to resume
Since we've our facts accum-
Ulated; we'll immediately
Our watch again assume.

Upon a parchment roll three names we see
Inscribed in solitary majesty.
What can we from these mystic words deduce
King Porter, Signor Swami, Baron Bruce.

Here a portion of the manuscript is unfortunately missing. It refers to King Porter.

This regal figure in high estate
I've nicknamed 'Frederick the Great';
He was a law-giver, equalled but by
The Babylonian, Hammurabi,
The author of a code of law,
Mercilessness its only flaw
The happy old days did not last
And many cruel laws were passed.

*Here is another large gap in the manuscript. It refers to Signor Swami, Baron Bruce,
and goes on to say a few words about the 'Servant of Two Masters'.*

Bravo! Bravo! Truffaldino!
The merriest rogue you've ever seen oh!
Putting his masters two to rights
With a leap and a kick of his coloured tights.
Gallant Gilliam, actor born,
Laughing Pantaloon to scorn.
Porter, Colin, now we meet,
Heroines coy with accents sweet,
And Pantaloon with small bonhomie
Is taken by the gifted Swami,
And others mentioned in these pages

Chronicled through difficult ages
Are factors in the worthy glory
Of 'The Servant of Two Masters' story.

*

Bravissimmo, Punchinollo!
What a jovial merry fellow!
Tragedy? No, that's just fun!
'Punch' not punches (what a pun).
Russell Thorndike, he who wrote it
Payed us tribute where he owed it,
(Compliments – a splendid show,
From the author-actor) so
We may judge this happy farce
The first and foremost of its class.

*

A good old English comedy
Is the next play on our list.
The rustic peer, Lord Duberley
Is fun not to be missed,
While Douglas Pangloss suave, polite,
Watches his blunders with delight;
Besides there is the sorry plight
Of sweet Miss Caroline.
Yet though sometime Vice stalks abroad
His downfall all can soon applaud –
To solemn Swami all the laud
For his performance fine.

Here again the manuscript is incomplete. Only the last stanza is left:

A close to all things there must be
In this our world so transitory;
And though we hope our glories last,
Those fair traditions of the past,
We see how other splendours wane
And all the last sad strife in vain . . .
Yet masters all, your glasses raise,
Remembering well those bygone days,
And shout, ere this late hour hath gone
To glorious Merrie Ingleton!

Note: The magazine – produced by Henderson and other residents at the orphanage – ends with this disclaimer: 'The editors wish to disclaim any responsibility for any slander that might inadvertently have crept into our pages. All those with impending libel actions should apply to the Commander, who is legally responsible for us.' [Editor]

[*Ingletonian Raconteur* – handmade. Vol. 1, No. 4, April 1936]

WELTSCHMERZ

[as Z. Marcas]

Where, world-weary from wandering, wandering,
    Stumbling and sleepridden, through the parched land,
Can a seared soul find rest, soft grass for slumbering
    Pastures and pleasant fruits in barren sand?

*

Oft in the gloaming, I, wandering, wandering
    Gazed at the vaulted sky, couch of the gods
Where, with unfeeling blade mortal lives sundering
    Atropes pierces, when mighty Zeus nods.

There alone, feeble, frail, glimmering, glimmering
    – For all she was weakly I knew she was kind –
One tiny star, I saw, palely was shimmering;
    Only in her a true friend did I find.

*

O ye souls sorrowfully pondering, pondering
    On the sick solitudes midst shadow mates
Seek not sour pleasures, sweet, spirit encumbering –
    Look to the heavens, – yet heed not the fates!

[*Alleynian*, Vol. 64, No. 454, June 1936]

THE GALLOWSMOUNTAIN
[Christian Morgenstern]

[as Agrippa]

To sightless, sensual churls incomprehensible
       We play the farce of life.
The swinging clods of sinning clay insensible
       Mock at your maze of strife.

Perched on your peak of folly intellectual
       Your answer: 'Childish spite
Of Death at Life.' *Your* life is ineffectual
       Until you learn we're right.

[*Alleynian*, Vol. 65, No. 459, March 1937]

THE SONG OF A GALLOWS BROTHER TO SOPHIE
THE HANGMAN'S DAUGHTER

[Christian Morgenstern]

[as Agrippa]

Come Sophie, buxom maiden;
Me bones wiv grief be laden –
     'Tis true me mouth
     Be black with drouth
What's that to be afraid on?

Come Sophie, buxom maiden,
One kiss, though lightsome laid on!
     Me head be bare
     Of every hair –
Kiss what the corbies preyed on!

Come Sophie, buxom maiden,
Here's nought to be afraid on!
     – Me eyes, m'sweet
     The eagles eat –
So show the stuff thou'rt made on.

[*Alleynian*, Vol. 65, No. 459, March 1937]

THE SPRING SONG OF A GALLOWS BROTHER
[Christian Morgenstern]

[as Agrippa]

To them upon this rosewood splinter
      Spring brings pleasure too.
A little leaf can laugh at winter –
      May's but half-way through.

And on *my* tree the leaves are merry –
      Who need seek the cause?
I almost feel – aye – happy, very,
      And the lad that once I was.

[*Alleynian*, Vol. 65, No. 459, March 1937]

HERR VON KORF'S WITTICISM
[Christian Morgenstern]

[as Agrippa]

Korf invents a joke of type peculiar –
Joke that takes effect a long while after
All have heard it with unbroken boredom.

Then – as when a dimly-glowing cinder
Flares – one chuckles, deep in cosy blankets,
Smiling like a satiated suckling.

[*Alleynian*, Vol. 65, No. 459, March 1937]

THE AESTHETE
[Christian Morgenstern]

[as Agrippa]

I do not wish to sit, dear heart,
As fleshly sitting-part desires;
My spiritual sitting-part
Can weave its own supporting wires.

But even so, its wants are few;
With *style* alone it has to do.
It leaves the vulgar *use* of chairs
To Philistines and Bulls and Bears.

[*Alleynian*, Vol. 65, No. 459, March 1937]

AMERICA
[as Polonius]

I
Where are the fair ones now, *(O, Pioneers!)*
    Where, Walt, your camerados gay and free
Redeemers of the indomitable years?

The scions stand in their pride, but the soul is far,
The wind-wild soul of the mountains that was so fair;
The soul is rouged and old and aweary of war.

O soon, how soon horizon-searching eyes
    Are bleared and blotched until they live for this:
The tinfoil-splashed, pin-table paradise
    Of gawdy ecstasy and bawdy bliss.
And where to find the gentle-eyed and wise?

Though Harper's Ferry welcomes the phantom throng
Who fired the North to war with a merry song,
I cannot away with the taste of their triumphing.

For old John Brown lies mouldering in the grave,
And who is there to redeem, ay, who to save?

II
    The wise old river under the drowsy night
When we lay in the reeds, Huck, Tom, you and I,
        remember?
We saw him fall and nod into sultry slumber
    And yawn his way to the stars and beyond man's
        sight . . .

The breeze in the reeds grew fresh and towzled our
      hair,
But it laughed in our wanton eyes and would not linger.
It fluttered the lazy waves till they stirred in anger,
  But silence and sleep hung near on the heavy air.

The firefly sparks still drift on the shrouded river,
And the son of man will wander and linger ever
    To feel the failing breeze on his cheek and brow.

But will not a sob rise up in the heart of thee
    And the mist of thine eyes grow thick for yestreen
      and now
As we sigh for the passing of faith, and the chivalry?

[*Alleynian*, Vol. 66, No. 466, June 1938]

A FELLOW TRAVELLER

(from the Gaelic)

Sunk in deep brooding thoughts, I strode a-main
O'er the rough track once cut deep in the moor
  – By the comman of Angus, long ago,
Before the Celtic power was crushed to nought; –
But now o'er grown with bracken and rank turf
And heather, dry and bloomless, it was scarce
Discernible e'en in that wilderness.

I lifted up mine eyes from time to time
To view the far blue hills of Fraoch Òg,
The longed-for goal of weary pilgrimage
Through this bleak, barren land toward the West.

At last I knew that, ere the moon was up
Shedding her soft, sweet radiance on the hills,
I would be climbing, joyful in my heart,
The first smooth, gentle slope of Ben na Craich;
And ere the first gleams of the dawn appeared,
In Kenneth's cave I, safe, would humbly kneel
And speak my mission to the forgotten seer
Who, once renowned throughout an hundred isles,
For weird sixth sight and many prophesies,
Had wandered, like our erstwhile lord, his king,
In the black vale of men's forgetfulness.
Since waning, Horror visited our land,
  – Beset by giant devils from the North
Who came in dragon-ships from o'er the sea,
And burned and razed each clachan to the dust,
Slaying the last of our great hero-kings –
I dreamt of all the glories old men tell
And heard the minstrels sing of ancient days
When Ian, Brude and Oscar of the Dirk

Built up that mighty empire – now destroyed –
Which made our Celtic fame ring through the world.

But one day, sick at heart, I heard a song,
A slow, sad ballad by the East sea's edge
Telling how, patiently, a hermit sat
In humble mountain cave far to the West
Awaiting who should come – as willed the Gods –
To beg his magic aid to make anew
The glory of the kingdom Angus ruled.
And ever in my head rang the refrain:

   'Come to the West, where great Kenneth awaiteth thee,
    Come to the Westerly isles of the sea;
    Over the moorland the seer's desire fateth thee
    On to the mountains of heather with me.'

Fired by the ballad's lilt, with zeal I searched
In ancient screeds, yet treasured by our priests
And found a tale like to the minstrel's lay
Promising great reward to him who sought
The distant cavern of one Kenneth Begh,
An aged, mighty seer, born in the days
When Seamus Ian slew the Picts, and yet
Alive! – I tarried not, but seized my staff
And spear, and started on my pilgrimage . . .

Thus thought I as, my journey's end in sight,
I gazed upon the hills, beyond whose ridge
Lay the blue waters of the Western sea; –
When suddenly I felt a presence near
And turning, saw a noble, upright man
Of comely countenance and raven beard,
A leathern, feathered bonnet on his head,
Stalking with heavy pace ten steps behind.
'Who art thou, friend, and whence has't come?' cried I

Gripping my spearshaft and the studded targe,
Advancing to my side, the stranger said:
'Continue not thy journey, foolish youth –
All is a dream, deceiving fantasy
Arising from thy restless, foolish brain.
The splendour of our race hath gone, hath gone,
And for no childish fretting may return.
Go back! Thou searchest for thy seer in vain.
There is no seer, enchantment, in the world
Can e'er restore the mountain glory more!
This land is drear and waste and nevermore
Can be aught else but hideous wilderness;
And only I remain to wail the past,
The dauntless spirit of the Celtic race!'

And with these awesome words, the demon wraith
Vanished, as melt the wisps of mountain mists.
Yet ever in my ears there ran anew
The plaintive, haunting ballad, which seemed now
To double its appeal and wistfulness.

   'Come to the West, where Great Kenneth awaiteth thee,
    Come to the Westerly isles of the sea.'

Then cast I off the spirit's powerful spell
Augering nought but horror and despair
And heeding but the lilting melody
Strove onwards o'er the moor through many hours –
At last with gladsome stride the uplands reached
And ran, such was my ardour, to the scarp –
How changed and fair the whole surroundings were!
Under my brogues the rich blue heather bent;
I passed midst leafy trees and heard a stream
Go rustling midst the ferns upon the slope.
I reached the crest – the moon already up –
And there in wide expanse before my eyes,

Bathed in the moonlight, by the Western sea,
And all the mighty company of the isles,
Here on this further slope the cavern lay!

Forgetful of my weary journey, I
Ran hard adown the hillside, and at last
Espied a hollow underneath a rock,
From which a glimmering light shone through the gloom.
With reverent steps the cavern I approached
And whispered: 'Holy seer: Thy wait is o'er!
'The Gods have willed a pilgrim youth to come
To beg the magic aid to make anew
The glory of the kingdom Angus ruled.'
I entered then the cave and knelt to wait
The longed-for charmed answer of the seer.
But nought but silence reigned within the cave,
The lighted bracket flick'ring eerily,
Then saw I at the blackest corner's edge
A fleshless skull and hideous skeleton,
And by its side a leathern bonnet lay.

[*The Raconteur*, Midsummer, 1937]

HOMAGE TO STEFAN GEORGE

[as Z. Marcas]

His creed of the Disciple englished

Ye speak of pleasures never for my proving;
In me love beats in longing for my King.
Ye know alone the lovely, I the loving.
    Still live I for my loving King.

Your days are sweet, your work is joyous, spacious.
I bow to work the purpose of my King.
I will not fail in it; my King is gracious
    And I will serve my gracious King.

I march with Hope for shield and Faith for visor
In lonely ways of night to meet my King.
The shadow foes are wise, but he is wiser
    And I will trust my wiser King.

Of flowers and wine and wild, wild love *thou* pratest.
My mede is in the mercy of my King.
Of shining kings: yet is my King the greatest.
    I follow still the greatest King.

[*Alleynian*, Vol. 66, No. 407, July 1938]

BALLADE DES NOMS DE PLUME

[Henderson, signing off as editor of the Alleynian, *catalogues the pseudonyms he has used whilst in post.]*

Marcas! Répétez-vous à vous-même ce nom composé de deux syllabes;
n'y trouvez-vous pas une sinistre signification? Ne vous semble-t-il pas que
l'homme qui le porte doive être martyrisé? Quoique étrange et sauvage,
ce nom a pourtant le droit d'aller à la postérité; il est bien composé, il se
pronounce facilement, il a cette brièveté voulue pour les noms
célèbres . . . Examinez encore une fois ce nom: Z. Marcas! Toute la
vie de l'homme est dans l'assemblage fantastique de ces sept lettres . . .
Z. Marcas! N'avez-vous pas l'idée de quelque chose de précieux qui se
brise par une chute avec ou sans bruit?

                         – *Honoré de Balzac*

Ho! Hearken how they thinly rave,
My ague-lank paralytics!
They 'lumed my blazoned architrave,
These bluely guttering candle-wicks!
Agrippa groans – his wounds he licks,
And Felix, too, has had his hour.
Yet though Old Time his guerdon picks
Z. *Marcas* was of all the flower.

To that bleak cross o'er yon waste grave
Prithee this rhyming scroll to fix:
'Toll for poor *Tusshe*; bemourn the brave;
In heavenly haunts his heels he kicks,
Who sang like Mother Carey's chicks
When 'fore the freezing blast they cower.'
Eke in dead *Tusshe's* gorge it sticks:
Z. *Marcas* was of all the flower.

His Yankee yawp *Polonius* gave,
And *Baralipton's* politics
Mid-way remained – mayhap to save
Indifferent demons' conscience-pricks.
Should speakers doubt a lad may mix
His words with theirs, they'll girn and glower,
      But safe from cranks and quartier-bricks
      Z. Marcas was of all the flower.

ENVOI

Prince Honoré, of roses six
Thine hath the most begraced my bower.
Though *Omega* sweeps up the tricks,
Z. Marcas was of all the flower.

Ω

Note: Henderson's successor as editor of the *Alleynian* concluded his first editorial with a clerihew for his predecessor:

      Z. Marcas – Agrippa – Hamish
      Found the *Alleynian* samish;
      Packed it with diversity –
      Packed off to the University.

[Editor]

[*Alleynian*, Vol. 66, No. 407, July 1938]

ACKNOWLEDGEMENTS

Special thanks are due to Hamish Henderson's family, Kätzel, Janet and Christine, for their generosity and their support for this project. Thanks to Polygon, and in particular, Edward Crossan, for proposing this collection. The bulk of the archival work for this volume was undertaken at the University of Edinburgh Centre for Research Collections, and I am very grateful for the support of all staff there. Librarians, curators and archivists at the University of Glasgow Library, the Janey Buchan Political Song Collection at the University of Glasgow, the National Library of Scotland and the University of South Carolina Irvin Department of Special Collections, have also been indispensable in tracking down these poems and songs. I also want to thank my colleagues in Scottish Literature and across the School of Critical Studies and the College of Arts at the University of Glasgow. Thanks, too, to Joy Hendry for her expertise and advice.

Many friends and colleagues have made important direct and indirect contributions to the development of this collection, including: Stewart Black, Rhona Brown, Gerard Carruthers, Sarah Dunnigan, Scott Hames, Theo van Heijnsbergen, Craig Lamont, Kirsteen McCue, Alasdair MacDonald, Pauline Mackay, Gerard McKeever, Helen McLaughlin, Beth Potter, John Purser, Alan Riach, Stewart Sanderson, Patrick Scott, Nikolas Stamatopoulos, Roy Thomas, Alex Thomson and Ronnie Young.

Heaps and heaps of love and thanks, finally, to my family. To Siobhan, Mamie, and Nora. To the Gibsons and to the Magees.

Some poems and songs that appear in this collection have been published in the following volumes and periodicals: *101 Scottish Songs* (ed. by Norman Buchan, Collins, 1961); *Aberdeen University Review*; *Atlantic Anthology* (ed. by Nicholas Moore, London, 1945); *Ballads of World War II* (The Lili Marleen Club of Glasgow, 1949); *The Best of Scottish Poetry* (ed. by Robin Bell, Chambers, 1989);

Broadsheet (ed. by Hayden Murphy, Dublin and Edinburgh); *Cencrastus* (Edinburgh); *Chapbook* (Edinburgh); *Chapman* (Edinburgh); *Citadel* (Cairo); *Conflict* (Glasgow University Socialist Club); *Ding Dong Dollar* (Glasgow Song Guild/Folkways, 1962); *Elegies for the Dead in Cyrenaica* (Lehmann, 1948; EUSPB, 1977; Polygon 1990, 2008);*The End of a Regime?* (Aberdeen University Press, 1991); *Englische Lyrik 1900–1980* (Reclam, Leipzig, 1983); *Favourite Scottish Song Lyrics* (Gordon Wright, 1983); *From Oasis Into Italy* (ed. by Victor Selwyn, Shepheard-Walwyn, 1983); *The Galliard* (Edinburgh); *Hamish Henderson: Collected Poems and Songs* (ed. Raymond Ross, Curly Snake, 2000); *Homage to John Maclean* (John Maclean Society, 1973); *Lines/Lines Review* (Edinburgh); *Modern Folk Ballads* (ed. by Charles Causley, Studio Vista, 1966); *Modern Scottish Poetry* (ed. by Maurice Lindsay, Carcanet, 1976); *The New Alliance* (Edinburgh); *The New Alliance & Scots Review* (Edinburgh); *The New Statesman* (London); *New Writing and Daylight* (London); *No Other Place* (ed. by Ian A. Olson, Tuckwell Press, 1995); *The Obscure Voice* (ed. by Alec Finlay, Morning Star, 1994); *Orientations* (Cairo); *Our Time* (London); *The Oxford Book of Scottish Verse* (ed. by J. MacQueen and Tom Scott, Oxford University Press, 1966); *Penguin New Writing* (ed. by John Lehmann); *The People's Past* (ed. by E.J. Cowan, Polygon, 1980); *Pervigilium Scotiae* (Etruscan Books, 1997); *Poeti della Scozia Contemporanea* (Supernova, Venice, 1992); *Poems Addressed to Hugh MacDiarmid* (ed. by Duncan Glen, Akros, 1967); *Poems of the Second World War* (ed. by Victor Selwyn, Dent, 1985); *Poetry Broadsheet* (Cambridge); *Poetry London*; *Poetry of the World Wars* (ed. by Michael Foss, Michael O'Mara, 1990); *Poetry of War 1939–1945* (ed. by Ian Hamilton, New English Library, 1972); *Poetry Scotland* (Edinburgh); *Poetry Quarterly* (Billericay); *The Rebels Ceilidh Song Book* (Bo'ness Rebel's Literary Society, 1951-3); *Return to 'Oasis'* (ed. by Victor Selwyn, Shepheard-Walwyn, 1980); *The Ring of Words* (ed. by Alan MacGillivray and James Rankin, Oliver and Boyd, 1970); *Scotland's Music* (Mainstream/BBC Scotland, 1992); *Scots on Scotch* (ed. by Phillip Hills, Mainstream, 1991); *The Scots Review* (Glasgow); *The Scottish Folksinger* (ed. by N. Buchan and P. Hall, Collins, 1978); *The Scottish Literary Revival* (ed. by

George Bruce, Macmillan, 1968); *Scottish Verse, 1851–1951* (ed. by Douglas Young, Nelson, 1952); *Seer* (Dundee); *Sing* (London); *The Terrible Rain* (ed. by Brian Gardner, Magnum Books, 1977); *Tocher* (Edinburgh); *Voice of Scotland* (Dunfermline); *The Voice of the Bard* (ed. by Timothy Neat and John MacInnes, Birlinn, 1999); *The Voice of War* (ed. by Victor Selwyn, Penguin and Salamander Oasis Trust, 1996)

INDEX OF TITLES

4 September 1939 195

A Fellow Traveller 384

A Pioneer Corps Ballad 79

A Translation of Nietzsche into
   Scots 219

A Voice Frae Yont the Grave 305

A Wife Ingenrit o the Sea 154

After Churchill 329

After the Battle of Trafalgar –
   A Thanks Giving Service 365

Alamein, October 23, 1942 198

America 382

Anti-Polaris 287

Anzio April 252

Army Life 246

As Burns Might Have Translated
   Catullus's Ode 369

Auld Reekie's Roses 352

Auld Reekie's Roses II 356

Auldearn 29

Back from the Island
   of Sulloon 180

Ballad of Anzio 81

Ballad of King Faruk and
   Queen Farida 69

Ballad of Snow-White
   Sandstroke 181

Ballad of the Banffies 74

Ballad of the Big Nobs 63

Ballad of the Creeping Jesus 175

Ballad of the D-Day Dodgers 61

Ballad of the Famous
   Twenty-Third 243

Ballad of the Men of
   Knoydart 277

Ballad of the Simeto 13

Ballad of the Stubby Guns 169

Ballad of the Taxi Driver's Cap 65

Ballad of the Twelve Stations of
   My Youth 177

Ballade des Noms de Plume 389

Bawdy Scrawled on a Postcard
   from Egypt 230

Billet Doux 324

Bridge St Blues 45

Brosnachadh 22

Brutality Begins at Home 229

Captain, Captain of the
   Guard 248

Chimaera 32

Clamavi (or, Serentis in Rebus) 151

Clanranald's Song to his Wife 347

Colour of Rain and Iron 312

Comrie Port a Beul 320

Dark Streets to Go Through 156

Death 152

Death or the Bed of Contention –
   MacDiarmid or Me? 328

Dialogue of the Angel and the
   Dead Boy 205

Eighth Elegy – Karnak 112

En Marche 225

Epigram – Z. Marcas 368

Epistill 130

Epistle to Mary 41

Epitaph 266

Epitaph for a Barn-Stormer 211

Fall of Tobruk 76

Fifth Elegy – Highland Jebel 99

First Elegy – End of a
   Campaign 91

For Colin Roy 366

Four Cambridge Poems 45

Fourth Elegy – El Adem 97

Francy 221

Freedom Becomes People 5

from The Gods from Greece 236

Fuck on, Fuck on, Verlaine, Rimbaud 28

Glasclune and Drumlochy 23

Goettingen Nicht 223

Good Germans 109

Greek Drinking Song 367

Hate Poem 165

Hate Song Against a Sergeant 228

Heine's Doktrin 350

Here's to the Maiden 210

Heroic Song for the Runners of Cyrene 121

Herr von Korf's Witticism 380

High Hedges 49

Homage to Stefan George 388

Honest Geordie 172

Hospital Afternoon 167

If You Sit Close Tae Me, I Winna Weary 290

In un Momento 314

Interlude – Opening of an Offensive 102

Into the Future 327

Inverey 30

Journey to a Kingdom 132

La Semana Nera 247

Lament for the Son 203

Leaving Brandenburg 1939 174

Letting Go of a Dove 315

Limericks 322

Lines to a Fool 186

Lost Love Blues 47

Love Song 241

Mains o' Rhynie 284

May's Mou for Jamie 297

Merrie Ingleton 370

Mr Jimmy Balgowrie Talking 160

My Way Home 245

Myself Answers 217

Nearly Xmas 1941 240

Ninth Elegy – Fort Capuzzo 117

Of Eros and Dust: Poems of C.P. Cavafy and Dino Campana 31

Oh, the Faded Churches 316

On Two Cambridge Professional Athletes 212

Paddy's Hogmanay 303

Patmos I 36

Patmos II 39

Peccadillo 346

Phoney War – Western Front 80

Picture in St Sebaldus Church, Nuremberg 9

Pioneer Ballad of Section Three 145

Piron's Epitaph on Himself 129

Poem 218

Poem for Silvano 168

Poem from the Diary of Corporal Heinrich Mattens 239

Primosole: Jul 42 242

Prologue to a Book of Ballads 325

Prologue to a Poem 7

Requiem for the Men the Nazis Murdered 189

Rivonia 298

Scottish Childhood 326

Seascape 155

Second Elegy – Halfaya 93

Sergeant Major Prick Talking 150

Seventh Elegy – Seven Good Germans 109

Sir Oriflamme Chammlinton 222

Sitzkrieg Fantasy 141

Sixth Elegy – Acroma 107

So Long 54

Socrates and Alcibiades 35

Soldat Bernhard Pankau 159

Song 323

Song for an Irish Red Killed in Sicily 140

Song of the Admiral Graf von Spree 77

Song of the Gillie More 280

Speech for a Sensualist in a Play 227

Strathspey 173

Tae Geordie Fraser on His Waddin Day 319

Tàladh Dhomnaill Ghuirm – Blue
    Donald's Lullaby 361
Tenth Elegy – The Frontier 118
The 51st Highland Division's
    Farewell to Sicily 67
The Aesthete 381
The Alpine Recruits 249
The Applause of Men 34
The Ballad o Corbara 254
The Ballad of Gibson Pasha 184
The Ballad of the Speaking
    Heart 300
The Ballad of Wadi Maktilla 59
The Ballad of Zem-Zem 232
The Belles o' Marchmont 282
The Blubbing Buchmanite 72
The Cell (1) 10
The Cell (2) 20
The Crowned Heads of
    Europe 273
The Druid and his Disciple 338
The Flyting o' Life and Daith 294
The Freedom Come-All-Ye 286
The Gallowsmountain 377
The Gods in Exile 234
The Guid Sodger Schweik 226
The Guillotine 200
The Highlanders at Alamein 196
The Highlanders of Sicily – A Pipe
    Tune 251
The John Maclean March 271
The Roads to Rome 64
The Salamander 163
The Serbian Spring, 1941 193
The Sleep of the Virgin 313
The Song of a Gallows Brother to
    Sophie the Hangman's
    Daughter 378
The Spring Song of a Gallows
    Brother 379
They've got 'ESS! 213
Third Elegy – Leaving
    the City 95
This is the Exile's Trouble 153
This Island a Fortress 214

Three Poems of Hölderlin 34
To a Free Kirk Minister 131
To Hugh MacDiarmid on
    Reading Lucky Poet 51
To Ledbury 366
To Stuart – On His Leaving
    for Jamaica 44
Tomb of Iases 31
Twa Blads frae Africa as Tae a
    Wheen Anglo-Cairenes 231
Two Poems 366
Two Renderings of Psalm 23 351
Under the Earth I Go 343
Unpublished haiku 330
Unpublished poem fragment 332
Unpublished poem
    fragment #2 333
Unpublished poem
    fragment #3 334
Unpublished poem
    fragment #4 335
Unpublished poem
    fragment #5 336
Unpublished quatrain 331
Untitled 224
Untitled 267
Verse of Good Wishes, collected
    from Catherine Dix of
    Berneray 337
Victory Hey-Down 263
Vivamus Mea Lesbia atque
    Amemus 349
We Show You That Death as a
    Dancer 171
Weltschmerz 376
When the Teased Idiot Turns 164
Wind on the Crescent [Eugenio
    Montale] 311
Written at a Conference 348
X Still = 0 48
You, My Poems, Are
    My Weapons 187